MYSTERIES BY ISAAC ASIMOV

NOVELS

The Caves of Steel (1954)
The Naked Sun (1957)
The Death Dealers (A Whiff of Death) (1958)
Murder at the ABA (1976)
The Robots of Dawn (1983)

SHORT STORY COLLECTIONS

Asimov's Mysteries (1968)
Tales of the Black Widowers (1974)
More Tales of the Black Widowers (1976)
The Key Word and Other Mysteries (1977)
Casebook of the Black Widowers (1980)
The Union Club Mysteries (1983)
Banquets of the Black Widowers (1984)
The Disappearing Man and Other Mysteries (1985)
The Best Mysteries of Isaac Asimov (1986)
Puzzles of the Black Widowers (1989)

ANTHOLOGIES (EDITED)

The Thirteen Crimes of Science Fiction (1979)
Miniature Mysteries (1981)
The Twelve Crimes of Christmas (1981)
Tantalizing Locked Room Mysteries (1982)
The Big Apple Mysteries (1982)
Show Business Is Murder (1983)
Murder on the Menu (1984)
Sherlock Holmes Through Time and Space (1984)
Hound Dunnit (1987)
The Best Crime Stories of the 19th Century (1988)

PUZZLES OF THE BLACK WIDOWERS

P U Z

OF THE

BLACK

DOUBLEDAY

NEW YORK LONDON TORONTO SYDNEY AUCKLAND

ZLES

WIDOWERS

ISAAC
ASIMOV

PUBLISHED BY DOUBLEDAY
a division of Bantam Doubleday Dell Publishing Group, Inc.
666 Fifth Avenue, New York, New York 10103

DOUBLEDAY and the portrayal of an anchor and a dolphin
are trademarks of Doubleday, a division of
Bantam Doubleday Dell Publishing Group, Inc.

Published in the UK in 1990 by Doubleday
A division of Transworld Publishers Ltd
61/63 Uxbridge Road, London W5 5SA

A CIP catalogue record for this book is available from the British Library

Library of Congress Cataloging-in-Publication Data
Asimov, Isaac, 1920–
    Puzzles of the black widowers / Isaac Asimov. —1st ed.
        p.   cm.
    ISBN 0-385-26264-7
    I. Title.
    PS3551.S5P8   1990
    813'.54—dc20   89-7814
                                                   CIP

BG

To the memory of Linwood V. Carter (1930–88),
and John D. ("Doc") Clark (1907–88),
who were the inspiration of Mario Gonzalo and
James Drake, respectively

ACKNOWLEDGMENTS

"The Fourth Homonym" originally published in
Ellery Queen's Mystery Magazine.
Copyright © 1984 by Isaac Asimov.
"Unique Is Where You Find It" originally published in
The Edge of Tomorrow (Tor Books).
Copyright © 1985 by Isaac Asimov.
"Triple Devil" originally published in *EQMM.*
Copyright © 1985 by Isaac Asimov.
"Sunset on the Water" originally published in *EQMM.*
Copyright © 1986 by Isaac Asimov.
"Where Is He?" originally published in *EQMM.*
Copyright © 1986 by Isaac Asimov.
"The Old Purse" originally published in *EQMM.*
Copyright © 1986 by Isaac Asimov.
"The Quiet Place" originally published in *EQMM.*
Copyright © 1987 by Isaac Asimov.
"The Envelope" originally published in *EQMM.*
Copyright © 1989 by Isaac Asimov.
"The Alibi" originally published in *EQMM.*
Copyright © 1989 by Isaac Asimov.

CONTENTS

INTRODUCTION

My first Black Widower story, "The Acquisitive Chuckle," was written in 1971 and was published in the January 1972 issue of *Ellery Queen's Mystery Magazine*. I had intended it as a one-shot, but Frederic Dannay (one of two authors who were Ellery Queen) had the idea that it would make a good series. So I kept on going and, as of now, I have written no fewer than sixty of these stories, and have put them into collections—twelve stories in each. This one, therefore, *Puzzles of the Black Widowers*, is the fifth collection.

Between the first story and the sixtieth, however, seventeen years have passed, and that means there have been changes. For instance, I think I am at least three or four years older than I was seventeen years ago, though that may just be my innate pessimism showing through. A much more serious change is that Fred Dannay died in

1982, to the loss of everyone in the field of mystery writing.

Other changes have involved the club on which this series is based. I have explained in earlier collections that there is a real-life organization called the Trap-Door Spiders which has been in existence for over forty years, and which is very like the Black Widowers. Indeed, I have modeled the latter, quite unashamedly, on the former.

I used six of the Spiders as models for my Black Widowers, choosing them more or less at random and making sure they didn't mind. I used them only as models for the physical appearance of my characters and for some of the conversational characteristics (such as Emmanuel Rubin's opinionativeness, Thomas Trumbull's short temper, Geoffrey Avalon's occasional, but lovable, pedantry, and so on.

For the record, here are the real people behind my Black Widowers:

Lester del Rey—Emmanuel Rubin

L. Sprague de Camp—Geoffrey Avalon

Don Bensen—Roger Halsted

Lin Carter—Mario Gonzalo

Gilbert Cant—Thomas Trumbull

John D. Clark—James Drake

The Trap-Door Spiders still exist after seventeen years and the club is going strong, but naturally, there have been changes in membership. Some old members have passed away and new members have been elected.

As it happens, and to my grief, three of those whom I saddled with Black Widowers alter egos have passed on to the Perpetual Banquet in the sky. They are Gilbert Cant, who died in 1982, and Lin Carter and John D. Clark, who each died in 1988.

Nevertheless, their alter egos remain Black Widowers and will continue to remain so as long as I myself continue to occupy my aging body. Nor will anyone grow older, or get sick, or become infirm. Within the Black Widower stories, time will not exist, and the puzzles will continue indefinitely.

I might add once again that Henry is not modeled on anybody but is my own creation (though more than one person has wondered whether I had P. G. Wodehouse's "Jeeves" in mind, and since I am a PGW idolator, who knows, I may have.) Henry also will not age, and, never fear, he will never be stumped, but will continue to solve each puzzle as it comes up, for as long as I live.

PUZZLES OF THE
BLACK WIDOWERS

THE FOURTH HOMONYM

"Homonyms!" said Nicholas Brant. He was Thomas Trumbull's guest at the monthly banquet of the Black Widowers. He was rather tall, and had surprisingly prominent bags under his eyes, despite the comparative youthfulness of his appearance otherwise. His face was thin and smooth-shaven, and his brown hair showed, as yet, no signs of gray. "Homonyms," he said.

"What?" said Mario Gonzalo blankly.

"The words you call 'sound-alikes.' The proper name for them is 'homonyms.' "

"That so?" said Gonzalo. "How do you spell it?"

Brant spelled it.

Emmanuel Rubin looked at Brant owlishly through the thick lenses of his glasses. He said, "You'll have to excuse Mario, Mr. Brant. He is a stranger to our language."

Gonzalo brushed some specks of dust from his jacket sleeve and said, "Manny is corroded with envy because I've invented a word game. He knows the words but he lacks any spark of inventiveness, and that kills him."

"Surely Mr. Rubin does not lack inventiveness," said Brant, soothingly. "I've read some of his books."

"I rest my case," said Gonzalo. "Anyway, I'm willing to call my game 'homonyms' instead of 'sound-alikes.' The thing is to make up some short situation which can be described by two words that are sound-alikes—that are homonyms. I'll give you an example: If the sky is perfectly clear, it is easy to decide to go on a picnic in the open. If it is raining cats and dogs, it is easy to decide *not* to go on a picnic. But what if it is cloudy, and the forecast is for possible showers, but there seem to be patches of blue here and there, so you can't make up your mind about the picnic. What would you call that?"

"A stupid story," said Trumbull tartly, passing his hand over his crisply waved white hair.

"Come on," said Gonzalo, "play the game. The answer is two words that sound alike."

There was a general silence and Gonzalo said, "The answer is 'whether weather.' It's the kind of weather where you wonder whether to go on a picnic or not. 'Whether weather,' don't you get it?"

James Drake stubbed out his cigarette and said, "We get it. The question is, how do we get rid of it?"

Roger Halsted said, in his soft voice, "Pay no attention, Mario. It's a reasonable parlor game, except that there don't seem to be many combinations you can use."

Geoffrey Avalon looked down austerely from his seventy-four-inch height and said, "More than you might think. Suppose you owned a castrated ram that was frisky on clear days and miserable on rainy days. If it were merely cloudy, however, you might wonder whether that ram would be frisky or miserable. That would be 'whether wether weather.' "

There came a chorus of outraged *What!*'s.

Avalon said, ponderously. "The first word is *w-h-e-t-h-e-r*, meaning if. The last word is *w-e-a-t-h-e-r*, which refers to atmospheric conditions. The middle word is *w-e-t-h-e-r*, meaning a castrated ram. Look it up if you don't believe me."

"Don't bother," said Rubin. "He's right."

"I repeat," growled Trumbull, "this is a stupid game."

"It doesn't have to be a game," said Brant. "Lawyers are but too aware of the ambiguities built into the language, and homonyms can cause trouble."

The gentle voice of Henry, that waiter for all seasons, made itself heard over the hubbub by some alchemy that worked only for him.

"Gentlemen," he said. "I regret the necessity of interrupting a warm discussion, but dinner is being served."

"Here's another one," said Gonzalo over the smoked trout. "Someone has written down all the digits and on all of them but one he has drawn a very clever face. A child watching this is delighted, but dissatisfied with the incompleteness of the project. What does he say?"

Halsted, who was spreading the horseradish sauce daintily over his trout, said, "The child says, 'Do that to two, too.' "

Gonzalo said in an aggrieved manner, "Have you heard that somewhere before?"

"No," said Halsted, "but it's a mathematical instance of the game. What's the use of teaching mathematics at junior high school, if I can't solve problems involving the number two?"

Gonzalo frowned. "You're trying to be funny, aren't you, Roger?"

"Who? Me?"

Trumbull said, "As host of the evening, I would like to recommend that we change the subject."

No one gave any sign of hearing. Avalon said, "Homonyms are usually the result of the accidents of language history. For instance, 'night,' by which I mean the opposite of day, is cognate to the German *Nacht*, while 'knight,' by which I mean a warrior of the Table Round, is cognate with the German *Knecht*. In English, the vowels changed and the *k* is invariably silent in an initial *kn*, so you end up with two words pronounced in identical fashion."

"The initial *kn* does not invariably have a silent *k*," said Rubin. "There are some words not yet sufficiently Anglicized. I have a Jewish friend who married a young lady of the Gentile persuasion. Anxious to please her new husband, she bought some ethnic delicacies for him, which she displayed proudly. Listing her purchases, she said, finally, 'And I also bought you this nish,' and was quite puzzled when he broke into hysterical laughter."

Drake said, "I don't get it."

Rubin said with a touch of impatience, "The word is 'knish'—with the *k* heavily pronounced. It is a ball of dough in whose interior one places spiced mashed potatoes, or possibly some other filling, with the whole then being fried or baked. Any New Yorker should know that."

Trumbull sighed and said, "Well, if you can't lick them, join them. Can anyone give me a group of four homonyms, four words all pronounced alike, with spelling and meaning different in each case? I'll give you five minutes in which I expect blessed silence."

The five minutes passed pleasantly enough, with only the sound of cracking lobster shells impinging upon the eardrums, and then Trumbull said, "I'll give you one of the words: 'right,' meaning the opposite of left. What are the other three?"

Halsted said, his mouth fairly full of lobster claw, "There's 'write,' meaning to inscribe words, and 'rite,' meaning a fixed religious procedure, but I don't think there's a fourth."

Avalon said, "Yes, there is. It's 'wright,' *w-r-i-g-h-t*, meaning a mechanic."

"That's archaic," protested Gonzalo.

"Not entirely," said Avalon, "We still speak of a 'playwright,' who would be someone who constructs plays."

Brant said, "My friend Tom mentioned 'right,' defining it as the opposite of left. What about 'right' meaning the opposite of wrong, and 'right' meaning perpendicular? Would that be a fifth and sixth homonym?"

"No," said Gonzalo, "the spelling has to be different for the words to be homonyms, at least as this game of mine is played."

Avalon said, "Not always, Mario. Two words can be spelled the same but have different meanings and have different etymological origins; they would count as homonyms. For instance, 'bear' meaning the animal, and 'bear' meaning to carry, have the same spelling and pronunciation but have different origins, so I would call them homonyms; along with 'bare' meaning unclothed, of course. The different uses of 'right,' however, as in 'right hand,' 'right answer,' and 'right angle,' all stem from the same root with the same meaning, so they would not be homonyms."

There were fifteen additional minutes before Trumbull felt justified in rattling his spoon against the water glass and bringing the conversation to a halt.

"I have never been so glad," he said, "at any of the banquets of the Black Widowers to put an end to a conversation. If I had absolute power as a host, I would fine Mario five dollars for starting it."

"You took part in it, Tom," said Gonzalo.

"In self-defense—and shut up," said Trumbull. "I would like to present my guest, Nicholas Brant, and Jeff, you seem civilized even if you were more homonymized than anyone else, so would you do the honors and begin the grilling?"

Avalon's formidable eyebrows lifted, and he said, "I scarcely think that 'homonymized' is English, Tom." Then, turning to the guest, he said, "Mr. Brant, how do you justify your existence?"

Brant smiled ruefully. "As a lawyer, I don't think I can. You know the old joke, perhaps, of the time God threatened to sue Satan, and Satan answered, 'How can you? I've got all the lawyers.' In my defense, however, I'm not the kind of lawyer who plays tricks in front of a judge and jury. Mostly I sit in my office and try to write documents that actually mean what they are supposed to mean."

Avalon said, "I'm a patent lawyer myself, so I ask the following question without evil intent. Do you ever try to write them so that they *don't* mean what they're supposed to mean? Do you try to build in loopholes?"

Brant said, "Naturally, I try to draw up a document

that leaves my client as much freedom of action as possible, and the other side as little freedom of action as possible. However, the other side has a lawyer, too, who is working hard for the reverse, and the usual result is that the contract ends up reasonably ironbound in both directions."

Avalon paused, then said, "In the earlier discussion on homonyms, you said, if I remember correctly, that homonyms are ambiguities that could cause trouble. Does that mean you ran into a homonym professionally, in your preparation of contracts, that brought about unexpected complications?"

Brant raised both hands. "No, no, nothing like that. What I had in mind when I made that statement was completely irrelevant to the subject now under discussion."

Avalon ran his finger around the rim of his water glass. "You must understand, Mr. Brant, that this is not a legal cross-examination. There is no particular subject under discussion, and nothing is irrelevant. I repeat my question."

Brant remained silent for a moment, then he said, "It's something that took place a little over twenty years ago, and that I have thought about only very occasionally since then. Mr. Gonzalo's game of homonyms brought it to mind, but it's . . . nothing. It doesn't involve any legal problems or any complications whatever. It's just a . . . puzzle. It's an insoluble matter that isn't worth discussing."

"Is it confidential?" put in Gonzalo. "Because if it is—"

"Nothing confidential about it," said Brant. "Nothing secret, nothing sensitive—and therefore nothing interesting."

Gonzalo said, "Anything that's insoluble is interesting. Don't you agree, Henry?"

Henry, who was filling the brandy glasses, said, "I find it so when there is at least room for speculation, Mr. Gonzalo."

Gonzalo began, "Well, then, if—"

Avalon said, "Mario, let me continue, please. —Mr. Brant, I wonder if you could give us the details of this insoluble puzzle of yours. We would greatly appreciate hearing it."

"You'll be very disappointed."

"That's a chance we will take."

"Well, then," said Brant, "if you'll just give me a chance to think back—"

He rested his face in one hand, thinking, while the six Black Widowers watched him expectantly, and Henry took his usual place by the sideboard.

Brant said, "Let me begin with Alfred Hunzinger. He was a poor boy of an immigrant family, and he had no education worth mentioning. I'm pretty sure he never went to high school. By the time he was fourteen, he was working. Those were the decades before World War I and education was by no means considered one's birthright, or even particularly desirable for what used to be called workingmen.

"Hunzinger wasn't your usual workingman, however. He was incredibly industrious and incredibly intelligent. Intelligence and education don't necessarily go hand in hand, you know."

Rubin said forcefully, "Indeed, they don't. I've known some very thoroughly educated jackasses."

"Hunzinger was the reverse," said Brant. "He was a very thoroughly uneducated business genius. He had a green thumb, but it was the green of dollar bills. Whatever he touched prospered, and he built a formidable business before he died.

"Nor was this enough for him. He always felt keenly his lack of education, and he embarked in a program of home study. It wasn't continuous, for his business was his first preoccupation and there were periods when he had little time. And it was spotty, for he read promiscuously and without outside guidance. Conversation with him was an exposure to a curious mixture of pedantry and naïveté."

Avalon said, "You knew him personally, I take it."

Brant said, "Not really. Not intimately. I did some work for him. Mainly, I prepared his will. This, when properly done, and when there are complex business matters to consider, takes a long time and produces a long document. Periodically, it must be updated or revised, and the wording considered carefully in the light of continually changing tax laws. Believe me, it was virtually a career in itself and I was forced to spend many hours in conference with him and to engage in extensive correspondence, too. However, it was a very limited and specialized relationship. I got to know the nature of his finances rather thoroughly, but to know him as a person only superficially."

"Did he have children?" asked Halsted.

"Yes, he did," said Brant. "He married late in life; at the age of forty-two, if I remember correctly. His wife was considerably younger. The marriage, while not idyllically happy, was a successful one. There was no divorce, nor any prospect of one at any time, and Mrs. Hunzinger died only about five years ago. They had four children, three boys and a girl. The girl married well;

she's still alive, still married, has children of her own, and is, and has been, very comfortably off. She scarcely figured in the will. Some investments were turned over to her during Hunzinger's lifetime, and that was it.

"The business was left on an equal basis, one-third each, to the three sons, whose names were Frank, Mark, and Luke."

"In that order of age?" asked Drake.

"Yes. The oldest is, to use his legal signature, B. Franklin Hunzinger. The middle son is Mark David Hunzinger. The youngest son is Luke Lynn Hunzinger. Naturally, I pointed out to Hunzinger that to leave his business in equal shares to his three sons was asking for trouble. The income might be divided equally, but the directing power, the decision-making power, had to be placed in the hands of one.

"He was very stubbornly resistant to that, however. He said he had brought up his sons in accordance with the ideals of the old Roman republic; that they were all faithful to him, the paterfamilias—he actually used the term, to my intense surprise—and to each other. There would be no trouble at all, he said.

"I took the liberty of pointing out that they might well be ideal sons while he was alive and with his forceful personality directing affairs. After he was gone, however, hidden rivalries might show up. Never, he insisted, never. I thought him blind, and wondered how anyone so alive to any hint of chicanery in business affairs, so realistic in matters of the world, could be so foolishly romantic where his own family was concerned."

Drake said, "What was the daughter's name?"

"Claudia Jane," said Brant. "I don't remember her married name at the moment. Why do you ask?"

"Just curious. She might have had ambitions, too, mightn't she?"

"I don't think so. At least not with respect to the business. She made it quite clear she neither expected nor wanted any share in it. Her husband was rich—old money—social position—that sort of thing. The last thing she wanted was to be identified with what was—in a manner of speaking—a giant hardware store."

"Well, I see that," said Drake.

"I must admit that the family seemed entirely harmonious," said Brant. "I met the sons at one time or another, singly and together, and they seemed fine young men, much at ease with one another, and obviously fond of their father. What with one thing and another, I reached the stage where it seemed to them appropriate to invite me to the festivities celebrating the old man's eightieth birthday. It was on that occasion that Hunzinger had the heart attack that carried him off. It was not entirely unexpected. He'd had a heart condition for years, but it was totally unfortunate for it to happen on his birthday.

"The party broke up, of course. He was laid, gently, on the nearest couch and doctors were called in. There was a kind of hushed pandemonium. The confusion was sufficient for me to be able to stay on. It may sound ghoulish, but I conceived myself to have a job to do. He had not yet assigned any son to be the head of the firm. It was too late to have anything in writing; but if he would say something, it might have some force.

"The sons, I suppose, did not know what I had in mind. They were there, of course. Their mother, half in shock, had been led away. No one seemed to notice I was present. I leaned across to the old man's ear and said,

'Which of your sons is to be the head of the firm, Mr. Hunzinger?'

"It was too late. His eyes were closed, his breathing was stertorous. I wondered if he had heard me. A doctor approached and I knew he would stop me, so I tried again quickly. This time, the dying man's eyelids fluttered, and his lips moved as though he were trying to speak. However, only one sound came out. It seemed to be the word 'to.' I heard nothing else. He lingered on for another hour but never said another word, and died, without regaining consciousness, on the couch on which he had been laid. —And that's it."

Gonzalo said, "What happened to the business?"

"Nothing," said Brant, with what seemed the residuum of a vast surprise. "The old man was right. The three sons get along famously. It's a sort of triumvirate. When a decision must be made, they get together and come to one quickly. It's really an amazing thing and if that sort of thing should become infectious, lawyers would all starve to death."

"Then it doesn't matter what the old man said, does it?" said Gonzalo.

"Not in the least, except that for a while it roused my curiosity. What was he trying to say? You see the difficulty, I suppose?"

"Of course," said Drake, fingering his small gray mustache. "You can't do much with the word 'to.'"

"It's worse than that," said Brant. "Which homonym? Was it *t-o*, or *t-o-o*, or *t-w-o*? There are *three* to's in the English language. Incidentally, how do you write that last sentence? I've often wondered. You can *say* 'three to's,' since all three are pronounced alike, but how do you write it, since each one of the homonyms is spelled differently?"

Avalon said, "I would say, 'There are three words pronounced *t-o-o*.' The double-*o* is the most unambiguous way of indicating the pronunciation that all three share, and you spell it out."

"Well, in any case, even if I knew which *t-o-o* it was, it wouldn't help me."

Trumbull said, "Might it not have been a word, Nick? Suppose he was saying a longer word such as 'constitution.' That's four syllables, and he managed to sound only the third. All you'd have would be *t-o-o*."

"Maybe," said Brant. "I can't prove that that's not so. Just the same, at the time, I got the impression that it was a word, one of the three *t-o-o*'s, however you want to spell it. I suppose I was desperately trying to read his lips and he might have said 'Headship to so-and-so' and all I got was the 'to.' Which leaves me with nothing. Of course, as I said, it doesn't matter. The sons are doing well. Still—"

Brant shook his head. "I'm a lawyer. It bothers me that I came so close to having it done *right*. Even if he was refusing to choose anyone. Even if he was saying 'Not to anyone,' he would have been expressing his last wish and that would have been better than just falling into a situation by default. So for a while I kept wondering, and now you've put it back in my head, and I'll keep on wondering for another while. —And getting nowhere because there's nowhere to be gotten."

A heavy silence descended about the table, one which was finally broken by Gonzalo, who said, "At least it's an interesting version of the game of homonyms. Which of the soundalikes was it?"

Trumbull said, "What's the difference? Not one of the three would help us make sense of what the old man was trying to say."

"I told you," said Brant glumly. "It's an insoluble problem. There just isn't enough information."

"We don't have to *solve* it," said Halsted, "since there's no crisis that has to be eased, or criminal on whom we must visit retribution. All we have to do is point out a reasonable possibility to ease your mind. For instance, suppose he was saying *t-w-o.*"

"Well, suppose he was," said Avalon.

"Then it may be that he was saying something like, 'Give it to son number two.'"

Brant shook his head and said, "The impression I got was that the *t-o* I heard was in the middle of the message. His lips moved before and after I heard the *t-o.*"

Rubin said, "I'm not sure you can go by that. His lips were scarcely under control. Some of what appeared to be movement might have been only trembling."

"Which makes it all the worse," said Brant.

"Now wait awhile," said Halsted. "My idea works even with the word in the middle of the message. It could have been something like 'Give it to number two son,' or 'Number two son gets it.'"

Trumbull growled, "Charlie Chan might say it, but was Hunzinger likely to do so? —Al, did you ever hear this man refer to his children by number?"

"No," said Brant. "I don't think I ever did."

"Well, then," said Trumbull, "why on earth should he start doing so on his deathbed?"

"I wonder," said Rubin. "Consider this. His second son is named Mark, which is also the name of the writer of the second gospel. His third son is named Luke, which

is the name of the writer of the third gospel. I'll bet that
if he had had a fourth son, that son's name would have
been John."

"What's the good of a bet like that?" said Gonzalo. "We
can't ever settle it and decide on a winner."

"Why wasn't the first son's name Matthew, then?"
asked Avalon.

Rubin said, "Maybe old Hunzinger didn't think of it
till after the first son was born. Maybe he simply didn't
like 'Matthew.' Anyway, it strikes me that if the word
was t-w-o, it would have a double meaning. It would refer
to the second son *and* the second gospel, and it would
mean Mark in either case."

Trumbull said, "There could be a million reasons why
the number two might point to Mark, but put them all
together and they wouldn't be any more likely to get him
to refer to 'my number two son' than just one reason
would. Why wouldn't he just say 'Mark,' if he meant
Mark?"

Brant said, "Well, he might have said 'to Mark' at that,
and all I heard was 'to.'"

Avalon said, "Mr. Brant, I wonder if you at any time
noted that old Mr. Hunzinger trusted one of his sons
more than another, valued more highly the business acumen of a particular son, loved one more."

Brant bent his head in thought. Then he shook it. "I
can't say I did. I have no recollection of anything of the
sort. Of course, as I said, my relationship with the family
was not a matter of warm personal friendship. It was
business, entirely. The old man never confided family
matters beyond anything that was relevant to the will."

Gonzalo said, "We keep talking about the sons. How
do you know the old man didn't give some thought to his

daughter? Suppose he left the business to his three sons, in thirds, but wanted his daughter to make crucial decisions. He might have thought she had the best business sense and should run the show even though she wouldn't want to be connected with the business in any open way."

"What gives you that idea, Mario?" asked Avalon.

"Suppose the word was *t-o-o*. He might have been saying, 'My daughter, too, should be involved.' Something like that."

"I don't think so," said Brant. "Mr. Hunzinger never mentioned his daughter in connection with the business. Remember, too, that his prejudices are pre–World War I, when women couldn't even vote. In no way was he a feminist. His wife was strictly a homebody, and that's the way he liked it. He took care to have his daughter marry a rich man, and as far as he was concerned, that was the limit of his responsibility toward her. At least, I am forced to that conclusion as I think of our various discussions of the will."

Again there fell a silence around the table, and finally Avalon said, with a rather theatrical sigh, "It doesn't matter what hypotheses we set forward. No matter how clever and ingenious they might be, there's no way in which we can show that they are true. I'm afraid that this once we have to decide that our guest is correct and that the problem, by its very nature, is insoluble."

Gonzalo said, "Not until we ask Henry."

"Henry?" said Brant in surprise. His voice dropped to a whisper. "Do you mean the waiter?"

Trumbull said, "No need to whisper, Nick. He's a member of the club."

"So I'll ask him," said Gonzalo. "Henry, do you have any ideas about this?"

From his place at the sideboard, Henry smiled very slightly and said, "I must admit, Mr. Gonzalo, that I've been wondering what the first name of the eldest son might be."

Gonzalo said, "Frank. Don't you remember?"

"I beg your pardon, Mr. Gonzalo, but I seem to recall the oldest son is B. Franklin Hunzinger. I wondered what the *B* stood for."

All eyes turned to Brant, who shrugged and said, "He's identified as B. Franklin even in his father's will. That's the legal form of his signature. I always assumed, however, that the *B* stood for Benjamin."

"It's a natural assumption," said Henry. "Any American named B. Franklin, it would seem, would be bound to be a Benjamin. But did you ever hear any member of the family—or anyone, for that matter—address him as Benjamin or Ben?"

Slowly, Brant shook his head. "I don't recall any such incident, but it was over twenty years ago and I was not really part of the family circle."

"Or since the death of the elder Hunzinger?"

"Oh, well, I've rarely had any contact with them at all since then, not even with respect to legal matters."

Trumbull said, "What's all this about, Henry?"

"Why, it occurred to me that there are, in a manner of speaking, four homonyms with the sound *t-o-o.*"

Avalon said in an astonished voice, "Four? You mean that one of the homonyms has two meanings of unrelated derivation, as in the case of *b-e-a-r?*"

"No, Mr. Avalon. I am referring to four homonyms with four different spellings."

Avalon thought briefly. "Impossible, Henry. Manny, can you think of a fourth homonym beyond *t-o*, *t-o-o*, and *t-w-o?*"

"No," said Rubin flatly, "there is no fourth homonym."

Henry said, "I said 'in a manner of speaking.' It all depends on the first name of B. Franklin."

Drake said, "Henry, you're being mysterious and you've got us all confused. Now *explain.*"

"Yes, Dr. Drake. Mr. Brant had said that the elder Hunzinger was self-educated, and he had indicated that he was particularly interested in Roman history. He raised his children in what he thought was the Roman tradition. He used terms such as 'paterfamilias,' and so on. And he gave his children traditional Roman names. His daughter he named Claudia; one son is Mark, from the Roman Marcus; another is Luke from the Roman Lucius.

"It is possible, in fact, that the original names were indeed Marcus and Lucius, and that the youngsters found Mark and Luke more palatable to their peers. Now what if the eldest had a Roman name also, which had no common Anglicized form? He might not have used it at all, but stayed with Franklin, which becomes the very common and acceptable Frank.

"One common Roman name beginning with *B* is Brutus, and that has no Anglicized form that is likely to be acceptable."

"Aha," said Rubin.

"Yes, Mr. Rubin," said Henry. "If the elder Mr. Hunzinger had picked up scraps of Latin, undoubtedly Julius Caesar's last words, one of the most famous of all Latin phrases, would be known to him. It contains the word 'tu,' which is Latin for the familiar form of 'you,' and is so well known among educated English-speaking people —if only from this phrase—that it might almost rank as a fourth homonym.

"Asked about which of his sons should head the firm, the dying man thought of the oldest, remembered the name he had given him as a child, and may have said something like 'all my sons share, and you, Brutus, will lead.' The phrase 'and you, Brutus' becomes the muttered Caesarian exclamation of 'et tu, Brute,' and only the 'tu' was loud enough to hear."

"Good God," muttered Brant, "who could possibly think of something like that?"

"But it's *most* ingenious," said Avalon. "I hope you're right, Henry. I'd hate to see that reasoning wasted. I suppose we could call Hunzinger and try to persuade him to give us his first name."

Gonzalo said excitedly, "Wait, Jeff, wouldn't it be in *Who's Who in America?* They usually include businessmen."

Avalon said, "They might well have only the legal version of his name—B. Franklin Hunzinger. Of course, they sometimes include the name beyond the period in parentheses to indicate it exists but is not to be used."

"Let's see," said Gonzalo. He took down the first volume of the tome and for a few moments there was the sound of flipping pages. Then it stopped and Gonzalo cried out in triumph, "Brutus Franklin Hunzinger, the *r-u-t-u-s* in parentheses."

Brant buried his head in his hands. "Twenty years, on and off, this has bothered me, and if I had looked him up in *Who's Who*— But why would it occur to me to look him up?" He shook his head. "I must tell them. They will have to know."

Henry said, "I don't think that would be wise, Mr. Brant. They get along well as it is, but if they find out that their father had chosen one of them to head the firm —which even as it is we can't be *certain* of—bad feelings might break out. Surely one shouldn't attempt to fix what isn't broken."

AFTERWORD

A number of my Black Widowers puzzles depend on the vagaries of the English language. I can't help this because I have a great interest in and admiration for the language.

I must admit, though, that I am uneasily aware that whenever too much depends on English, I throw barriers in the way of translators and may diminish my chances of getting foreign editions. It's not just that foreign editions bring in money (it is well-known that my character is entirely too refined and noble for me to be interested in money), but that they introduce my work to audiences that would otherwise be unable to read me. And being widely read *does* interest me.

However, I must admit that when a point of language strikes me as being a useful gimmick, as in the story you have just read, I can never resist.

The story first appeared in the March 1985 issue of *Ellery Queen's Mystery Magazine*.

UNIQUE IS WHERE YOU FIND IT

Emmanuel Rubin would have fought to the death rather than admit that the smile on his face was a fatuous one. It was, though. Try as he might, he could not conceal the pride in his voice or the pleased gleam in his eye.

"Fellow Widowers," he said, "now that even Tom Trumbull is here, let me introduce my guest of the evening. This is my nephew, Horace Rubin, eldest son of my younger brother and the shining light of the new generation."

Horace smiled weakly at this. He was a full head taller than his uncle and a bit thinner. He had dark, crisply curled hair, a prominent, well-beaked nose, and a wide mouth. He was definitely not handsome and Mario Gonzalo, the artist of the Black Widowers, was fighting hard not to exaggerate the features. Photographic accuracy was caricature enough. What didn't get into the drawing, of course, was the unmistakable light of quick intelligence in the young man's eyes.

"My nephew," said Rubin, "is working toward his Ph.D. at Columbia. In chemistry. And he's doing it now, Jim, not in 1900 as you did."

James Drake, the only Black Widower with a legitimate doctorate (although all were entitled to be addressed as "Doctor" by the club rules), said, "Good for him—and my own degree was earned just before the war; World War II, that is." He smiled reminiscently through the thin column of smoke curling upward from his cigarette.

Thomas Trumbull, who had, as usual, arrived at the preprandial cocktail hour late, scowled over his drink and said, "Am I dreaming, Manny, or is it customary to elicit these details during the grilling session after dinner? Why are you jumping the gun?" He waved his hand petulantly at the cigarette smoke, and stepped away from Drake in a marked manner.

"Just laying the foundation," said Rubin indignantly. "What I expect you to grill Horace about is the subject of his coming dissertation. There's no reason the Black Widowers can't gain a little education."

Gonzalo said, "Are you going to make us laugh, Manny, by telling us you understand what your nephew is doing in his laboratory?"

Rubin's scanty beard bristled. "I understand a lot more about chemistry than you think."

"You're bound to, because I think you understand zero." Gonzalo turned to Roger Halsted and said, "I happen to know that Manny majored in Babylonian pottery at some correspondence college."

"Not true," said Rubin, "but still a step above your major in beer and pretzels."

Geoffrey Avalon, who listened with disdain to this exchange, detached his attention, and said to the young student, "How old are you, Mr. Rubin?"

"You'd better call me Horace," said the young man, in an unexpected baritone, "or Uncle Manny will answer and I'll never get a word in edgewise."

Avalon smiled grimly. "He is indeed our conversational monopolist when we allow him to be. But how old are you, Horace?"

"Twenty-two, sir."

"Isn't that rather on the young side for a doctoral candidate, or are you just beginning?"

"No. I should be starting my dissertation about now and I expect to be through in half a year. I'm rather young, but not unusually so. Robert Woodward got his Ph.D. in chemistry when he was twenty. Of course, he nearly got kicked out of school at seventeen."

"Twenty-two isn't bad, though."

"I'll be twenty-three next month. I'll be getting it at that age—or never." He shrugged and looked despondent.

The soft voice of Henry, the perennial and irreplaceable waiter at all the Black Widower banquets, made itself heard. "Gentlemen, dinner is served. We are going to have curried lamb and our chef, I'm afraid, believes that curry was made to be tasted, so if any of you would prefer something rather on the blander side, tell me now and I will see to it that you are obliged."

Halsted said, "If any faint-heart would rather have scrambled eggs, Henry, just bring me his helping of curried lamb in addition to my own. We must not waste it."

Unique Is Where You Find It 27

"Nor must we contribute to your overweight problem, Roger," growled Trumbull. "We'll all have the curry, Henry, and bring in the accompanying condiments, especially the chutney and coconut. I intend to be heavy-handed myself."

"And keep the bicarbonate handy, too, Henry," said Gonzalo. "Tom's eyes are more optimistic than his stomach lining is."

Henry was serving the brandy when Rubin clattered his spoon against the water glass and said, "To business, gentlemen, to business. My nephew, I have observed, has wreaked havoc on the comestibles and it is time that he be made to pay for that in the grilling session. —Jim, you'd be the natural grill-master, since you're a chemist of sorts yourself, but I don't want you and Horace to get into a private discussion of chemical minutiae. Roger, you're a mere mathematician, which puts you sufficiently off the mark. Would you do the honors?"

"Gladly," said Halsted, sipping gently at his curaçao. "Young Rubin—or Horace, if you prefer—how do you justify your existence?"

Horace said, "Once I get my degree and find myself a position on a decent faculty, I'm sure that the work I do will be ample justification. Otherwise—" He shrugged.

"You seem doubtful, young man. Do you expect to have trouble finding a job?"

"It's not something one can be certain about, sir, but I've been interviewed here and there, and, if all goes well, it seems to me that something desirable should solidify."

"If all goes well, you say. Is there some hitch in your research?"

"No, not at all. I had enough good sense to pick a fail-safe problem. Yes, no, or maybe—any of the three possible answers—would earn me a degree. As it happens, the answer is yes, which is the best of the alternatives, and I consider myself set."

Drake said suddenly, "Whom are you working for, Horace?"

"Dr. Kendall, sir."

"The kinetics man?"

"Yes, sir. I'm working on the kinetics of DNA replication. It's not something to which physical chemical techniques have hitherto been rigorously applied, and I am now able to build computerized graphics of the process, which—"

Halsted interrupted. "We'll get to that, Horace. Later. For now, I'm still trying to find out what's bugging you. You have the prospect of a job. Your research has gone well. What about your coursework?"

"Never any problem there. Except—"

Halsted endured the pause for a moment, then said, "Except what?"

"I wasn't that good in my lab courses. Especially organic lab. I'm not . . . deft. I'm a theoretician."

"Did you fail?"

"No, of course not. I just didn't cover myself with glory."

"Well, then, what *is* bugging you? During dinner I overheard you tell Jeff that you'd be getting your Ph.D. when you're twenty-three—or never. Why never? Where does that possibility come in?

The young man hesitated. "It's not the sort of thing—"

Rubin, clearly flustered, frowned and said, "Horace, you've never told *me* you were having problems."

Horace looked about as though searching for some hole through which he could crawl. "Well, Uncle Manny, you've got *your* troubles and you don't come to *me* with them. I'll fight this out on my own—or not."

"Fight *what* out?" said Rubin, his voice growing louder.

"It's not the sort of thing—" began Horace again.

"Number one," said Rubin vigorously, "anything you say here is completely, *totally* confidential. Number two, I told you that at the grilling session you would be expected to answer all questions. Number three, if you don't stop playing games, I'll kick your behind into raspberry gelatin."

Horace sighed. "Yes, Uncle Manny. —I just want to say," he looked about the table, "that he's threatened me like this since I was two and he's never laid a hand on me. My mother would take him apart if he did."

"There's always a first time, and I'm not afraid of your mother. I can handle *her*," said Rubin.

"Yes, Uncle Manny. —All right, then. My problem is Professor Richard Youngerlea."

"Uh-oh," said Drake softly.

"Do you know him, Dr. Drake?"

"Well, yes."

"Is he a friend of yours?"

"Well, no. He's a good chemist but, as a matter of fact, I despise him."

Horace's homely face broke into a wide smile, and he said, "Then I can speak freely?"

"You could anyway," said Drake.

"Here it is," said Horace. "I'm sure Youngerlea is going to be on my examining board. He wouldn't miss the chance and he swings enough weight to get on if he wants to."

Avalon said in his deep voice, "I take it, Horace, that you dislike him."

"Very much," said Horace in a heartfelt voice.

"And I imagine he dislikes you."

"I'm afraid so. I had my organic lab under him and, as I said, I didn't shine."

Avalon said, "I imagine a certain number of students don't shine. Does he dislike them all?"

"Well, he doesn't *like* them."

"I gather you suspect that he wants to be on your examining board in order to cut you down. Is that the way he reacts to every student who doesn't shine in his laboratory?"

"Well, he does seem to think that lab work is motherhood and apple pandowdy and everything that's good and noble, but no, it's not just that I didn't shine."

"Well, then," said Halsted, taking over the grilling again, "we're getting to it. I teach in a junior high school and I know all about obnoxious students. I am sure that the professor found *you* obnoxious. —In what way?"

Horace frowned. "I am *not* obnoxious. Youngerlea is. Look, he's a bully. There are always some teachers who take advantage of the fact that they are in an unassailable position. They excoriate students; they brutalize them verbally; they hold them up to ridicule. They do this although they know full well that the students are reluctant to defend themselves for fear of getting a poor mark. Who's to argue with Youngerlea if he hands out a C, or, for that matter, an F? Who's to argue with him if he expresses his very influential opinion at a faculty conference that such and such a student doesn't have what it takes to make a good chemist?"

"Did he hold *you* up to ridicule?" asked Halsted.

"He held *everybody* up to ridicule. There was one poor guy who was British, and when he referred to aluminum chloride, which is used as a catalyst in the Friedel-Crafts reaction, he referred to it as 'aluminium' chloride, with the accent on the third syllable and the first *u* as 'yoo' instead of 'oo.' It was just the British pronunciation, after all, but Youngerlea chewed him out. He denounced all this crap—his expression—of having an unnecessary extra syllable, five instead of four, and so on, and the stupidity of making any chemical name longer than necessary, and so on. It was *nothing* and yet he *humiliated* the poor man, who didn't dare say a word in his own defense. And all the damned sycophants in the class laughed."

"So what makes you worse than the rest?"

Horace flushed, but there was a note of pride in his voice as he replied. "*I* answer back. When he starts on me, I don't just sit there and take it. In fact, I interrupted him in this aluminum-aluminium business. I said in a good, loud voice, 'The name of an element is a human convention, professor, and not a law of nature.' That stopped him, but he did say in his sneering way, 'Ah, Rubin, been dropping any beakers lately?' "

"And the class laughed, I suppose?" said Halsted.

"Sure they did, the pimple-heads. I dropped one beaker all course. One! And that was only because someone jostled me. —And then, once, I came across Youngerlea in the chem library looking up some compound in Beilstein—"

Gonzalo asked, "What's Beilstein?"

"It's a reference book of about seventy-five volumes, listing many thousands of organic compounds, with references to the work done on each, all of them listed in order according to some logical but very complicated system. Youngerlea had a couple of volumes on his desk and was leafing through first one, then the other. I was curious, and asked him what compound he was searching for. He told me and I was overcome with ecstasy when I realized he was looking in the wrong volumes altogether. I moved quietly to the Beilstein shelves, took down a volume, found the compound Youngerlea wanted—it took me thirty seconds—came back to his table, and put the volume in front of him, open to the correct page."

"I suppose he didn't thank you," said Drake.

"No, he didn't," said Horace, "but at that, he might have if I didn't have the world's biggest grin on my face. At the moment, though, I would rather have had my revenge than my Ph.D. —And that may be the way it will work out."

Rubin said, "I've never considered you the most tactful person in the world, Horace."

"No, Uncle Manny," said Horace sadly, "my mother says I take after you—but she only says that when she's really annoyed with me."

Even Avalon laughed at that, and Rubin muttered something under his breath.

Gonzalo said, "Well, what can he do to you? If your marks are all right, and your research is all right, and you do all right on the exam, they've *got* to pass you."

"It's not that easy, sir," said Horace. "In the first place, it's an oral exam and the pressures are intense. A guy like Youngerlea is a past master at intensifying the pressure, and he can just possibly reduce me to incoherence, or get me into a furious slanging match with him. Either way he can maintain I don't have the emotional stability to make a good chemist. He's a powerful figure in the department and he might swing the committee. Even if I pass and get my degree, he has enough influence in chemical circles to blackball me in some very important places."

There was silence around the table.

Drake said, "What are you going to do?"

"Well . . . I tried to make peace with the old bastard. I thought about it and thought about it, and finally asked for an appointment so that I could eat a little crow. I said I knew we had not gotten along, but that I hoped he didn't think I would make a bad chemist—that really, chemistry was my life—well, you know what I mean."

Drake nodded. "What did *he* say?"

"He enjoyed himself. He had me where he wanted me. He did his best to make me crawl; told me I was a wise guy with an ungovernable temper, and a few other things designed to make me go out of control. I held on, though, and said, 'But, granted I've got my peculiarities, would you say that necessarily makes me a bad chemist?'

"And he said, 'Well, let's see if you're a good chemist. I'm thinking of the name of a unique chemical element. You tell me what the element is, and why it's unique, and why I should think of it, and I'll admit you're a good chemist.'

"I said, 'But what would that have to do with my being a good chemist?' He said, 'The fact that you don't see that is a point against you. You ought to be able to reason it out, and reasoning is the prime tool of a chemist, or of any scientist. A person like you who talks about being a theoretical scientist and who therefore scorns little things like manual dexterity should have no trouble agreeing with this. Well, use your reason and tell me which element I am thinking of. You have one week from this moment; say, five P.M. next Monday; and you only have one chance. If your choice of element is wrong, there's no second guess.'

"I said, 'Professor Youngerlea, there are over a hundred elements. Are you going to give me any hints?'

" 'I already have,' he said. 'I told you it's unique, and that's all you're going to get.' And he gave me the same kind of grin I gave him at the time of the Beilstein incident."

Avalon said, "Well, young man, what happened the next Monday? Did you work out the problem?"

"It isn't next Monday yet, sir. That's coming three days from now, and I'm stuck. There's no possible way of answering. One element out of over a hundred, and the only hint is that it's unique."

Trumbull said, "Is the man honest? Granted that he is a bully and a rotter, do you suppose he is really thinking an element and that he'll accept a right answer from you? He wouldn't declare you wrong no matter what you say, would he, and then use that as a weapon against you?"

Horace made a face. "Well, I can't read his mind, but as a scientist, he's the real thing. He's actually a great chemist and, as far as I know, he's completely ethical in his profession. What's more, his papers are marvelously well written—concise, clear. He uses no jargon, never a long word when a shorter one will do, never a complicated sentence when a simpler one will do. You have to admire him for that. So if he asks a scientific question, I think he will be honest about it."

"And you're really stuck?" asked Halsted. "Nothing comes to you."

"On the contrary, a great deal comes to me, but too much is as bad as nothing. For instance, the first thought I had was that the element had to be hydrogen. It's the simplest atom, the lightest atom, atom number one. It's the only atom that has a nucleus made of a single particle —just a proton. It's the only atom with a nucleus that contains no neutrons, and *that* certainly makes it unique."

Drake said, "You're talking about hydrogen-1."

"That's *right,* " said Horace. "Hydrogen is found in nature in three varieties, or isotopes: hydrogen-1, hydrogen-2, and hydrogen-3. The nucleus of hydrogen-1 is just a proton, but hydrogen-2 has a nucleus composed of a proton and a neutron, and hydrogen-3 has one composed of a proton and two neutrons. Of course, almost all hydrogen atoms are hydrogen-1, but Youngerlea asked for an element, not an isotope, and if I say that the *element* hydrogen is the only one with a nucleus containing no neutrons, I'd be wrong. Just wrong."

Drake said, "It's still the lightest and simplest element."

"Sure, but that's so obvious. And there are other possibilities. Helium, which is element number two, is the most inert of all the elements. It has the lowest boiling point and doesn't freeze solid even at absolute zero. At very low temperatures, it becomes helium-II, which has properties like no other substance in the Universe."

"Does it come in different varieties?" asked Gonzalo.

"Two isotopes occur in nature, helium-3 and helium-4, but all those unique properties apply to both."

"Don't forget," said Drake, "that helium is the only

element to be discovered in space before being discovered on Earth."

"I know, sir. It was discovered in the Sun. Helium can be considered unique in a number of different ways, but it's so obvious too. I don't think Youngerlea would have anything obvious in mind."

Drake said, after blowing a smoke ring and regarding it with some satisfaction, "I suppose if you're ingenious enough, you can think up something unique about each element."

"Absolutely," said Horace, "and I think I've just about done it. For instance, lithium, which is element number three, is the least dense of all the metals. Cesium, element number fifty-five, is the most active of all the stable metals. Fluorine, element number nine, is the most active of all the nonmetals. Carbon, element number six, is the basis of all organic molecules, including those that make up living tissue. It is probably the only atom capable of playing such a role, so that it is the unique element of life."

"It seems to me," said Avalon, "that an element that is uniquely related to life is unique enough—"

"No," said Horace violently, "it's the answer least likely to be true. Youngerlea is an organic chemist, which means he deals with carbon compounds only. It would be impossibly obvious for him. Then there's mercury, element number eighty—"

Gonzalo said, "Do you know all the elements by number?"

"I didn't before last Monday. Since then, I've been poring over the list of elements. See?" He pulled a sheet of paper from his inside jacket pocket. "This is the periodic table of elements. I've just about memorized it."

Trumbull said, "But it doesn't help, I gather."

"Not so far. As I was saying, mercury, element number eighty, has the lowest melting point of any metal, so that it is the only metal that is a liquid at ordinary temperatures. That's certainly unique."

Rubin said, "Gold is the most beautiful element, if you want to get into aesthetics, and is the most valued."

"Gold is element number seventy-nine," said Horace. "It's possible to argue, though, that it's neither the most beautiful nor the most valued. Many people would say a properly cut diamond is more beautiful than gold, and, weight for weight, it would certainly be worth more money—and a diamond is pure carbon.

"The densest metal is osmium, element number seventy-six, and the least active metal is iridium, element number seventy-seven. The highest melting metal is tungsten, element number seventy-four, and the most magnetic metal is iron, element number twenty-six. Technetium, element number forty-three, is the lightest element that has no stable isotopes. It is radioactive in all its varieties, and it is the first element to be produced in the laboratory. Uranium, element number ninety-two, is the most complicated atom to occur in substantial quantities in the Earth's crust. Iodine, element number fifty-three, is the most complicated of those elements essential to human life, while bismuth, element number eighty-three, is the most complicated element that has at least one isotope that is stable and not radioactive.

"You can go on and on and on and, as Dr. Drake said, if you're ingenious enough, you can tag each and every element with a unique characteristic. The trouble is that there's nothing to say which one Youngerlea is thinking of, which uniqueness is *his* uniqueness, and if I don't come up with the right something, he's going to say that that proves I don't have the capacity to think clearly."

Drake said, "If we put our minds together right now—"

Trumbull interrupted, "Would that be legitimate? If the young man gets the answer from others—"

"What are the rules of the game, Horace?" Avalon said. "Did Professor Youngerlea tell you that you could not consult anyone else?"

Horace shook his head emphatically. "Nothing was said about that. I've been using this periodic table. I've been using reference books. I see no reason why I can't ask other human beings. Books are just the words of human beings, words that have been frozen into print. Besides, whatever you may suggest, it's I who will have to decide whether the suggestion is good or bad, and take the risk on the basis of that decision of mine. —But will you be able to help me?"

"We might," said Drake. "If Youngerlea is an honest scientist, he wouldn't give you a problem that contains within it no possibility of reaching a solution. There must be some way of reasoning out an answer. After all, if you can't solve the problem, you could challenge him to give you the right answer. If he can't do that, or if he makes use of an obviously ridiculous path of reasoning, you could complain loudly to everyone in the school. *I* would."

"I'm willing to try, then. Is there anyone here, besides Dr. Drake, who is a chemist?"

Rubin said, "You don't have to be a professional chemist at the Ph.D. level to know something about the elements."

"All right, Uncle Manny," said Horace. "What's the answer, then?"

Rubin said, "Personally, I'm stuck on carbon. It's *the* chemical of life and, in the form of diamond, it has another type of uniqueness. Is there any other element that, in its pure form, has an unusual aspect—"

"Allotrope it's called, Uncle."

"Don't fling your jargon at me, pip-squeak. Is there any other element that has an allotrope as unusual as diamond?"

"No. And aside from human judgments concerning its beauty and value, the diamond happens to be the hardest substance in existence, under normal conditions."

"Well, then?"

"I've already said that it's too obvious for an organic chemist to set up carbon as a solution to the problem."

"Sure," said Rubin. "He chose the obvious because he thinks you'll dismiss it *because* it's obvious."

"There speaks the mystery writer," grumbled Trumbull.

"Just the same, I reject that solution," said Horace. "You can advise me, any of you, but I'm the one to make the decision to accept or reject. Any other ideas?"

There was complete silence about the table.

"In that case," said Horace, "I'd better tell you one of my thoughts. I'm getting desperate, you see. Youngerlea said, 'I'm thinking of the name of a unique chemical element.' He didn't say he was thinking of the element, but of the *name* of the element."

"Are you sure you remember that correctly?" said Avalon. "You didn't tape the conversation, and memory can be a tricky thing."

"No, no. I remember it clearly. I'm not the least uncertain. Not the least. —So yesterday I got to thinking that it's not the physical or chemical properties of the element that count. That's just a red herring. It's the *name* that counts."

"Have you got a unique name?" asked Halsted.

"Unfortunately," said Horace, "the names give you as much oversupply as the properties of the elements do. If you consider an alphabetical listing of the elements, actinium, element number eighty-nine, is first on the list, and zirconium, element number forty, is the last on the list. Dysprosium, which is element number sixty-six, is the only element with a name that begins with a *D*. Krypton, element number thirty-six, is the only one with a name that begins with a *K*. Uranium, Vanadium, and Xenon, which are elements numbers ninety-two, twenty-three, and fifty-four, respectively, are the only elements to begin with a *U*, *V*, or *X*. How do I choose among these five? *U* is the only vowel, but that seems weak."

Gonzalo said, "Is there any letter that doesn't start the name of any element at all?"

"Three. There is no element that starts with *J*, *Q*, or *W* —but what good is that? You can't claim an element is unique just because it doesn't exist. You can argue that there are an infinite number of elements that don't exist."

Drake said, "Mercury has, as an alternative name, 'quicksilver.' That starts with a *Q*."

"I know, but that's feeble," said Horace. "In German, *I* and *J* are not distinguished in print. The chemical symbol of iodine is *I*, but I've seen German papers in Latin print, in which the symbol of the element is given as *J*, but that's even feebler.

"Speaking of the chemical symbols, there are thirteen

elements with symbols that are single letters. Almost always that letter is the initial of the name of the element. Thus, carbon has the symbol C; oxygen, O; nitrogen, N; phosphorus, P; sulfur, S; and so on. However, the element potassium has the symbol K."

"Why?" asked Gonzalo.

"Because that's the initial of the German name, *Kalium*. If potassium were the only case, I might consider it, but tungsten has the symbol W, for the German name, *Wolfram*, so neither is unique. Strontium has a name that starts with three consonants, but so do chlorine and chromium. Iodine has a name that starts with two vowels, but so do einsteinium and europium. I'm stopped at every turn."

Gonzalo said, "is there anything about the spelling of the element names that is the same in almost all of them?"

"Almost all of them end in *ium.*"

"Really?" said Gonzalo, snapping his fingers in an agony of thought. "How about the element the British pronounce differently. They call it 'aluminium' with the *ium* ending, but we say 'aluminum' so that it has only a *um* ending, and the professor made a fuss about it. Maybe it's aluminum that's unique, then."

"A good thought," said Horace, "but there's lanthanum, molybdenum, and platinum, each with a *um* ending. There are also endings of *ine, en,* and *'on',* but always more than one of each. Nothing unique. Nothing unique."

Avalon said, "And yet there must be something!"

"Then tell me what it is. Rhenium was the last stable element to be discovered in nature; promethium is the only radioactive rare earth metal; gadolinium is the only stable element to be named after a human being. Nothing works. Nothing is convincing."

Horace shook his head dolefully. "Well, it's not the end of the world. I'll go to Youngerlea with my best guess and, if that's wrong, let him do his worst. If I write a crackerjack dissertation, it may be so good they couldn't possibly flunk me, and if Youngerlea keeps me from getting a place at Cal Tech or M.I.T., I'll get in somewhere else and work my way up. I'm not going to let him stop me."

Drake nodded. "That's the right attitude, son."

Henry said softly, "Mr. Rubin?"

Rubin said, "Yes, Henry."

"I beg your pardon, sir. I was addressing your nephew, the younger Mr. Rubin."

Horace looked up. "Yes, waiter. Is there something else to order?"

"No, sir. I wonder if I might discuss the matter of the unique element."

Horace frowned, then said, "Are you a chemist, waiter?"

Gonzalo said, "He's not a chemist, but he's Henry and you had better listen to him. He's brighter than anyone in the room."

"Mr. Gonzalo," said Henry, in soft deprecation.

"It's so, Henry," insisted Gonzalo. "Go ahead. What do you have to say?"

"Only that in weighing a question that seems to have no answer, it might help to consider the person asking the question. Perhaps Professor Youngerlea has some quirk that would lead him to attach some importance to a particular uniqueness, which, to others, might be barely noticed."

"You mean," said Halsted, "uniqueness is where you find it?"

"Exactly," said Henry, "as is almost everything that allows for an element of human judgment. If we consider Professor Youngerlea, we know this about him. He uses the English language carefully and concisely. He does not use a complicated sentence when a simpler one will do, or a long word where a shorter word will do. What's more, he was furious with a student for using a perfectly acceptable name for aluminum, but a name which added a letter and a syllable. Am I correct in all this, Mr. Rubin?"

"Yes," said Horace, "I've said all that."

"Well, then, on the club's reference shelf, there is the World Almanac, which lists all the elements, and we have the Unabridged, of course, which gives the pronunciations. I've taken the liberty of studying the material during the course of the discussion that has been taking place."

"And?"

"It occurs to me that the element praseodymium, which is number fifty-nine, is uniquely designed to rouse Professor Youngerlea's ire. Praseodymium is the only name with six syllables. All other names have five syllables or less. Surely, to Professor Youngerlea, praseodymium is bound to seem unbearably long and unwieldy; the most irritating name in all the list, and unique in that respect. If he had to use that element in his work, he would probably complain loudly and at length, and there would be no mistake in the matter. Perhaps, though, he does not use the element?"

Horace's eyes were gleaming. "No, it's a rare earth element and I doubt that Youngerlea, as an organic chemist, has ever had to refer to it. That *would* be the only reason we haven't heard him on the subject. But you're right, Henry. Its mere existence would be a constant irritant to him. I accept that suggestion, and I'll go to him with it on Monday. If it's wrong, it's wrong. But"—and he was suddenly jubilant—"I'll bet it's right. I'll bet *anything* it's right."

"If it should be wrong," said Henry, "I trust you will keep your resolve to work your way through in any case."

"Don't worry, I will, but praseodymium is the answer. I know it is. —However, I wish I had gotten it on my own, Henry. *You* got it."

"That's a small item, sir," said Henry, smiling paternally. "You were considering names and, in a very short time, I'm sure the oddity of praseodymium would have struck you. I got to it first only because your labors had already eliminated so many false trails."

AFTERWORD

"Unique Is Where You Find It" and the following story, "The Lucky Piece," were both written, by request, for a magazine that was to be devoted to mystery short stories. Both stories were paid for generously, and then, as sometimes happens in publishing, something went wrong and the magazine never appeared.

I therefore placed "Unique Is Where You Find It" in a collection containing both my science fiction and my science essays in alternation (thus encouraging readers to read both and, if they were only acquainted with me in one of my incarnations, to rush out and buy the other with mad abandon). "Unique Is Where You Find It" represented the only brand-new item in the book, which is entitled *The Edge of Tomorrow* and was published by Tor Books in 1985.

This is one of the not-so-rare cases where something in the story is based on an actual event in my life. When I was in graduate school, I had a professor much like Youngerlea, and my own reaction to him was very much like Horace Rubin's. The Beilstein incident, described in the story, really happened exactly as described and I really seized the opportunity to humiliate the professor even at the risk of damage to my grades and considered the opportunity well worth the risk.

THE LUCKY PIECE

"Mr. Silverstein," said Thomas Trumbull, "how do you justify your existence?"

Albert Silverstein was the guest of James Drake at that month's banquet of the Black Widowers. He was a rather shriveled-looking gentleman, small of body, with a good-natured, gnomelike face, a tanned complexion to the bald dome of his head, and an easy smile.

He was smiling now as he said, "I suppose you might say that I add to the feeling of security of many people."

"Indeed?" said Trumbull, creasing his own tanned forehead into a washboard effect. "And how do you do that?"

"Well," said Silverstein, "I own a chain of novelty stores—perfectly innocent novelties, you understand, though some tend to be in questionable taste—"

Mario Gonzalo straightened his delicately striped

jacket and said, with a touch of sarcasm, "Like the clay representations of dog excrement that you carefully place on your host's living-room carpet when you've brought your hound with you on a visit?"

Silverstein laughed. "No, we've never handled that. However, one popular item in my father's time was the upset ink bottle and the apparently spreading ink stain in hard rubber that you put on your friend's best tablecloth. Of course, the coming of the ballpoint pen wiped out ink bottles *and* that particular novelty. Our industry has to keep up with technological change."

"Where does the feeling of security come in?" asked Trumbull doggedly.

"The point there is that one of our biggest perennials is the sale of lucky pieces—like this one." He reached into his jacket pocket and withdrew a small plastic square. Embedded in it was a four-leaf clover. "One of our steady sellers," he said. "We sell thousands each year."

Geoffrey Avalon, who sat next to Silverstein, took the object from him and stared at it with a mixture of puzzlement and contempt on his stiffly aristocratic face. He said disapprovingly, "Do you really mean that thousands of people believe that a clover mutation will affect the Universe in their favor, and are willing to pay money for something like this?"

"Of course," said Silverstein cheerfully. "Thousands every year, year in and year out. These days, of course, they hesitate to admit their superstition. They buy it for their children, supposedly, or as a gift, or as a curio, but they buy it and hang it up in their car or keep it on their key ring. That thing sells for up to five dollars."

"That's revolting," said Trumbull. "You make money out of their folly."

Silverstein's smile vanished. "Not at all," he said seriously. "It is not that object I sell, but a feeling of security, as I said, and that is a very valuable commodity which I sell for far less than it is worth. For as long as someone owns that four-leaf clover, a weight of fear is lifted from his or her mind and soul. There is less fear of crossing the street, of encountering a mugger, of hearing bad news. There is less concern if it should happen that a black cat ran across one's path, or if one should carelessly walk beneath a ladder."

"But the sense of security they get is a false one."

"It is *not*, sir. The sense of security they experience is very real. The *cause* may be unreal, but it brings the desired result. Consider, too, that most fears that people have are unreal in the sense that they do not tend to happen. You do *not* get mugged every time you take a walk. You do *not* get bad news every time you pick up a letter. You do *not* break a leg every time you fall. Misadventures are, in fact, quite rare. If my lucky pieces remove, or at least lessen, these unnecessary fears, and lighten the load of apprehension each of us carries about, then I perform a useful service. The price of that four-leaf clover, which will soothe you for as long as you own it, would buy you only five minutes or less of a psychiatrist's time."

Roger Halsted was now regarding the lucky piece. As he passed it to Emmanuel Rubin, he said, "Where do you find thousands of four-leaf clovers every year? Do you pay an army of assistants to comb the clover patches of the world?"

"Of course not," said Silverstein. "That thing would

cost a couple of thousand dollars if I had to pay an army, and I doubt that anyone would be superstitious enough to submit to that kind of financial sacrifice. What those are—" He paused, and said, "Jim Drake told me that everything said at these meetings was strictly under the rose."

"Absolutely, Al," said Drake in his softly hoarse cigarette voice.

Silverstein's eyes drifted to the waiter and Halsted intervened quickly. "Our waiter, Henry, is a member of the Black Widowers, sir, and as quiet about anything he hears as a mummy would be."

"In that case," said Silverstein, "four three-leaf clovers, which are almost as common as sand grains, make three four-leaf clovers. What you're holding is a three-leaf clover with an added leaf held in place by the plastic. You'll see the join-point under a magnifying glass, but no one has ever returned it on that account."

"What if someone did?" asked Gonzalo.

"We'd explain that sometimes a leaf breaks off in the plastic-embedding process, and give him his money back."

"But this is fraud," said Trumbull violently. "You're not really selling them lucky pieces."

Silverstein said, "Think of what you're saying, Mr. Trumbull. There are no lucky pieces outside the mind of the owner. A four-leaf clover does not really bring luck, and a three-leaf clover, with a fourth leaf added, can do no worse. If the owner *believes* it to be a lucky piece, that is all that counts.

"We can argue similarly," he went on, "for the aluminum horseshoes we sell, and the cat's-fur rabbit's feet, and the cheap rings with lover's knots twined around them, which are *said* to insure the fidelity of a loved one. We never guarantee anything, or say that anything *will* do something. Nothing can stop us, however, from saying that something is *said* to do something, because that's true.

"One big item in my grandfather's day was a cheap brass coin with a swastika on it and the words 'Good Luck' on the other side. The swastika was a good luck symbol since ancient times, you know. My grandfather stopped selling them in 1928, however, for obvious reasons. The industry has to keep up with social change, too, and I suppose the swastika will never again be used as a good luck symbol."

For a moment there was silence in the room and Silverstein's generally sunny expression turned solemn and unhappy. —But then he shrugged and said, "Well, we can only hope that nothing like that ever happens again. —And meanwhile, I am reminded of a peculiar example of the force of a good luck piece. I'm not referring to its force as a bringer of good luck, but it's force in inspiring belief. However, I mustn't forget that this is a grilling, and a long-winded story might not fit in with the occasion."

"Wait," said Gonzalo in sudden urgency. "How peculiar was the peculiar example?"

"In my opinion, very peculiar."

"In that case, would you tell us about it?"

"Oh, for the love of Mike," said Trumbull, grimacing. "I want to find out about additional aspects of the novelty business."

"No," said Gonzalo, managing a frown worthy of Trumbull himself. "Mine is a legitimate question. Am I a Black Widower or am I not? —Jim?"

Drake stared thoughtfully through the smoke of his cigarette and, as host, made the decision. "Mario has put the question and deserves a response. Tell us about it, Al. I'm curious, too."

Silverstein said, "Gladly. It was—let's see—nine years ago. The wife and I were at a small summer resort and she had gone off to see some summer-stock performance in which I was totally uninterested. Fortunately, she didn't mind going alone, so I was spared.

"I spent the evening in the living room of the place, with about a dozen others who were likewise not caught up in the stampede to see a third-rate play just because, like Mount Everest, it was there. Besides me, there was a man, his wife, and their son, who figured in what was about to happen. The man was a rather stiff, unsociable fellow, his wife was passive and quiet, and his son was about twelve years old, well-behaved, and clearly very bright. Their name was Winters.

"Then there was a woman who my wife and I referred to, in private, as 'the Tongue.' Her name, if I remember correctly, was Mrs. Freed. She seemed a good-natured woman and had a rather lively mind, but what was most noticeable about her was her perpetual stream of talk. She never seemed to stop except when someone else managed to insert a remark by main force. Hers wasn't an unpleasant voice; it wasn't rasping, or shrill, or hectoring. It might even have been considered a pleasant voice, if there had been less of it.

"Her husband walked with a slight stoop, I remember, as though he were forever breasting the wind of that unceasing vocal current. Needless to say, he rarely spoke.

"There were six other people, if I remember correctly, two couples and two spare men who were either single or, like me, with their wives at the play. I don't remember which.

"The Tongue was knitting skillfully, and I sat watching her fingers as they kept time with her words, and between the two I was hypnotized into a semi-coma that was not at all unpleasant. Periodically, as she pulled at her yarn, her large ball of wool rolled to the floor, and each time she scrambled after it. One time it rolled in the direction of the Winterses, and the young boy leapt for it and returned it to her. She thanked him effusively and patted him and smiled. It occurred to me at the time that she had no children of her own and that her heart yearned when she saw those of others.

"Then at one point she reached into her purse for a mint—I suspect she needed a steady supply to keep her tongue lubricated—and the zipper on the purse opened with a rasp. There were, in fact, several rasps, for it was a multicompartment purse and, of course, she had to find which compartment contained the mints.

"One of the other women managed to insert a statement of marvel at what an unusual purse it was. It was, too, for it was quite thick. The Tongue said, as near as I can get across her way of speaking, 'Unusual indeed I bought it in a little store in New Orleans and now the store is gone and the company that made it is out of business and really whenever I find something I like they stop making it at once you see this purse has seven zippers and seven compartments three of the zippers are inside a bit and I can have a different compartment for my lipsticks and my money and my papers and my letters I have to mail and so on they're all lined with slick material so I can empty any or all the compartments when I have to and nothing ever stays behind when I change purses though heaven knows I never want to change this one I'll show you, let's see—'

"That's the way she spoke, you understand, making no use of punctuation. Then, in her effort to show how her purse worked, she started rasping the zippers again, looking for a compartment she could empty without creating too much trouble for herself, I suppose.

"When she finally decided, she turned the purse upside down, gave it a shake, and out came flying a small shower of coins and costume jewelry.

" 'Nothing left behind,' she said triumphantly, spreading the opening apart and showing it to the woman who had asked. She then put everything back, and again there was the rasp of zippers as she tried to decide on another compartment to empty, but apparently thought the better of it. She put the purse down and continued talking.

"I remember this incident well and repeated it to show you that in the novelty business, we have to keep our ears and eyes open. Listening to her talk about her purse gave me an idea for a novelty I called 'the bottomless purse.' It was a real purse, with three zippers above and a hidden zipper below. Two zippers above were straightforward and opened into two compartments, but they were unobtrusive. The middle zipper above had a very noticeable handle in colored glass and was usually the only one the victim saw.

"The owner of the purse would fill it with unimportant objects and would then give it to some innocent and easily embarrassed man or woman at a party. 'Would you hold this for me for a moment?' Then, a while later, she would say, 'Would you reach into my purse for my compact? It's right on top.' The victim would, of course, pull the noticeable zipper and that would activate the hidden zipper below. With both compartments open, everything would drop out all over the floor, to the utter confusion and horror of the victim."

Avalon said disapprovingly, "And another old friendship would come to an end."

"Not at all," said Silverstein. "Once the joke became obvious, the victim usually laughed harder than anyone, especially since he or she had the pleasure of sitting back while the perpetrator had to go through the trouble of collecting everything that had fallen.

"We had it on the market the next spring and it did pretty well. It wasn't a world-beater but it did pretty well. It was a woman's item, of course, but it's a mistake to think women are not interested in novelties. You have to—"

Trumbull interrupted. "Was that the peculiar event? Emptying the purse?"

Silverstein seemed to have been brought up with a jerk. He flushed, then laughed in an embarrassed way. "Well, no. Actually, I haven't come to that part yet. —I'm afraid I have a little of the Tongue in me, especially when it comes to a discussion of my profession.

"It was some time after the purse incident that the Winters boy caught my eye. He had been watching and listening to everything with a look of deep interest, but now he suddenly seemed concerned. He seemed to hesitate a moment and then turned to his father and spoke rapidly in a very low voice. As he listened, the father stiffened and his face went a dead white. He muttered something to his wife, and then all three began to peer about the floor, to move their chairs and look beneath. They looked very anxious, the father particularly so.

"I did what anyone would do. I said, 'Have you folks lost something?'

"The father looked up, seemed for a moment to be lost in thought, then, as though he had come to a difficult decision, rose to his feet and said in a stiff and pedantic way, 'I'm afraid that my son has lost a lucky piece that he greatly valued, though of course it has no intrinsic worth. It looks like a rather large coin with good luck symbols of various kinds on each side. It may have rolled somewhere. If anyone sees it—'

"We were all moved by the same kindly impulse or, if you wish to be cynical about it, each of us thought it would be fun to look for something that was lost when we were in no personal agony at the loss. Either way, the room was at once put under an unsystematic, but thorough search. Two men moved the couch, searched amid the dust beneath, then put it back in place. The material in the unused fireplace was looked through. The carpet was lifted all around the edges. It was all to no avail.

"I felt rather guilty. The lucky piece, as described, was certainly not one of ours, but I felt somehow responsible. I said to the boy softly, 'You know, son, these lucky pieces don't really bring good luck. If it doesn't show up, that doesn't mean you're in for trouble.'

"The boy looked at me in his quick, intelligent way and said, 'I know that. I just hate to lose anything.'

"But he looked very troubled just the same and it's an axiom in my business that to deny superstition doesn't mean a thing. The deniers are quite as likely to believe as the admitters are.

"We were all taking our seats again. Someone said to the boy, 'Maybe you lost it before you came into the room, sonny.'

"Mr. Winters turned to the son. 'Is that possible, Maurice?'

"Maurice looked more frightened than ever, but his high-pitched voice was firm. He said, 'No, Father, I had the lucky piece when I entered this room. I'm sure of that.'

"Winters clearly accepted his son's word as putting the matter beyond dispute. He cleared his throat and looked, somehow, both embarrassed and determined. He said, 'Ladies and gentlemen, it may be that one of you has picked up this valueless object a little while ago and put it away without thinking and that you are now reluctant to admit it. Please don't let embarrassment stand in the way. This means a great deal to my little Maurice.'

"No one said a word. Each one looked from neighbor to neighbor as though expecting someone to produce the lucky piece and curious to see who would. Winters, face red with mortification, allowed his eyes to rest for a moment on the Tongue's thick purse. As they did so, I couldn't help remembering the coins that had rolled out of it when she demonstrated how it might be emptied.

"The Tongue had participated in the search and had been unusually quiet since. She caught the look and had no trouble interpreting it. Her lips tightened a bit, but she showed no open sign of offense. She said, 'Well I don't suppose it would be convincing if I told you I didn't have the thing in my purse you would really want to see for yourself so let's just empty the whole thing on the table.'

"It was really quite an impressive and convincing performance. She put the purse on the table before her and said, slowly, 'One—two—three—four—five—six—seven.' With each count, there was the sound of a zipper

being rasped open. She then turned the purse upside
down and a cascade of items tumbled out upon the table.
You wouldn't believe one woman could have so many
items of so many different kinds in one purse. Some
items rolled off the table, but she didn't try to stop them.
She shook the purse to show nothing else was falling out
and then tossed it to one side.

"She said kindly, and with no trace of ill temper,
'Sonny, you know what your lucky piece looks like so
just rummage through everything on the table and look
at whatever rolled on the floor. Go ahead, you can look
through my wallet, and any envelope you see. I know
you won't take anything but what is yours.'

"The boy took her at her word and looked through and
at everything thoroughly, while his father remained at
his side, watching the process sharply. Finally, the boy
said, 'Father, it isn't here.'

"Winters nodded gloomily and the Tongue began putting the objects back into her purse, carefully choosing
which of the seven compartments was the correct one for
each item, and carrying on a running commentary as she
did so. The boy picked up the items on the floor for her.

"After that, of course, the other two ladies had to follow suit and empty their purses, but with less good grace
than the Tongue had. I was the first man to turn out my
pockets and then the other men did the same.

"The good luck piece was nowhere to be found—not
in any purse, not in any pocket. And still Winters stood
there, clearly unwilling to give up but uncertain as to the
next step.

"I still felt a bit of responsibility, but I also felt irri-
tated, so I said, 'If it will make you feel any better, Mr.
Winter, you and I can step into the library, lock the door,

and pull down the blinds. I'll take off my clothes and you can search them for hidden pockets and lucky pieces. You can also see if I have it glued to my skin.'

"I didn't think for one moment that he'd take me up on it, but damned if he didn't. I had a most embarrassed and uncomfortable five minutes as I stood there totally bare while he went over my clothes and studied me narrowly front, side, and back.

"I was beginning to worry that he'd suggest inspecting my various apertures, but the lucky piece was undoubtedly too large to make them reasonable hiding places.

"One by one, the other men followed my lead. One made as though he were going to refuse, but when every eye turned on him with clear suspicion, he gave in. But he left in a fury as soon as the search was completed. Perhaps he was wearing dirty underwear.

"When that was done, the Tongue rose to her feet and said, 'Well if Mrs. Winters will do the honors I'll stand still to be searched after all I might have slipped it into my bra there'd be plenty of room there and it wouldn't show through this dress the way I drape my shawl over it.'

"Off she marched and, eventually, back she came, and the other two women had to agree to be searched as well."

Silverstein paused in his tale to sip at his neglected brandy, and Halsted said, "I take it the lucky piece wasn't found on anyone."

"That's right," said Silverstein, "it wasn't. Apparently, though, Winters didn't give up easily. He got in touch with the manager of the hotel and persuaded him to detail two employees to help Winters look through the room even more carefully, to say nothing of the passages adjoining, the grounds outside the windows, and so on. At least, that's the story that went round the next day."

"And did they find it?" asked Halsted.

"No," said Silverstein. "Winters looked like death warmed over the next day. In the evening, he took what I was sure was an early departure, and I myself heard the manager feverishly assuring him that the search would continue and that as soon as the lucky piece was found it would be forwarded to him."

"And was it found thereafter?"

"No, it wasn't. At least, no word reached us to that effect up to the time my wife and I left a week later. —But you see the peculiar angle, don't you?"

Gonzalo said, "Sure. The thing disappeared into nothingness."

"Of course not," said Avalon sharply. "What evidence do we have that the lucky piece existed in the first place? The whole thing may have been a charade."

"To what end?" said Drake, making a face.

Avalon said, "To demonstrate that it was gone, of course."

"But why?" said Drake again. "If it were something intrinsically valuable, I can see that Winters might be laying the groundwork for an insurance claim—but a lucky piece worth, what? seventy-five cents?"

"I don't know the motive," said Avalon in exasperation, "but I can only suppose that Winters had one. I'd certainly sooner believe in the existence of an unknown motive than in the total disappearance of a material object."

Silverstein shook his head. "I don't think it was a charade, Mr. Avalon. If Winters was playing an elaborate game, it was one in which his wife and son were part.

About the wife I can't say for certain, but that boy, Maurice, was not acting. I cannot doubt for a moment that he was really scared.

"Then, too, if it were really all play-acting, why would Mr. Winters feel it necessary to go to such extremes? A much simpler search would have been sufficient to establish that the lucky piece was missing, if that were all he wanted to do. *That* was the peculiar thing to me. Why should Winters have searched with such extreme assiduity, and why should young Maurice have look frightened rather than merely unhappy? Don't you see the explanation? It seems obvious to me."

There was silence among the Black Widowers for a few moments and then Rubin said, "Suppose you tell us your explanation, Mr. Silverstein, and I'll then tell you if it is correct or not."

Silverstein smiled. "Oh, you'll agree with me. Once the matter is explained, it will seem as obvious to you as it does to me. —That was *not* the boy's lucky piece, it was his father's. Winters had allowed his son to have it for a while and the boy had lost it. I'm sure the boy knew how intensely his father valued the lucky piece, so he looked scared, *very* scared, and I don't blame him. And it is only by realizing that Winters was looking for his *own* lucky piece that you can rationalize the nature of his search."

Halsted said, "He insisted it was his son's lucky piece."

"Of course! People are quite apt to deny their superstitions, as I told you earlier—especially if they are intelligent and educated and in the presence of other educated people—and most especially if the grip of the superstition is pathologically strong. They are intelligent enough to be bitterly ashamed of their madness and yet still be helpless in its grip. I'm a professional in such matters and

I tell you it's so. Of course, he would pretend the lucky piece was his son's and I believed that, at first. However, as I watched Winters I eventually recognized his emotions to be those of someone terrorized in the belief that his luck had vanished forever. He was as much a victim of an irresistible craving for that vanished security as a drug addict would be for the heroin he lacked."

Trumbull said, "And yet you sell this druglike thing to people."

Silverstein shook his head. "A vanishingly small percentage are affected so extremely. Is a manufacture of penicillin to be blamed for the death of a few who develop a fatal sensitivity to it? —Well, Mr. Rubin, am I right or wrong?" He smiled confidently.

Rubin said, "Wrong, I'm afraid. You're having Winters behave in two irreconcilable ways. If he is so in the grip of the lucky piece mania that he would carry on a psychotically intense search for it, then, surely, he would never have given it to his boy to play with. No, I find it impossible to believe in the lucky piece story either for the son or the father."

Silverstein said, in the offended tone of one whose clever idea, triumphantly produced, is cavalierly dismissed, "I would like to hear an alternate explanation that makes any sense."

"No problem," said Rubin. "I would suggest that the so-called lucky piece was, in actual fact, a very valuable item."

"Do you mean it was actually a piece of gold, or contained real jewels, or was a work of art?" said Silverstein, with what was almost a sneer. "If so, the objection you raised still stands. Why give it to the boy to play with? And, for that matter, why call it a lucky piece? If Winters had mentioned its value, we'd have looked harder and submitted to a search with better grace."

"It might be," said Rubin, "that the value rested in something unmentionable. Suppose it was a device of some sort, or carried a message—a coded carving, or microfilm in a tiny inner compartment—"

Silverstein frowned. "Do you mean Winters was a spy?"

"Consider it as a hypothesis," said Rubin. "Winters, having reason to feel there were others on his track and that an effort would be made to relieve him of the object he carried, had his son carry it instead, feeling that boy would go unsuspected."

Avalon harrumphed disapprovingly. "A rather heartless thing for a father to do."

"Not at all," said Rubin. "Winters himself would still be the one liable to be attacked, if there were danger of that sort of thing. But then they wouldn't find the object upon him. If they failed to suspect the boy of being the carrier, the youngster would not be in danger at any time. At least, that must have been his hope. And if there *was* danger for the boy, it might be that he was the sort of patriot who felt that his country and his task came first.

"When the object turned out to be missing, Winters' first thought must have been that it had been accidentally dropped, but when it was not found at once, Winters would have come to the frightening conclusion that it had been stolen by an enemy. He then carried through a major search in the hope that his adversary, whoever it might prove to be, would be uncovered at the same time the object was found. Naturally, he had to pretend it was something trivial he was searching for. But since it wasn't found, he was forced to leave, his mission destroyed, his own cover blown, his enemy secure. I don't envy him his situation. And I don't wonder his son was frightened, if he was intelligent enough to have an inkling of what was going on."

The Black Widowers showed no particular enthusiasm over this. Drake shook his head solemnly.

Rubin said indignantly, "What do you think, Tom? This is your kind of baby."

Trumbull shrugged. "I don't know everything that goes on. This happened nine years ago, you say, Silverstein?"

"Yes, sir."

"It may be that there was something, then, that involved South Africa and its attempts to develop a nuclear bomb— The American government was not involved in that, though, in any way."

"It didn't have to be," said Rubin, "from anything we heard. But I take it, Tom, that my interpretation is possible."

"Possible, sure, but I don't commit myself to more than that."

Gonzalo said, "You're all missing the point. You're talking about motivations, and why a kid should look frightened, and why a guy should search madly. No one seems to be the least interested in the real puzzle. What's the difference whether it's a lucky piece or a key to a nuclear bomb? What happened to it? Where did it go?"

Avalon said heavily, "I see no mystery there. The only way the object could disappear into nothingness was for it not to have been brought into the place to begin with. Despite the young man's denial, he must have lost it before he ever entered the room and was afraid to admit it —assuming it existed in the first place. After all, intelligent or not, he was twelve years old. He couldn't resist playing with it and he may have dropped it somewhere irretrievable, perhaps. He would then have been afraid to say anything about it, for he knows it is important to his father. In the room, later, his father asks him if it is safe, and he has to admit it's gone, but can't possibly say he lost it some time before and dared not own up to it."

"No!" said Silverstein violently. "He just wasn't that kind of youngster. You could see he had been brought up to meet rigid grown-up standards. The father didn't ask him for the lucky piece. The boy went up to him to volunteer the information that it was gone. If he had lost it earlier, he would have reported it earlier. I'm sure of that."

Drake said, "Suppose the loss were accidental. He might have pulled a handkerchief out of his pocket an hour earlier somewhere else and the object might have come out and fallen in the grass, let us say. He may never have noted the loss till he was in the room."

"No!" said Silverstein again. "The boy said he had it when he came into the room and his father believed him and didn't question the matter. He knew his son."

Avalon said, "Well, Mr. Silverstein, if you insist the object really existed and was really lost in the room, do you have any idea where it went to?"

Silverstein shrugged. "I don't know. Maybe it fell through a crack into the cellar. Maybe it was in some perfectly ordinary place and for some reason everyone overlooked it. Many a time I've scoured my apartment for something that seemed to have vanished, and then, when I found it, it proved to be in plain sight all along."

"Yes, after you *found* it," said Avalon. "One always

finds it, even without a search as prolonged and intense as Winters' search."

A momentary silence fell and then Trumbull said, "We seem to be at an impasse. The puzzle is an interesting one, but I don't see that it's anything that can be solved. We just don't have enough information."

Gonzalo said, "Well, wait. We haven't heard from Henry."

Trumbull said, "Don't wish it on Henry. If a puzzle is inherently insoluble, it is insoluble even for Henry."

Gonzalo said, "Is that a fact? Well, I want to hear Henry say that. —Henry?"

Henry, who from the sideboard had listened carefully to all the proceedings, smiled a small smile in an avuncular fashion, and said, "As a matter of fact, Mr. Gonzalo, I can't help but think that a solution may be suggested. The object need not be considered to have vanished mysteriously."

Trumbull's eyebrows climbed. "Really, Henry? What do you suggest?"

"Well, sir, consider Mr. Silverstein's comment to the effect that he had designed a trick purse through the inspiration of the one belonging to Mrs. Freed, the woman who talked a great deal."

Silverstein stared. "Do you mean the Tongue had a trick purse?"

"No, sir. But it did occur to me that tricks could be done with even a legitimate purse if it had seven zippers and seven compartments."

"You had better explain, Henry," said Drake.

Henry said, "This is all supposition, gentlemen, but suppose Mrs. Freed talked endlessly for a purpose. One who earns the sobriquet 'Tongue' is bound to seem silly to anyone less penetrating than Mr. Silverstein, and is sure to be underestimated—which is an advantage for a spy.

"Suppose she had learned of the existence of the object and, for some reason, suspected it was in the possession of the boy, Maurice. Her ball of yarn fell to the floor several times, and at least once, according to Mr. Silverstein, it rolled in the direction of Maurice. He sprang to help her; she petted him and, in this way, distracted him by touching him—an old pickpocket's trick. A moment later, the object was not in the boy's pocket but in Mrs. Freed's hand.

"Next she reached for a mint. In doing so, the object was dropped into a compartment that was already open and contained nothing. She had to fiddle with the zippers, searching for the mints, and when she was done, all the compartments were closed, including the one with the object.

"She then displayed how easily and surely the purse might be emptied by opening one compartment and turning the purse upside down. Having made that demonstration, intended to impress everyone, she fiddled with the zippers again, according to Mr. Silverstein, as though she were searching for another compartment with which to demonstrate, but apparently deciding against it. When she was done fiddling, however, all the compartments were closed, except the one with the object. That was open. She had then only to wait. If the object was not noticed to have been lost, fine. If the loss were noticed, she was ready.

"The loss *was* noticed and Winters' eye fell on her purse. She at once volunteered to empty it, and pulled every zipper, counting ostentatiously from one to seven as she did so. When she was done, the six compartments which had been closed were open, and the one compartment, with the object and nothing else inside, which had been open, was *closed*.

"She then upended the purse and out of it dropped every last thing it contained *but* the object. And because she had worked very hard to seem nothing but a chatterbox, because she had laid such a careful background, and because she had complied cheerfully with the search, no one gave any thought to investigating the apparently empty purse. In the end, therefore, the object seemed to have vanished into thin air."

Mr. Silverstein, whose mouth had dropped open as Henry had talked, closed it with what seemed to be an effort, then said, "It might have happened exactly like that. It seems to fit perfectly what I saw, and I've told the story so many times in the past nine years, there is no question of my having forgotten what I saw. Still, I don't suppose we can ever know for sure."

"No," said Trumbull, "but I'll bet on Henry, and from now on, I think my people will be on the watch for harmless chatterboxes with intricate purses."

"Only if they are zippered, sir," said Henry. "Purses with catches and clasps open quietly, but close with a loud snap, whereas the sounds of a zipper opening and of a zipper closing are indistinguishable."

AFTERWORD

As explained in the previous Afterword, "The Lucky Piece" was bought and paid for, but the magazine that was to publish it never appeared. The story therefore makes its first appearance in this book. That doesn't bother me. In each of my Black Widowers collections, I have managed to include some stories that have not appeared elsewhere. I consider it a bonus to those who are generous enough to buy these books.

Incidentally, it is necessary for me occasionally to include some graphic details of some facet of the human experience as part of the background to these stories. In "The Lucky Piece," for instance, I discuss the novelty business to some extent. You may have admired the neatness of my research into the matter, but please don't. I am far too lazy (and far too busy writing a million other things) to waste time on research. When I need details on the novelty business, I just make them up out of my ever-fevered imagination. Consequently, if you run a novelty business yourself and feel I have made a mistake, write and enlighten me.

TRIPLE DEVIL

It was not surprising that at this particular banquet of the Black Widowers, the conversation turned on the subject of self-made men.

After all, Mario Gonzalo, host of the evening, was bringing as his guest the well-known retired owner of a chain of bookstores, Benjamin Manfred. It was also well known that Manfred had delivered newspapers as a young lad, more than half a century before, and was the son of poor but honest parents—very honest, and very, very poor.

And now here he was, not exactly a Getty or an Onassis, but very comfortably situated. And with four children and a number of grandchildren all engaged in dealing with one portion or another of the chain, he was even the founder of a dynasty.

Since Manfred had phoned to say, with many regrets,

that he would be a little delayed, but would certainly be there before the actual banquet was begun, it meant that the cocktail hour was taking place in his absence and the conversation could continue freely without the inhibition produced by the very presence of one of those who was the subject of discussion.

Nor was it surprising that the loudest of the pontificators was Emmanuel Rubin.

"There is no such thing as a self-made man—or woman, for that matter—anymore," said Rubin with passion, and when he spoke with passion, there was no choice but to listen. If his sixty-four inches made him the shortest of the Black Widowers, his voice was undoubtedly the loudest. Add to that the bristling of his sparse gray beard, and the flashing of his eyes through the thick lenses that served to magnify them almost frighteningly, and he was not to be ignored.

"Ben Manfred is a self-made man," said Gonzalo defensively.

"Maybe he is," said Rubin, reluctant to make any exceptions to any generalization he had launched, "but he self-made himself in the 1920s and 1930s. I'm talking about *now*—post–World War Two America, which is prosperous and welfare-minded. You can always find help making your way through school, tiding yourself over unemployment, getting grants of some sort to help you get started. Sure you can make it, but not by yourself, never by yourself. There's a whole set of government apparatuses helping you."

"Perhaps there is something in what you say, Manny," said Geoffrey Avalon, looking down with a somewhat distant amusement. His seventy-four inches made him the tallest of the Black Widowers. "Nevertheless, wouldn't you consider yourself a self-made man? I never heard that you inherited or married wealth, and I don't see you, somehow, accepting government handouts."

"Well, I haven't gotten anything the easy way," said Rubin, "but you can't be a self-made man until you're *made*. If I didn't have a rich father, and don't have a rich wife, neither am I exactly rich myself. I can afford some of the niceties of life, but I'm not *rich*. What we have to do is define the self-made man. It's not enough that he's not starving. It's not enough that he's better off than he used to be. A self-made man is someone who starts off poor, without any money above the subsistence level. Then, without getting large slabs of money from the outside, he manages, through hard work and shrewd business acumen, or through enormous talent, to become a millionaire."

"How about luck?" growled Thomas Trumbull. "Suppose someone enters a sweepstakes and wins a million dollars, or suppose he consistently backs winners at a racetrack."

Rubin said, "You *know* that doesn't count. You're just a luck-made man then. That goes if you pull an old man from under a hackney coach and he calls down heaven's blessing on you and gives you a million dollars. And I'm not counting those people who get rich by illegal activity. Al Capone, from a standing start, was making sixty million dollars a year before he was thirty, at a time when the dollar was worth a dollar and not twenty-two cents. He paid no taxes on it, either. You can call him self-made, but not by my definition."

"The trouble with you, Manny," said Roger Halsted, "is that you want to restrict the term to people you approve of morally. Andrew Carnegie was a self-made man and he was a great philanthropist after he had made his millions, and, as far as I know, he was never put in jail. Still, on his way up, I'll bet he engaged in questionable business activities and that he managed to grind the faces of the poor when that was necessary."

Rubin said, "Within the law is all I ask for. I don't expect people to be saints."

Gonzalo said, with a totally unconvincing air of innocence, "What about your friend, Isaac Asimov, Manny—"

And, of course, Rubin rose to the bait at once. "My *friend?* Just because I lend him a few bucks now and then to help him pay the rent, money that I don't ever expect to see again, he goes around telling everyone he's my friend."

"Come on, Manny. No one's going to believe that libel. He's well-heeled. And according to his autobiography, he started with nothing. He worked in his father's candy store, and he delivered newspapers, too. He's a self-made man."

"Is that so?" said Rubin. "Well, if he's a self-made man, all I can say is that he certainly worships his creator."

There was no telling how long Rubin would have gone on to improvise variations on this theme, but it was at this moment that Benjamin Manfred arrived, and conversation stopped at once while Gonzalo made the introductions.

Manfred was of average height, quite thin, with a lined but good-natured face. His hair was sparse and white, his clothing neat and old-fashioned. He wore a vest, for instance, and one was surprised that the chain of a pocket watch was not looped from one side to the other. He wore a wristwatch instead, but it was so old-fashioned that it had a stem-winder.

He acknowledged the introductions with a pleasant smile, and when he shook hands with Rubin, said, "I'm so pleased to meet you, Mr. Rubin. I read your mysteries with such pleasure."

"Thank you, sir," said Rubin, trying manfully to be modest.

"In my stores, I can always count on good sales for your books. You almost match Asimov."

And he turned away to greet James Drake, while Rubin slowly turned a furious magenta, and the five other Black Widowers suffered substantial internal pain in their desperate efforts not to laugh.

Henry, the perennial waiter of the Black Widowers, having seen to it that the old man was supplied with a generous dry martini, announced that dinner was served.

Drake stubbed out his cigarette and looked at the small mound of caviar on his plate with pleasure. He helped himself to the condiments being passed around by Henry, hesitating at the chopped onion and then firmly taking two helpings.

He whispered to Gonzalo, "How come you can afford caviar, Mario?"

Mario whispered back, "Old man Manfred is paying me very nicely for a portrait he's sitting for. That's how I know him, and I might as well show him a bit of a good time with his money."

"It's nice to know people still want their portraits painted."

"Some people still have good taste," said Gonzalo.

Drake grinned. "Would you care to repeat that loudly enough for Manny to hear it?"

"No, thanks," said Gonzalo. "I'm host and I'm responsible for the decorum of the table."

The table, as it happened, was perfectly decorous. Rubin seemed subdued and let pass a dozen opportunities to tell Manfred what was wrong with the bookselling business and how it contributed to the impoverishment of worthy young authors.

If the Black Widowers were quieter for Rubin's withdrawal from the fray, they were happy enough, and loud in their praise of the courses as they passed—the turtle soup, the roast goose with the potato pancakes and red cabbage, the baked Alaska—and perhaps just a trifle less than tactful in their clear surprise that a dinner hosted by Gonzalo should have such Lucullan overtones.

Gonzalo bore it with good humor and, when it was time to tinkle the water glass melodiously with his spoon, he even made a noble attempt to mollify Rubin.

He said, "Manny, you're the book person here and, as we all agree, the best in your class, bar none. Would you please do the honors in grilling Mr. Manfred?"

Rubin snorted loudly, and said with only his normal supply of grumpiness, "I might as well. I doubt that any of the rest of you are literate enough."

He turned to Manfred and said, "Mr. Manfred, how do you justify your existence?"

Manfred did not seem surprised at the question. He said, "If there's one person who shouldn't have trouble justifying his existence, it is someone whose business it is to purvey books. Books, gentlemen, hold within them the gathered wisdom of humanity, the collected knowledge of the world's thinkers, the amusement and excitement built up by the imaginations of brilliant people. Books contain humor, beauty, wit, emotion, thought, and, indeed, all of life. Life without books is empty."

Halsted muttered, "These days there's movies and TV."

Manfred heard. He said, with a smile, "I watch television also. Sometimes I will see a movie. Just because I appreciate a meal such as the one we have just had doesn't mean that I may not eat a hot dog now and then. But I don't confuse the two. No matter how splendid movies and television may seem, they are junk food for the mind, amusement for the illiterate, a bit of diversion for those who are momentarily in the mood for nothing more."

"Unfortunately," said Avalon, looking solemn, "Hollywood is where the money is."

"Of course," said Manfred, "but what does that mean? Undoubtedly, a chain of hamburger joints will make more money than a four-star restaurant, but that doesn't convert hamburger to Peking duck."

"Still," said Rubin, "since we are discussing money, may I ask if you consider yourself a self-made man?"

Manfred's eyebrows lifted. "That is rather an old-fashioned phrase, is it not?"

"Right," said Rubin, with a stir of enthusiasm. "I maintained exactly that over the cocktails. It is my opinion that nowadays it is impossible for anyone to be a truly self-made man. There is too much routine government help."

Manfred shook with silent laughter. "Before the New Deal, that was not so. The government in those days was a highly moral and neutral referee. If a large corporation had an argument with a small employee, the government's job was to see that both sides had only the help they could afford. What could be fairer than that? Of course the rich always won, but that was just a coincidence, and if the poor man didn't see that, the government sent in the National Guard to explain things to him. Those were great days."

"Nevertheless, the point is that you were poor when you were young, were you not?"

"Very poor. My parents arrived in the United States from Germany in 1907 and brought me with them. I was three at the time. My father was employed at a tailor shop and made five dollars a week to begin with. I was the only child then, but you can imagine how it improved his economic position when he later had three daughters one after the other. He was a Socialist, and a vocal one, and as soon as he became a citizen he voted for Eugene V. Debs. This made some people, whose views on freedom of speech were strictly limited to freedom of *their* speech, feel he ought to be deported.

"My mother helped out by part-time work in between babies. From the age of nine, I delivered papers in the morning before school and had odd jobs after school. Somehow my father managed to accumulate enough money to make a down payment on a small tailor shop of his own, and I worked with him after school. Once I turned sixteen, I didn't have to stay in school anymore, so I quit at once to work in the shop full-time. I never finished high school."

Rubin said, "You don't sound like an uneducated man."

"It depends on how you define education. If you are willing to allow the kind of education you pick up for yourself in books, then I'm educated, thanks to old Mr. Lineweaver."

"This Mr. Lineweaver gave you books?"

"Only one, actually. But he got me interested in books. In fact, I owe nearly everything to him. I couldn't have gotten my start without him, so that maybe I'm *not* a self-made man. And yet, he didn't *give* me anything. I had to work it out for myself, so maybe I *am* a self-made man. You know, I'm honestly not sure."

Drake said, "You've got me confused, Mr. Manfred. What was it you had to work out for yourself? A puzzle of some sort?"

"In a way."

"Is it a well-known episode in your life?"

Manfred said, "There was some mention in newspapers at the time, but it was a long time ago and it has been forgotten. Sometimes, though, I wonder how fair the whole thing was. Did I take advantage? I was accused of undue influence and who knows what, but I won out."

Rubin said, "I'm afraid, Mr. Manfred, I must ask you to tell us the story in detail. Whatever you say will be held completely confidential."

Manfred said, "So Mr. Gonzalo told me, sir, and I accept that." But, for a moment, Manfred's eyes rested on Henry, who stood, with his usual air of respectful attention, at the sideboard.

Trumbull caught the glance and said, "Our waiter, whose name is Henry, is a member of the club."

"In that case," said Manfred, "I will tell you the story. And if you find it dull, you have only yourselves to blame."

"But wait," interjected Gonzalo eagerly, "if there's

some kind of puzzle or mystery involved, I figure you solved it. Right?"

"Oh, yes. There is no mystery waiting to be solved." He waved his hands, as though in erasure. "No puzzle."

"In that case," said Gonzalo, "when you tell the story about Mr. Lineweaver, don't tell us the answer to the puzzle. Let us guess."

Manfred chuckled. "You won't guess. Not correctly."

"Good," said Rubin, "please continue with the story, and we will try not to interrupt."

Manfred said, "The story starts when I was not quite fifteen, just after the end of the war—the first one, World War I. It was Saturday, no school, but I still had papers to deliver, and the last stop on the route was an old mansion. I left the paper in a little hook on the side of the door, and once a week, I rang the bell and a servant came out and gave me the money for the papers and would hand me a quarter as a tip. The general payment was a dime, so I was always grateful to this particular place.

"Saturday was collection day, so I rang the bell, and this time, for the first time I could remember, out came old Mr. Lineweaver himself. Maybe he just happened to be near the door when I rang the bell. He was about seventy and I thought he was just another servant—I had never seen him before.

"It was a bitterly cold day in January—1919, it was—and I was inadequately dressed. I wore the only coat I had and it was rather thin. My hands and face were blue and I was shivering. I wasn't particularly sorry for myself, because I had delivered papers on many cold days and that was the way it was, that's all. What could I do about it?

"Mr. Lineweaver was perturbed, however. He said,

'Come inside, boy. I'll pay you where it's warm.' His air of authority made me realize he was the owner of the house, and that scared me.

"Then, when he paid me, he gave me a dollar as a tip. I had never heard of a dollar tip. Next he brought me into his library—a large room, with bookshelves from floor to ceiling on every wall, and a balcony with additional books. He had a servant bring me hot cocoa, and he kept me there for almost an hour, asking me questions.

"I tried to be very polite, but I finally told him I had to go home or my parents would think I was run over. I couldn't call to reassure them, for, in 1919, very few people had telephones.

"When I came home, my parents were very impressed, especially with the dollar tip, which my father took and put away. It wasn't cruelty on his part; it was merely that there was a common coffer for the earnings of the entire family, and none of us could hold out any of it for themselves. My allowance for the week was exactly zero.

"The next Saturday, old Mr. Lineweaver was waiting for me. It wasn't nearly as cold as the week before, but he invited me in for hot cocoa again. When he offered me another dollar, I followed my father's instructions and told him that it was too much, and that a quarter would be enough. My father, I'm afraid, had learned from life to distrust unexplained generosity. Mr. Lineweaver laughed and said he had nothing smaller and that I must take it.

"I suspect he noticed the curious looks I was giving the books, for he asked if I had any books at home. I said my father had a couple, but they were in German. He asked if I went to school and, of course, I said yes, but that as soon as I was sixteen I would have to quit. He asked if I went to the public library, and I said that I did sometimes, but what with the newspaper delivery and the tailor shop, I didn't really have much chance to do so.

" 'Would you like to look at these books?' he asked, waving his hands toward the walls.

" 'I might get them dirty, Mr. Lineweaver,' I said diffidently, looking at my hands, which were black with newspaper ink, of course.

"He said, 'I tell you what. On Sundays, when you have no school and the tailor shop is closed, you come here after you've delivered your papers and you can wash your hands and stay in the library as long as you want and read some of those books. Would you like that?'

" 'Oh, yes,' I said.

" 'Good,' he said. 'Then you tell your parents you'll be spending the time here.'

"I did and, for ten years, I was there faithfully every Sunday except when I was sick or he was away. Eventually, when I grew older, I came by on Saturday afternoons, and even on a few weekday evenings.

"He had a wonderfully wide variety of books for me to choose from, and was strong on British fiction. I read Thackeray and Trollope and puzzled over *Tristram Shandy*. I remember being fascinated by Warren's *Ten Thousand a Year*. It was a mixture of humor and incredibly reactionary politics. The antihero was Tittlebat Titmouse and there was a very effective villain named Oily Gammon. I eventually learned, from my reading, that 'gammon' was a slang term equivalent to our present slang term of 'boloney.'

"I read Pope, Byron, Shelley, Keats, Tennyson, Coleridge—didn't like Wordsworth or Browning, for some reason. There was lots of Shakespeare, naturally. I wasn't strong on nonfiction, but I remember trying to read Darwin's *Origin of Species* and not getting very far. There was a new book, *Outline of History* by H. G. Wells, that fascinated me. I read some American writers, too. Mark Twain and Hawthorne, but I couldn't stay with *Moby Dick*. I read some of Walter Scott. All this was spread out over years, to be sure."

Trumbull, at this point, stirred in his seat and said, "Mr. Manfred, I take it this Lineweaver was a wealthy man."

"Quite well-to-do, yes."

"Did he have children?"

"Two grown sons. A grown daughter."

"Grandchildren?"

"Several."

"Why did he make a surrogate son of you, then?"

Manfred considered. "I don't know. The house was empty except for servants. He was a widower. His children and grandchildren rarely came to visit. He was lonely, I suppose, and liked having a youngster in the house, now and then. I'm under the impression he thought I was bright and he certainly enjoyed my pleasure in the books. He would occasionally sit and talk to me about them, ask me what I thought of this book or that, and suggest new ones I might read."

"Did he ever give you any money?" asked Trumbull.

"Only that dollar a week, which he handed me without fail each Saturday. Eventually, I dropped the paper route, but he didn't know that. I kept on delivering his paper every day. I'd buy it myself and deliver it."

"Did he feed you?"

"The hot cocoa. When I stayed through lunch, a servant would bring me a ham sandwich and milk, or the equivalent."

"Did he give you books?"

Manfred shook his head slowly. "Not while he was alive. Never. He wouldn't give me one, or let me borrow one. I could read whatever I liked, but only as long as I sat in the library. I had to wash my hands before I walked into the library and I had to put each book back on the shelf in the place where I had got it before taking another."

Avalon said, "I should think Mr. Lineweaver's children would resent you."

"I think they did," said Manfred, "but I never saw them while the old man was alive. Once he said to me, with a little chuckle, 'One of my sons said I must keep an eye on you, or you'll take some of my books.' I must have looked horrified at the insult to my parents. Would that be the kind of son they would bring up? He laughed and tousled my hair and said, 'I told him he didn't know what he was talking about.'"

Rubin said, "Were his books valuable?"

"At the time, it never occurred to me that they might be. I had no idea what books cost, or that some might be worth more than others. I found out, eventually, though. He was proud of them, you see. He told me he had bought every one of them himself. I said that some of them looked so old he must have bought them when he was a little boy.

"He laughed, and said, 'No, I bought many of them in secondhand bookstores. They were old when I got them, you see. If you do that, sometimes you can pick up some very valuable books for almost nothing. Triple devil,' he said. 'Triple devil.'

"I thought he was referring to himself and how clever he was to find these valuable books. Of course, I didn't know which ones might be the valuable ones.

"As the years passed, I developed an ambition. What I wanted was to own a bookstore someday. I wanted to be surrounded by books and sell them till I had made enough money to build a library of my own, a collection of books I wouldn't have to sell and that I could read to my heart's content.

"I told this to Mr. Lineweaver once, when he questioned me. I said I was going to work in the tailor shop and save every cent till I had enough to buy a bookstore —or maybe an empty store and then buy the books.

"Lineweaver shook his head. 'That will take a long time, Bennie. The trouble is I've got children of my own to take care of, even though they're a selfish lot. Still, there's no reason I can't help you out in some sneaky way that they won't be able to do anything about. Just remember I own a very valuable book.'

"I said, 'I hope it's hidden away, Mr. Lineweaver.'

" 'In the best place in the world,' he said. 'Do you remember your Chesterton? What's the best place to hide a pebble?'

"I grinned. The Father Brown stories were new then, and I loved them. 'On the beach,' I said, 'and the best place to hide a leaf is in a forest.'

" 'Exactly right,' said Mr. Lineweaver, 'and my book is hidden in my library.'

"I looked about curiously. 'Which one?' I asked, and was instantly sorry, for he might have thought I would want to take it.

"He shook his head. 'I won't tell you. Triple devil! Tri-

ple devil!' Again, I felt he was referring to his own slyness in not revealing his secret.

"In early 1929, ten years almost to the day after I had
first met him, he died, and I received a call from the
lawyers to attend a reading of the will. That astonished
me, but my mother was in seventh heaven. She felt I
would inherit a great deal of money. My father frowned
and worried that the money belonged to the family, and
that I would be a thief to take it from them. He was that
kind of person.

"I attended, dressed in my best clothes, and felt incredibly ill at ease and out of place. I was surrounded by the
family, the children and grandchildren I had never before seen, and their looks at me were the reverse of lov-
ing. I think they, too, thought I would get a great deal of
money.

"But they didn't have to worry. I was left one book—
one—from his library. Any book I wished. It was to be
my free choice. I knew he wanted me to have the valuable one, but he had never told me which one that was.

"The bequest did not satisfy the family. You would
think they could spare one book out of perhaps ten thousand, but they apparently resented my even being mentioned in the will. The lawyer told me I could make my
choice as soon as the will was probated.

"I asked if I might go into the library and study the
books in order to make that choice. The lawyer seemed
to think that was reasonable, but this was objected to at
once by the family, who pointed out that the will said
nothing about my going into the library.

" 'You have been in the library often enough and long
enough,' said the older son. 'Just make your choice and
you can have it when the will is probated.'

"The lawyer wasn't exactly pleased by that and he said that he would seal the library till probation, and no one could go in. That made me feel better, because I thought that perhaps the family knew which book was valuable and would remove it themselves.

"It took time for the will to be probated, so I refused to make the choice immediately. The family grumbled at that, but the lawyer held his ground there. I spent the time thinking. Had old Mr. Lineweaver ever said anything to me that was puzzling and that might have been intended as a hint? I could think of nothing but the 'triple devil' he used to call himself when he wanted to praise his own slyness. —But he only said that when he discussed the valuable book. Could the phrase refer to the book, and not to himself?

"I was twenty-four now, and far from the innocent child I had been ten years before. I had a vast miscellany of information at my fingertips, thanks to my reading, and when the time came for me to make my choice, I did not have to walk into the library. I named the book I wanted and explained exactly where it would be on the shelves, for I had read it, of course, though I had never dreamed it was valuable.

"The lawyer himself went in and got it for me, and it was the right book. As a book dealer, I now know why it was valuable, but never mind that. The point is that I had the lawyer—a good man—arrange to have it appraised, and then to have it sold at a public auction. It brought in seventy thousand dollars, a true fortune in those days. If it were offered for sale now it would bring in a quarter of a million, but I needed the money *then*.

"The family was furious, of course, but there was nothing they could do. They brought suit, but the fact they had not let me enter the library and study the books lost them a great deal of sympathy. In any case, after the legal hassle was over, I bought a bookstore, made it pay through the Depression, when books were one form of relatively cheap amusement, and built things up to where they now are. —So am I a self-made man?"

Rubin said, "In my opinion, this doesn't come under the heading of luck. You had to pick one book out of ten thousand on the basis of a small and obscure hint, and you did. That's ingenuity, and, therefore, you earned the money. Just out of curiosity, what was the book?"

"Hey," said Gonzalo angrily.

Manfred said, "Mr. Gonzalo asked me not to give you the solution. He said you might want to work on it yourselves."

The smoke from Drake's cigarette curled up toward the ceiling. He said, in his softly hoarse voice, "One out of ten thousand on the basis of 'triple devil.' We never saw the library and you did. You knew what books were present and we don't. It's scarcely a fair test."

"I admit that," said Manfred, "so I'll tell you if you wish."

"No," said Gonzalo. "We've got to have a chance. The book must have had 'devil' in the title. It might have been 'The Devil and Daniel Webster,' for instance."

"That's a short story by Stephen Vincent Benét," said Manfred, "and wasn't published till 1937."

Halsted said, "The usual image of the devil, with horns, hooves and a tail, is drawn, actually, from the Greek nature god, Pan. Was it a book about Pan, or with the word 'Pan' in the title?"

"Actually," said Manfred, "I can't think of one."

Avalon said, "The witch goddess, Hecate, is often

thought of as triple—maid, matron, and crone—because she was a Moon goddess, too, and those were the phases —first quarter, full, and last quarter. As a witch goddess, she might be looked at as a triple devil. *Memoirs of Hecate County* was published too late to be the solution, but is there something earlier with Hecate in the title?"

"Not that I know of," said Manfred.

There was a silence about the table, and Rubin said, "We just don't have enough information. I think the story was interesting in itself, and that Mr. Manfred can now tell us the solution."

Gonzalo said, "Henry hasn't had his chance. Henry— have you any idea what the book might be?"

Henry smiled. "I have a small notion."

Manfred smiled, too. "I don't think you will be correct."

Henry said, "Perhaps not. In any case, people are often afraid to mention the devil by name, lest they call him up in the process, so they use numerous nicknames or euphemisms for him. Very frequently, they use the diminutive of some common masculine name as a kind of friendly gesture that might serve to placate him. 'Old Nick' springs to mind."

Manfred half rose from his seat, but Henry paid no attention.

"Once one thinks of that, it is simple to go on to think of *Nicholas Nickleby* which, so to speak, is old Nick twice, and is therefore 'double devil.' "

"But we want 'triple devil,' Henry," said Gonzalo.

"The diminutive of Richard gives us 'dickens,' a very well known euphemism for 'devil,' as in 'What the dickens?' and the author of *Nicholas Nickleby* is, of course,

Charles Dickens, and there is the 'triple devil.' Am I right, Mr. Manfred?"

Manfred said, "You're completely right, Henry. I'm afraid I wasn't as ingenious as I've thought these past fifty-five years. You did it in far less time than I did, and without even seeing the library."

Henry said, "No, Mr. Manfred. I deserve far less credit than you. You see, you gave the solution away in your account of events."

"When?" said Manfred, frowning. "I was careful not to say anything at all that would give you a hint."

"Exactly, sir. You mentioned so many authors and never once mentioned the outstanding English novelist of the nineteenth century, or probably any other century, or even, perhaps, any other language. Your failure to mention him made me think at once there was particular significance to the name Charles Dickens, and 'triple devil' then had no mystery to me."

AFTERWORD

You may have noticed that in this story, Isaac Asimov is mentioned as a friend of Emmanuel Rubin, who instantly seizes the opportunity to revile and libel poor Asimov.

I do that about once every ten stories or so because I enjoy doing it, but, of course, it is poor Rubin I am being unfair to and not myself.

Rubin in his real-life incarnation is Lester del Rey, who *is* a good friend of mine and has been for nearly fifty years. We squabble lovingly in public (which is what gave me the idea of having Rubin act as he does) but, in actual fact, we are each ready to give the other the shirt off our backs, if necessary. Lester is, in fact, one of the straight-arrows I have been fortunate enough to know, absolutely honest and absolutely reliable—but idiosyncratic, as I am.

Lester consistently denies there is any resemblance between himself and Rubin, even though I assure him that strangers often stop me in the street and say, "Hey, that guy Rubin in your stories—he's an awful lot like Lester del Rey."

This story first appeared in the August 1985 issue of *Ellery Queen's Mystery Magazine*.

SUNSET ON THE WATER

It didn't take much to make Emmanuel Rubin indignant so that his beard (what there was of it) bristled. It didn't take much more to make him furious and have his eyes flash behind his thick-lensed spectacles.

He was somewhere between indignation and rage now, and the upstairs room at the Milano, where the Black Widowers met for their monthly banquets, rang with his voice.

"I get this fan letter from California," he said, "and after the usual bosh about how good my books are—"

"Bosh is right," said Mario Gonzalo, staring complacently at the sketch he was making of the banquet guest, a sketch that seemed all eyebrows.

Rubin went right on with his sentence, not bothering to stop to demolish the other—unusual for him and indicative of the concentrated nature of his anger. "—he writes to me that if I'm ever on the Coast, I should drop in and he'll put me up."

"Kindly meant, I'm sure," said Roger Halsted, nibbling at a sausage roll—one of the hot appetizers that the inestimable Henry had put out this time as an accompaniment to the drinks.

"No one can be kind and stupid at the same time," said Rubin, inventing a cosmic law on the spot. "I wrote back and said, 'I am *already* on the Coast, thank you.'"

"Good Lord," said Thomas Trumbull, who had arrived three minutes before and had accepted a scotch and soda from Henry with his usual affectation of having just returned from Death Valley and being in the last extremity of thirst. "Is *that* what you're furious about? So what if Californians talk about their coast as though it were the only one in the world? It's just a way of speaking."

"As a matter of fact," said James Drake, who was born in Alaska, "the West Coasters, if you'll excuse that expression, are not the only offenders. As soon as an East Coaster has been in California for five minutes, he begins saying, 'Here on the Coast—' In the same way, you can get a guy from Ohio who has called his native land 'the United States' all his life, put him in Europe for five minutes, and he begins to talk about the 'States.'"

Geoffrey Avalon, host of the banquet on this occasion, and noted for his annoying ability to see both sides of a question, said, "Provincialism is not the monopoly of anyone. There is the story of the two Boston dowagers who found themselves in Los Angeles early in October, with the temperature at one hundred and five degrees. Said one, "My goodness, Prudence, it is certainly hot here." Said the other, "What do you expect, Hepzibah?

We are, after all, nearly three thousand miles from the ocean."

Avalon then took a sip of his drink in his usual grave way and said, "Tom, you haven't had a chance to meet my guest, Chester Dunhill. Chester, this is Tom Trumbull, who has some sort of sensitive job with the government. He's never specific about it."

Trumbull said, "Glad to meet you, Mr. Dunhill. If our doings here puzzle you, I must explain that it is customary for the Black Widowers to debate furiously over trifles."

Dunhill was a tall man with a thick head of white hair and eyebrows of a startling and bushy black. He said, in a booming bass voice, "We can survive catastrophes. It's the trifles that kill us."

Gonzalo looked startled and seemed about to say something, but Henry announced, with quiet finality, "Gentlemen, dinner is served."

Rubin did well with the ham and pea soup, and wreaked havoc on the broiled sole, and on the rather plain salad. He drew up short, however, at the individual pies handed out in all the pride of their crisp, golden crust.

"Henry," said Rubin in a slow rumble, "what exists under this crust?"

Henry said, "I fear, Mr. Rubin, that Mr. Avalon, in a British mood, has asked that we serve steak and kidney pie."

"Kidney? *Kidney?*" Rubin looked outraged. "That's liver squared. Jeff, I wouldn't have thought you capable of such a lapse in taste."

Avalon looked pained. He said, "Steak and kidney pie, properly prepared, is a great delicacy—"

"For whom? Vultures?"

"For every one of us at this table. Why don't you try it, Manny?"

Rubin said intransigently. "Kidney tastes like urine."

Gonzalo said, "So does your favorite brand of beer, Manny, but you guzzle it down."

"For God's sake," said Trumbull, "what kind of dinner conversation is this? Manny, if you can't eat what's set before you, then I'm sure Henry can get you scrambled eggs."

Rubin sneered and said, "I'll eat the steak," and sat sulkily through the main course, the treacle tart, the sardine-on-toast savory, and the strong tea. It made for a quiet dinner and, as Gonzalo pointed out in dumb show, Rubin did manage to eat the entire pie, kidney included.

Eventually, Avalon rang his spoon against the water glass and said, "Gentlemen, I call on Mario to grill our honored guest, my good friend, Chester Dunhill. I've explained the rules of the game to him and he is quite prepared to answer truthfully and completely."

Gonzalo said, "Mr. Dunhill, how do you justify your existence?"

Dunhill blinked, then said, "Well, I try to keep the past alive for the general public. Considering that we can't possibly order the present intelligently unless we learn the lessons of the past, I think I earn my place on Earth."

Gonzalo said, "How do you keep the past alive?"

"By writing about it. I suppose I could call myself a historian for the layman."

"Can you make a living from that?" asked Gonzalo.

Halsted put in at once, "Will Durant did, and Barbara Tuchman still does."

Dunhill smiled, with an air of diffidence that did not sit comfortably upon him. "I don't exactly put myself in their class. Still, I *do* make a living."

Avalon cleared his throat with vehemence. "May I interrupt? My friend, Charles, is being needlessly modest. In addition to his histories, he also writes historical novels for teenagers, mostly set in the Greece of the Peloponnesian War and the Rome of the Second Punic War. These are both critical and popular successes."

Gonzalo said, "Why those periods in particular, Mr. Dunhill?"

Dunhill said, "Both were periods of epic conflict between two nearly equally matched powers: Athens and Sparta in one case; Rome and Carthage in the other. Both wars are well documented; both were filled with great battles, with dramatic triumphs and disasters, with generals and politicians, some brilliant and some idiotic. Both periods, in short, are dead ringers for the period we're living in now. We can understand, sympathize, and see the lessons I try to make plain. What's more, we can't even draw an overall conclusion, because in one case the adversary we admire won out over the other, Rome defeating Carthage. In the other, the adversary we admire lost, Athens succumbing to Sparta. Of course, I've always had a personal soft spot in my heart for the Carthaginian general, Hannibal. He's one of three great generals in history who ended a loser without that in the least tarnishing his reputation."

Rubin said, "Napoleon was a second. Who was the third?"

"Robert E. Lee, of course," said Dunhill, his voice booming again.

Rubin looked discomfited but recovered and said, "I thought you were going to say Charles XII of Sweden, and that would have been wrong."

"That's right," said Dunhill, "it would have been wrong. Charles XII lacked prudence."

"How about generals who never lost?" asked Drake.

"There are quite a few of them," said Dunhill. "Genghis Khan, Cromwell, Alexander the Great, Julius Caesar, the Duke of Marlborough, and so on. Their reputations depend on the manner of their victories and the quality of their adversaries. At least two generals I can think of almost always lost but remained great considering what they did with what they had. There's George Washington, of course, and General Giap of North Vietnam."

Gonzalo said, "I suppose that in your history books and novels, you deal with the catastrophes that people survive. What are the trifles that can kill you?"

Everyone turned to look at Gonzalo, who grew restive under the communal stare. "What's wrong with the question? Mr. Dunhill said that catastrophes could be survived, but trifles kill you."

"Did I?" said Dunhill, frowning.

"Yes, you did. You said it to Tom Trumbull." He turned to Trumbull, who was nursing his brandy. "Tom, didn't he say that?"

Trumbull nodded. "You said that, Mr. Dunhill."

"Well, then," said Gonzalo. "What trifles did you have in mind?"

"Actually," put in Avalon, "every defeat suffered by a competent general might be blamed on some trifle. In fact, in *War and Peace* Tolstoy argued, in what I found to be tedious detail, the thesis that no general controls a battle, but that trivialities decide it all.''

Gonzalo said, "Come on, Jeff, you're trying to get your guest off the hook, and that's unethical. I don't think Mr. Dunhill was thinking about big battles. I think he had something personal in mind. That's the way it sounded to me and that's what I want to know about."

Dunhill shook his head. "It was just a remark. We all make remarks."

Gonzalo said, "Remarks aren't made out of nothing. You must have had something in your mind."

Dunhill shook his head again.

Trumbull sighed and said, "It seemed to me, too, Mr. Dunhill, that when you made that remark something was tearing at you. Jeff said he explained the game to you. You've agreed to answer all questions and we agree, in return, to hold everything you say absolutely confidential. If you're willing to state flatly that the statement had no personal meaning to you then and that you spoke idly, we will have to accept that, but please don't say that unless it is the truth."

Avalon said, in a tone of deep discomfort, "I did tell you that this would all be confidential, Chet."

Dunhill said, with a touch of anger in his voice, "There's nothing involved here but a deep personal disappointment that I can hardly bear to think of, let alone discuss. The trouble is that it is a matter of no moment to anyone but me, and others will only laugh at the whole thing. It involves a ridiculous trifle that places all the blame squarely on me. That's the unbearable part. If I could blame it on the government, on Fate, on the Universe, it wouldn't be so—" He stopped, broodingly.

"May we hear about it?" said Gonzalo stubbornly.

"I warn you," said Dunhill. "It's a long story of no interest whatever except to me."

"That's beside the point," said Gonzalo.

"Very well, but you asked for it. —During World War II, I was a young chap who missed actual army service (for a few years, anyway) because I was working for the Navy as a chemist. This was in Philadelphia. I was rather an unsocial creature in those days and my chief amusement lay in making my way out to the main branch of the Free Library and reading whatever I came across. And one of the things I came across was *The Historians' History of the World* in twenty-four volumes. It was published in 1902, with a second edition in 1907, with two supplementary volumes carrying things through World War I, and an index volume—twenty-seven altogether. Did any of you ever hear of it?"

There was silence. Dunhill went on, "I'm not surprised. To most people, it would be a deadly work. It was long out of print even at the time I came across it forty years ago, and now—"

He shrugged, and went on. "The volumes are a cut-and-paste job. Sections from the Greek and Roman historians and from the modern historians of the eighteenth and nineteenth centuries were included in the proper order in a series of histories dealing with the various nations separately. Volumes three and four were on Greece; volumes five and six were on Rome; and so on. There is a great deal of overlapping, of course, but that just meant that the same events are described from the viewpoints of different historians, possibly of different nationalities.

"The general editor, Henry Smith Williams, filled in

gaps with essays of his own. He was a humane person of liberal views and almost every time I read what I thought was a particularly telling passage, it proved to be one of his. You must understand that it was edited to read as connectedly as possible. There was just an occasional unobtrusive superscript which guided you to the end of the volume, where you found out that you were reading Gibbon or Prescott or Bury or Macaulay or Thucydides or whoever.

"The library had the set in double volumes and I picked them out one and by one and quickly found I could not bear to stop reading them for anything as dull as my daily work. I took them to the lab with me and read them during lunch or through a partially open desk while I had something boiling slowly under a reflex condenser. My memories of that entire period are vague except for those volumes.

"I had always been interested in history, but it was those volumes that converted that interest into an obsession. The volumes were all terribly old-fashioned, of course, for prior to the twentieth century, history was almost exclusively a matter of battles and court intrigue. Still, that was what I loved and my own histories are just as old-fashioned. I dwell very little on social and economic issues."

Rubin said, "The social and economic issues would make your histories more valuable."

"And more dull, perhaps," said Dunhill. "I don't omit such things altogether but I always remember I am writing for the general public, not for scholars. In any case, by the late 1950s, nearly ten years after I had held those library books in my hands for the last time, I abandoned chemistry and began to spend my full time on histories and historical novels."

Dunhill paused and seemed to brood awhile.

Drake chuckled as he stubbed out a cigarette. He said, "Unless you're telling the story with a total absence of art, which I cannot believe of a novelist, that *Historians' History* is going to turn up again."

Dunhill nodded vigorously. "You are quite correct. A few years ago, I made a new acquaintance, and my wife and I visited his house and had dinner there with several other couples. After dinner, I wandered over to his bookshelves and studied them—a bad habit that exasperates my wife but of which even she cannot cure me.

"And there, filling an entire shelf, was the *Historians' History*. I hadn't thought of it in years, had all but forgotten it. The instant I saw it, however, everything flooded back. The memory of reading those volumes at a terrible time in modern history, memories gilded and made more wonderful by the passage of years, were achingly sweet and intense.

"I was no longer the impecunious lad of decades ago. I am quite well off now and can afford to cater to my whims. I approached my host at once, therefore, and offered to buy his set. I couldn't believe that it had any attraction to anyone but myself and I was ready to pay far more than it was worth. Unfortunately, my host, for some reason he never explained, would not sell. He was quite emphatic about it.

"I tell you, gentlemen, if there were a million dollars on this table, and I knew I could take it without danger of detection, I would not touch it, out of a simple sense of honesty. But I actually thought of *stealing* those volumes that my friend would not sell me. It was only the thought of being caught if I tried breaking and entering that held me back. My sense of ethics simply shattered under the strain and I ended the new friendship rather than expose myself to the bitterness of seeing those volumes in some-one else's possession.

"I began visiting such secondhand bookstores as I could reach, and calling those I could not reach, asking them if they had or could get a set of the volumes. I even advertised in the *New York Times Book Review*, in general magazines, and in periodicals of interest to history buffs. The longer I waited the more I was willing to pay if I had to. —And this brings me down to the present."

Halsted said, "I hope you're not going to tell us you drew a complete blank and that that's the end of the story."

Dunhill frowned at him, his eyebrows hunching low. He said bitterly, "How I wish I could tell you exactly that. I gave a box number in the advertisement and the booksellers all had my home address, but I got nothing in either case. Nothing. Nil. Zilch.

"One week ago, however, I picked up a letter at my publisher's. I see them once a week and they usually hold any letters for me that are written care of them. They're never important, and usually they're from people who nitpick some historical point I make, something that must be dealt with, but always depresses me.

"I was holding the letter in my hand as I left my pub-lisher's and walked down the street to Grand Central. Idly, I glanced at the envelope and noted that it was ad-dressed in pen and ink in a spidery hand, which I ac-cepted as a bad sign. I decided it was from an elderly man who would raise some faint and querulous point con-cerning some pet theory of his. In a bad temper, I ripped open the envelope and removed the sheet of paper inside. At that point, I passed a garbage truck and tossed the envelope into its yawning maw, like a good citizen. But then I had to cross the street, which takes all one's concentration in Manhattan, and shoved the note into my pocket.

"I didn't remember it till I was in my commuter train and, taking out the note, I read it and a sudden rush of ecstasy filled me. —Here, I have the letter. Let me read it to you."

Dunhill unfolded a letter and read its crabbed handwriting aloud and with ease, as though he had memorized it.

Dear Mr. Dunhill,

I am a great fan of your books and I read your ad and would like to tell you that I have a complete set of "The Historians' History of the World" that I would be delighted to let you have. My father bought it for me when I was quite young and I enjoyed it greatly. It is still in very good shape and if you are willing to pay me a reasonable price plus all mailing costs, I would have it sent to you by insured express mail.

I would never dream of selling the set but I am quite old now and will be moving to a little place near my daughter's home, and there will be no room for the set there. I am a widower and I'm afraid I cannot live alone any longer. I just can't cope with the harsh winters.

It means having to live in a small town instead of in a sizable city. It also means giving up my apartment on the shore where, on clear evenings, I have often watched the sun set into the endless stretch of water so that I almost imagined I could hear it hiss.

Still, if I must give up these books, I can't think of anyone I'd rather give it up to than you. I hope you have many years of pleasure with it. Please let me hear from you soon.

> Sincerely,
> Ludovic Broadbottom

Rubin said, "Congratulations, Mr. Dunhill. Is everything arranged, or is that where the trivialities come in?"

Dunhill said grimly, "That is where the trivialities come in. Here, take this letter and look at it and tell me where to write."

Rubin took the letter, and glanced over the writing which filled one side of the sheet. He turned it over and looked at the totally blank other side. He said, "There's no return address on it."

"No, there isn't," said Dunhill indignantly. "Can you imagine the stupidity of people who don't put return addresses on their letters and then expect an answer?"

Avalon said, "People who don't put return addresses on their letters usually do put it on their envelopes—oh," he concluded, remembering.

"That's right," said Dunhill. "I threw the damned envelope away. There are your trifles. Here's a guy who reads an ad that clearly has a box number attached, yet he writes in care of my publisher instead. That not only means a delay of several days, but deprives me of the chance of knowing at once that the letter is important.

"Then I decide, of all things, to open the letter on the street and to discard the envelope into a handy garbage truck without really looking at it. If I had only just noted the name of the city and nothing more, I could have got his address from the city directory. There can't be more than one Ludovic Broadbottom in any one city. And to top it all off, he doesn't include his return address in the body of the letter. What's the result of all these trivialities? I have an offer of my *Historians' History* and I can't reach out and take it."

Gonzalo said, "Is there a bright side, Mr. Dunhill? Can you get other reference books for your histories and novels."

Dunhill said, with real anguish, "Get other books? I *have* other books. I have two large rooms crammed with historical reference material of the finest sort, to say nothing of the resources of the New York Public Library and of Columbia University. You don't get the point. I want a copy of *Historians' History* for *myself*, for sentimental reasons, for what it's *done* for me, for what it's *meant* to me. And I *have* it, and can't get it."

For a moment, what was almost a child's whine entered his deep voice. He must have recognized that himself, if belatedly, for he threw himself back in his chair, took a deep breath, and said, "Pardon me, gentlemen, I don't mean to rail uselessly at Fate."

"Why not?" said Avalon. "We all do it from time to time. But look here, we usually see more than we think we do. You glanced at the envelope long enough to see that it was addressed to you and to note that it was an old man's handwriting—"

"Yes," said Dunhill vehemently, "another trifle. The handwriting threw me off, too, and added to my conviction the letter was unimportant. If he had only typed my address on the envelope, I would surely have treated it with more respect."

"Yes," said Avalon, ploughing on, "but the point is that you must have glanced at the return address, too. If you concentrate quietly, you may remember something about it."

"No," said Dunhill hopelessly. "I've been trying for days. It's useless."

Trumbull said, "Why don't we work from what he says in his letter? He lives in a sizable city on the shore, and sees the sunset over the ocean. That means he's on the West Coast, or 'the Coast,' to quote Manny's fan. Here in New York, we can see sunrise out of the water, but never sunset into the water. Can we make a start with that?"

Dunhill seemed to have recovered his self-control. He said quietly, "Gentlemen, I have been a chemist, and I am a historian. I am used to the process of reasoning. Please note, however, that he talks of the harsh winters he experiences and that he can no longer endure. Neither Los Angeles nor San Francisco can possibly be considered as having harsh winters. No city on the West Coast can."

Gonzalo said, "Seattle is pretty damned rainy. I was there once, and you can believe me. That might sicken anyone."

"Then he would speak of rainy weather. No one speaks of harsh winters unless they mean cold and snow. That eliminates the West Coast, and Hawaii, too, but—"

"Wait," said Rubin, "how do you know it was from the United States? The letter is written in English, but it could be from Canada, Scotland, Australia. For that matter, almost any educated, non-Anglophone foreigner can write in English these days."

Dunhill flushed. "Well, then, I did notice *something* about the envelope. It had an American stamp. I know because I save foreign stamps for a friend of mine and I automatically watch for one on all envelopes. Had there been a foreign stamp on the envelope I would have torn it off and discarded the rest. I think I would even have noticed a foreign postal-meter mark. —As I say, then, we can eliminate California, Oregon, Washington, and Hawaii. That leaves Alaska."

"I wouldn't have thought of Alaska," muttered Gonzalo.

"I would," said Drake, smiling. "I was born there."

"In any case," said Dunhill, "the only town in Alaska that even an Alaskan would think of as sizable is Anchorage. It's on the coast but not on the open ocean. It's on Cook Inlet. The inlet is to the west of Anchorage, however, and perhaps you can see the sun set into it. Perhaps. I didn't take chances. I called the Anchorage phone exchange and the post office. There's no Ludovic Broadbottom in the city. In fact, just to play it safe, I called Juneau and Sitka. Juneau is on another inlet farther south, and Sitka has a population of less than ten thousand. But I called them—and nothing doing."

Halsted said thoughtfully, "If you're going to count cities on inlets, what about the East Coast? The ocean may be to the east, but there may be inlets to the west."

"I know," said Dunhill. "Florida has a long western coast and someone living on the shore in Tampa or Key West could watch the sunset on the water as the sun dives into the Gulf of Mexico. However, where would the harsh winters come in?

"There's a long peninsula that forms the eastern shore of Chesapeake Bay. The largest city on the western shore of that peninsula is Cambridge. It has a population of about eleven or twelve thousand, but from it you can watch the sunset on the water, since Chesapeake Bay is a broad stretch. So I called the town and drew a blank there, too.

"Besides, the only harsh winters on the East Coast would be from Philadelphia northward—New England particularly. Any city on the northeast coast, however, faces an ocean on the east or south. Even Provincetown, at the tip of Cape Cod, which could face west to the ocean, faces south. Falmouth faces west but it is a small town. Absolutely no town that could conceivably be considered sizable has a western exposure to the ocean."

Gonzalo said, more to himself than to anyone else, "From Manhattan you can see the Sun tumble into the Hudson."

"No, you can't," said Drake. "It squats down on New Jersey."

Halsted rubbed his high, pinkish forehead and said, "You don't suppose your letter writer got his directions twisted, do you? Not long ago an American delegate to the United Nations invited any nation which was dissatisfied with American hospitality to leave. He said he would be delighted to wave farewell to them as they sailed off into the sunset. He didn't bother to explain how one can sail into the sunset from New York."

Dunhill snorted loudly. "I remember that incident. He was simply using a metaphor stupidly. Besides, we're not talking about any member of the present administration. We're talking about an average American of, presumably, average intelligence."

"Besides," pointed out Avalon, "a man can mistake east and west, but if he's describing solar motions there is no way in which he can confuse sunset and sunrise. No, we need a sizable city with the ocean to the west and with a harsh winter. I confess I can't think of one that fills the bill."

Gonzalo said, "How about American islands that aren't part of states? Puerto Rico, Guam. They would still use American stamps, wouldn't they?"

"Yes, they would," said Dunhill, "and they're all tropical islands, too. —Believe me, gentlemen, I'm at the end of my rope."

Halsted said, "You don't think this whole thing might be a gag, do you? Maybe Ludovic Broadbottom is a made-up name, and he deliberately sent you clues that lead nowhere. Maybe there was no return address on the envelope, either. Or a fake one."

Slowly, Dunhill said, "Why should anyone bother? I'm a harmless person and my request is harmless, too. What would be the point of a practical joke of this nature?"

"The confirmed practical joker," said Avalon, "doesn't have to have a point—except on top of his head, of course."

Halsted said, "Do you have any friends who are practical jokers?"

"Not that I know of," said Dunhill. "I select my friends with reasonable care."

Gonzalo said, "Maybe Henry has some idea." He turned in his seat and said, puzzled, "Where's Henry? He was here a moment ago, listening to us." He raised his voice. "Henry!"

Henry emerged from the cloakroom and said, imperturbably, "I am here, gentlemen. I was merely engaged in a small task. —Mr. Dunhill, I have Mr. Ludovic

Broadbottom on the telephone. He is anxious to speak to you."

Dunhill's eyes bulged. He said in a choked voice, "Mr. Ludovic— Are you serious?"

"Quite," said Henry, with a bland smile. "Perhaps you had better not delay. And I might advise you to offer a generous sum. He's moving next week, and there will be no time to bargain."

Dunhill rose, appearing dazed, and vanished into the cloakroom toward the phone booth located there.

The Black Widowers sat in shocked silence for a few moments, and then Rubin said, "All right, Henry, what kind of magic did you use?"

Henry said, "No magic, gentlemen. It was Mr. Rubin who gave me the idea when he initiated the discussion of provincial attitudes toward coasts—the manner in which Americans on one coast sometimes forget, or ignore, the other.

"It seems to me that Americans on all three seacoasts— the Pacific, the Atlantic, and the Gulf, too, if you want to count that separately—tend altogether to ignore America's fourth coast, which is quite a long one, too."

"The fourth coast?" said Avalon, frowning.

"Of course," said Rubin, shaking his head in disgust.

"Yes, Mr. Rubin," said Henry. "I'm thinking of the Great Lakes. We don't think of it as a coastline but Mr. Broadbottom didn't refer to it as that. He spoke of the 'shore,' and the Great Lakes certainly have a shore. We very commonly speak of a lakeshore. And anyone living in a place on the shore of any one of the Great Lakes would perceive the same effect as would be obtained if one were overlooking an ocean. Those are large lakes, gentlemen.

"However, all the sizable cities on the lakeshores have their lakes to the east, south, or north. We can even include the Canadian cities, if we wish. Duluth has Lake Superior on the east. Milwaukee and Chicago have Lake Michigan on the east. Gary has Lake Michigan on the north. Detroit has Lake St. Clair on the east—tiny by Great Lake standards but large enough to give the effect of sunrise out of the water. Toledo has Lake Erie on the east. Cleveland and Erie have Lake Erie on the north, though Erie gets some western view. Hamilton has Lake Ontario on the east, while Toronto has that lake on the south and east, and Rochester has it on the north.

"The only really sizable city that looks west to a Great Lake is Buffalo, New York. It has Lake Erie to the west. From a proper location in Buffalo one can see the Sun set into Lake Erie—and Buffalo is notorious for its snowy winters. So I tried that first. I phoned Buffalo, obtained Mr. Broadbottom's number, called it, and he answered at once. He was quite concerned at not having heard from Mr. Dunhill. He is as anxious to sell as Mr. Dunhill—"

At this point, Dunhill emerged from the cloakroom, his face alight with joy. "All arranged," he said. "I will pay five hundred dollars plus shipping costs and I hope to have it in just a matter of days."

He reached for his wallet before a horrified Avalon could stop him. "Henry, you deserve a ten percent finder's fee for this," Dunhill said. "How did you do it?"

Henry raised his hand in a gentle gesture of rejection.

"Mr. Dunhill," he said with quiet firmness, "as a member of the Black Widowers, I cannot accept a fee in connection with my club duties."

Dunhill hesitated, then replaced his wallet in his pocket. "But how did you do it, man?"

Henry said, "Just a matter of thinking of the Great Lakes as small oceans. It's not worth discussing. The important thing is that you'll have your books."

AFTERWORD

Notice that Dunhill lusted for *The Historians' History of the World*. It was *I* that lusted for it. It was *I* who had read it as a youngster, taking it volume by volume from the public library, and it was *I* who noticed it in a friend's library. And it was *I* who would have stolen it if I had been able to think of a way. It was the only thing that I was *ever* tempted to steal.

However, my own story ended quite happily. I tried to find a copy that I could buy legitimately for money, and failed. My friend, however, managed to get another copy and *presented* it to me. After long persuasion, I managed to get him to accept a pittance in exchange. I still own the set and it is one of the apples of my eye.

But as a matter of conscience, I must make a confession to you. My friend's set was missing a volume. The set he presented to me was not. For a while I tried to persuade myself to offer him the volume he was missing—*but I just could not make myself do it.* How's that for being a mean bum?

This story first appeared in the January 1986 issue of *Ellery Queen's Mystery Magazine.*

WHERE IS HE?

When Roger Halsted introduced his guest as his investment broker, the members of the Black Widowers, assembled at their monthly banquet, responded at first with a stunned silence.

Halsted ignored that, and went about the room, introducing the members methodically.

"As I said, this is W. Bradford Hume, folks. —Brad, I want you to meet Emmanuel Rubin, who writes mysteries; Mario Gonzalo, who will be doing your portrait soon; James Drake, who's coughing over his cigarette, and was a chemist before he retired; Geoffrey Avalon, a patent attorney, though I've never found out what they do; and Thomas Trumbull, who works for a hush-hush branch of the government. —And this is our waiter, Henry, who's also a member, and who has just brought you your drink."

Hume acknowledged all the introductions with grace and a smile. He took his martini with a "Thank you, Henry," and by that time the assemblage had recovered.

Rubin, his eyes wide behind his thick glasses, said, "Are you telling us this is *your* investment broker?"

"That's exactly what I'm telling you," said Halsted, haughtily.

"Have they given you a raise in salary? Quintupled it?"

Halsted said, "No need to assume I'm a beggar, Manny, just because I teach mathematics at a junior high school. I've got seniority, security, and a reasonable salary; neither rich nor gaudy, but reasonable. Besides, Alice works also and makes more than I do, and I have a small inheritance from my mother, rest her soul—so Brad takes care of a few bucks for me, and very well, too."

Hume smiled appreciatively, and said, "Not that I'm trying to drum up business, gentlemen. It's my understanding that this is a purely social evening."

"Purely!" growled Trumbull.

Avalon cleared his throat. "I should think, Mr. Hume, that being a financial adviser in these unsettled times makes for a tense life."

"So it does, Mr. Avalon, but all times are unsettled, and that makes it particularly difficult for a financial adviser, since he is expected to see the future—the immediate future, at any rate."

"What stocks go up? What stocks go down?" murmured Gonzalo. He was already working at Hume's caricature and had put in the shock of dark hair under which he intended to hang an almost cherubic face.

"That, certainly," said Hume, "but a little more than that, too. You have to be able to judge what will be useful as a long-term investment, to anticipate changes in tax—"

At this point, Halsted put his hand on Hume's arm. "Don't talk about it now, Brad. They're going to grill you after the meal, and until then you have a right to relax."

"That suits me," said Hume. "What's on the menu for tonight, or am I not supposed to ask?"

"Why shouldn't you ask?" said Halsted. "Henry, what's on?"

Henry's smooth, sixtyish face crinkled slightly. "There will be grilled salmon tonight, Mr. Halsted, and I think you will find it most unusual. The lobster sauce is a private recipe of the chef's."

"Trying it out on us, is he?" said Drake, in his hoarse voice.

"You will not be disappointed, Dr. Drake. It will be preceded by a Portuguese fish chowder, which you may find a bit spicy."

"That won't bother *me*," said Avalon, his bushy eyebrows hunching low and giving his face an amiably Satanic look.

As it turned out, Henry was quite right. From soup through the rum chocolate cake, there were sounds of approval. Even Rubin's stout assertion that the "now-fashionable exercise of futurism" was empty of content did not rouse much in the way of clamorous opposition.

"All you have to do," said Rubin, "is to go back and read the predictions for the present time handed out by the charlatans of half a century ago. You'll find that they saw a million things that didn't happen, saw almost nothing of what *did* happen."

Hume listened gravely to the discussion that followed, but said nothing.

Gonzalo said, with obvious mischief in his eyes, "Your good friend, Asimov, is a futurist, isn't he?"

"He?" said Rubin, every hair in his sparse beard seeming to bristle. "He describes the future in what he *calls* science fiction, but the only points he gets right are those that are painfully obvious to anyone. And I wouldn't call him my *friend*. I just help him with the plot of a story now and then, when he's stuck."

Halsted patted his stomach with a satisfied smile and tapped his water glass with his spoon. "Gentlemen, it is time for Brad to pay for his excellent meal by facing a grilling. Manny, since you have so low an opinion of futurism, would you serve as grill-master? And please remember to maintain an elementary level of courtesy to one who is our honored guest."

Rubin snorted. "I'll let you know, Roger, when I need lessons in manners. —Mr. Hume, how do you justify your existence?"

"If you expect me to say," said Hume, "that I justify it by making people rich through clever investments, you'll be disappointed. The justification comes from my skill as an after-dinner speaker."

"It does, does it? I take it you consider yourself good at it?"

"Yes, I do. I've been doing it for fifteen years and by now I've reached a routine fee of seventy-five hundred dollars for an hour talk. I think that's an adequate measure of my skill."

"Huh," said Rubin, seeing no immediate opportunity for a riposte. "Why do you bother doing anything else?"

Hume shrugged. "I don't particularly like to travel, so

I want to be in a position to be able to pick and choose—
to turn down any talk, regardless of fee. I can do that best
if I have a regular job as a financial cushion. And that's
why I don't have an agent. They put pressure on you—
and they take thirty percent."

Rubin said, "If you don't have an agent, how do you
get speaking engagements?"

"Word of mouth. If you can give a good talk, the world
will beat a path to your door."

"What's your subject?"

"Futurism, Mr. Rubin—which you don't think much
of. Despite your comments on the subject, everyone
seems interested these days in what the future holds.
What's the future of education? Of robots? Of interna-
tional relations? Of space exploration? You name it—
they're interested."

"And you speak on all of that?"

"I do."

"How many different talks do you have prepared?"

"None. If I had to prepare my talks, I'd have to neglect
my brokerage work, and I can't do that. I speak extemporaneously and I don't need preparation. Call out your
subject and I'll stand up and talk for an hour—but you'll
have to pay me my fee."

Halsted said, "Listen, I've heard him speak. He *is*
good."

Gonzalo said, "Have you had any funny experiences in
your speaking career, Mr. Hume?"

"Funny?" said Hume, leaning back in his chair, and
looking completely comfortable. "I've had some memora-
ble introductions, which I *didn't* think were funny,
though others might laugh. I once had someone object to
my fee and write me a letter saying that it was four times

as much as they had ever paid anyone. I wrote back and said, 'I'm four times as good—at least.' In introducing me, he read the correspondence, and the audience, a professional engineers organization, suddenly realized they were being soaked four times the usual by an arrogant bum. I could feel the north wind blow as I rose and it took me half the talk to win them over.

"Another time, a woman introduced me in a thoroughly pedestrian way—which I'm used to. Mild applause came and I rose, in order to begin right after it had peaked so that I could start with the audience's self-hypnosis in my favor. Except that the woman who introduced me—and may she have a special place in hell someday—began to call out to latecomers that there were seats on the side. She kept it up till the applause died, and I had to rise and address a dead audience. I never did quite liven them up.

"Then there's the funny man. I had one give a fifteen-minute talk as an introduction. Fifteen minutes! I timed it on my watch. And he was funny, *really* funny. He had the audience rolling and he wasn't charging a penny. I had to follow him, and I knew that the audience was going to consider me far less funny—and at an exorbitant price. I was considering forfeiting the money and leaving, when my introducer concluded by saying, 'But don't let me give you the impression that Mr. Hume can do *anything*. I happen to know that he has never sung the role of the Duke in *Rigoletto*,' and sat down to loud laughter.

"What he didn't know was that he had handed it to me on a plate. I got up, waited for the routine applause to die all the way down, and in the dead silence I belted out, in my best tenor voice, *'Bella figlia dell'amore,'* the first notes of the Duke's contribution to the famous Quartet, and the audience rocked with the loudest laugh of the evening, and I *had* them.

"I had to give a talk twelve hours before I had a heart attack, and then another twelve hours after the attack. Fortunately, I didn't know it was a heart attack at the time. The second talk was to a bunch of cardiologists, and not one of them—"

Gonzalo said, "Hold on for a minute. *Hold on!*"

Hume rather skidded to a halt, and looked surprised. "I beg your pardon."

Gonzalo said, "I *believe* you when you say you can speak for an hour extemporaneously without notice, but you didn't get my question."

"You asked me if I had had any funny experiences, didn't you?"

"Yes, but I didn't mean funny—humorous. I meant funny—odd or puzzling. I meant *funny.*"

Hume rubbed his nose and said, "Could you explain that at greater depth, Mr. Gonzalo?"

"I meant something you couldn't explain. A puzzle. A *mystery.*"

Avalon brought the palm of his hand down on the table with a loud slap. "Mario, I move we eject you from membership."

"You can't," said Gonzalo angrily. "There are no restrictions on the questions we ask."

"Except the canons of good taste, for heaven's sake."

"What's in bad taste about asking for a mystery? I like mysteries. If he doesn't have any, he can say so." He turned to Hume, frowning, and, in a distinctly self-righteous voice, said, "Well, have you had any kind of mystery in connection with your speaking engagements?"

He then brushed the sleeves of his red velvet jacket, as though sweeping away all petty objections to the question.

Hume was smiling delightedly. "Well, yes! As a matter of fact, I did have. How odd that you should ask. It was years ago, of course, but it was a real mystery. We didn't have the slightest idea where the fellow had gone. —Do you want to hear it?"

Gonzalo rose from his seat and said, "*I* do, but I'll be glad to put it to a vote. Is there anyone here who *doesn't* want to hear it?"

There wasn't a sound, and then Avalon said, "Well, Mario, we'll listen."

Gonzalo nodded his head emphatically. "All right, then. Mr. Hume, you have the floor."

Hume said mildly, "I'll be glad to. But are you going to stop me midway, or will I be allowed to talk freely?"

Avalon said, "I assure you, Mr. Hume. You will be allowed to talk. Roger as host will have absolute control over the conversation and when he sayeth 'Speak' we will speak, and when he sayeth 'Speak not,' we will remain silent. —Right, Roger?"

"Right," said Halsted.

"I will begin," said Hume, "and take my chance."

The story begins [said Hume] some years ago when I was invited to give a talk in Seattle. It meant I would have to fly, obviously, and I'm not keen on flying. I never do it voluntarily; certainly not in January. What's more, the fee offered was considerably less than I liked. So, to put it all into one tightly crumpled ball, I said no.

And it was a good thing I said no, because, as it happened, the Northwest was visited by a tenacious fog on just the day I would have arrived. Even assuming I would have landed safely, very few planes left Seattle for a week thereafter, and I would have been stranded. That would have annoyed me, since I had work to do at home, and it would have annoyed my employer, too. The firm doesn't mind my speaking, since I generally give it a plug or two, and it looks good for them to be concerned with, and involved in, the future. Still, my staying away a week would have been pushing them a little far.

All that is irrelevant, however. The important thing is that the gentleman at the other end didn't accept my no. He and his associates took advantage of the miracle of modern communication and came back at me with the suggestion that I sit right in New York and submit to a twenty-minute interview on television. The interview would be taped and eventually played for a presumably eager audience in Seattle.

The fee was still less than I would have liked, but I was flattered at their persistence. Then, too, I wouldn't have to travel. The interview would take place at a midtown location within walking distance of my apartment, if the weather was passable, which is, of course, by no means a foregone conclusion in December. Anyway, I accepted.

The gentleman inviting me—I forget his name, but that's immaterial, so I'll call him Smith—sensed a residium of unenthusiasm about me and tried to reassure me that all would be made as simple as possible for me. He told me that he would come and get me in a taxi at nine-twenty A.M. in order to get me there at nine-thirty. The cameraman, scheduled to get there shortly after nine A.M., would be all set up and ready when I arrived.

That was an important point to me. I'd done television work—cameras being set up for an interview in some hotel room, for instance—and let me tell you that there's no easier way to be driven crazy. Television has been around for forty years and the cameramen still haven't worked out a system for setting up lights in such a way that the subject is well-illuminated and with no distracting shadows.

Besides, they all consider themselves artists and there's some sort of law, apparently, that compels artists never to be satisfied. Every adjustment here throws out something there. It takes hours for them to reach a point of near-satisfaction, and then when you sit down, they become aware for the first time that you wear glasses, and that those glasses cast an undesirable reflection—and so all the weary work must be gone through again.

I said, "Are you sure the cameraman will be ready, that all I'll have to do will be to sit down?"

"Positive," he said, and that swung it.

Came the day. Smith pulled up in his taxi on time and off we went. We arrived at the proper place within ten minutes, and, as we went up, Smith said to me, "He'll be all ready for us."

I tried not to let my cynicism show. I'm convinced that cameramen are not ready for anything at any time for anyone. "Fine," I said.

We rose to one of the upper floors and swung into the office just before nine-thirty A.M. We had entered the offices of quite a large law firm, in which an old army buddy of Smith's was a senior partner. Let's call him Jones, because I don't remember his name, either. They were lending us the use of a conference room.

Smith said jovially to the receptionist, "Hello, I'm Smith and this is Mr. Hume. We're here for the television taping. I suppose the cameraman has arrived and is set up."

The receptionist said, rather indifferently, "I didn't see any cameraman, sir."

"What? No cameraman?"

"No, sir."

Smith frowned but decided to be invincibly optimist. "It can't be," he said. "He's waiting for us."

But he wasn't. We walked into the conference room and it was as bare as a Shakespearean stage.

"Where is he?" I asked.

"I don't know," said Smith.

Down came Smith's buddy, Jones, who shook hands with me, and said to Smith, "Well, where is he?"

"I don't know," said Smith again.

I said, "Better call his office."

Smith said, "His office is in Indianapolis."

Whereupon I said, rather nonplussed, "Aren't there any cameramen in New York? Why send in one from Indianapolis?"

Smith shrugged. "It's a firm we always work with."

Jones pointed to a telephone in the corner. He said to Smith, "Push any button at the bottom that's not lit up, then push 8 and wait for another dial tone, push 1, the area code, and the number."

I waited patiently. It's an amazing thing. Usually, the one thing that brings out the fury in me is having to wait. All sorts of things can go wrong and I am patience itself. Everyone remarks on what a sweet fellow I am. But if someone doesn't appear at the agreed-upon instant, a frown creases my brow. Let five minutes pass, and smoke is curling out of my ears. But time was passing and it was almost the moment at which I was counting on having *finished* the interview, and the cameraman hadn't even showed up, and I wasn't in the least perturbed. There was a mystery about it, and I was interested.

Smith had returned from the telephone. "He left yesterday," he said, "and the manager says he had the right name, the right address, and everything was as it should be. What's more, the manager says the cameraman assigned to us is known as 'Old Reliable.' He's worked all over the world, and he never misses an appointment."

I said, "He's missed this one. Where's he supposed to be today, then, if he left yesterday?"

"At a hotel," said Smith.

"Did he ever get there?" I asked.

It was back to the telephone and, after a while, Smith said, "He registered last night."

Jones said, "All right, then. He took a taxi and the taxi driver spotted him for an out-of-towner and took him to this place by way of Yonkers. Taxi drivers have been known to do that."

"That's impossible," said Smith with intense irritation. "He's staying at the New York Hilton. Isn't that right in the neighborhood?"

"The New York Hilton?" Jones sounded nonplussed. "Yes, it is. It's right across the street. All he has to do is cross Fifty-fourth Street."

"Yes. So he wouldn't take a taxi, would he?"

"I guess not. The hotel's address is 1335 Sixth and we're at 1345 Sixth. The biggest greenhorn in the world wouldn't take a taxi to go ten numbers along a particular street, and this guy is a world traveler who's called Old Reliable."

I felt cynicism rising as high as my nostrils and said,

"So Old Reliable is here in the big city. He's gone on a toot, brought home an amiable young woman, and he's sleeping it off."

Smith looked indignant. "Come on, the manager said he's forty-eight years old. He's no wild kid."

"He's no dead hulk, either," I said. "I'm older than he is and I could do it easily. I mean, I don't, but I could if I wanted to."

"Well, he wouldn't do it, if he had a date to keep in the morning. He's a professional man."

"All right," I said. "You're talking me into wondering if he didn't have a heart attack in the night; if he might not be lying in that hotel bed right now, dying, or maybe dead."

Smith and Jones both looked uneasy. Smith said uncertainly, "Do you think we ought to call the police?"

Jones said, "Not before we have someone look into his room."

Jones went to the phone this time. He spoke crisply into it, then hung up. We all maintained a worried silence for a while.

Smith said, "Do you suppose he came to this building and couldn't get in? I imagine the security is tight, and he may be wandering about the lobby right now."

"Security is tight, sure," said Jones, "but a pass was delivered to him last night. He should have had no trouble getting in."

"Maybe it never got to him," I said, ever the pessimist, "and he never got past the lobby."

Jones said, "I'll send someone to the lobby to look."

By that time the phone was ringing. Jones answered it, talked awhile, and came back to say, "Hotel security went into his room. His baggage is there, but he isn't.

And there's no camera equipment. So he left with his cameras."

"Then where is he?" I asked.

There was no answer, of course. Jones thought awhile and said, "I suppose they looked in the bathroom."

Smith shrugged. "I assume the security people know their business."

By now I had been there nearly an hour and word came up that there was no sign of any cameraman wandering about the lobby. Obviously, if he was carrying camera equipment about with him, he would be easily spotted. For that matter, the security man downstairs had not seen anyone with such equipment come in, with or without a pass.

I said, "Did they check as to whether he had signed in?"

Jones shook his head. "He wouldn't have to sign in, if he had a pass. They'd just wave him through."

Smith said, "You don't suppose he got off the elevator on the wrong floor, do you? He couldn't be wandering about helplessly?"

Jones looked at his watch. "He was due here an hour and a half ago. How could he be wandering around on the wrong floor for an hour and a half? There's not a floor in this building which doesn't have security guards. No one would be allowed to wander about anywhere. —And he wouldn't, anyway. He'd ask. After all, he knew the name of this firm. For that matter, he knew the correct floor."

There was a sticky silence and we all took turns looking at our watches. Finally, Jones muttered an "Excuse me" and left. He was back in three minutes and said, "I just talked to Josie—"

"Who's she?" I asked.

"The receptionist. She swears no cameraman came in. In fact, no one, *no one* came in who wasn't a member of the firm, except you, Smith, and you, Mr. Hume."

Smith said, "Was she at her desk the whole time?"

"The receptionist insists she was."

"You mean she didn't go out to powder her nose, or whatever?"

"She says she didn't. She says she was on the job and alert all morning, and she says no one could possibly have gotten into the place without her seeing him."

I said, "Is she a truthful woman?"

Jones frowned at me. "We can trust her. We've had her on the job nearly five years now and if she says no one got in, no one got in."

Smith said, "Then where is he? How could he have gotten lost just crossing the street?"

I said, "We're eliminating everything, except the possibility that he might have had an accident crossing the street."

Smith said shakily, "You mean he might have been hit by a car?"

"It's been known to happen," I said.

"It would have to be pretty serious," said Jones. "Being a professional, he would call us, or the home office. Even if he were immobilized he would tell someone else to call us."

I said, "If he were conscious. If he were alive."

Jones said, "If it was a really serious accident in the street just outside, they'd known about it downstairs."

I said, "Did anyone ask?"

Jones hesitated about two seconds and called downstairs. It didn't take long. He shook his head. "No one down there knows anything about any accident."

Smith said, "Call the police. They would have to have a record."

Jones didn't seem to want to, but he did. That took longer, but the result was the same. He said, "The police say there is no record of any accident at any time this A.M. at Fifty-fourth Street and Sixth Avenue."

Smith said, "Then where is he?"

I got up. "Gentlemen," I said, "I don't know where he is, but I can wait no longer. I've got other appointments to meet, other work to do. I'm terribly sorry but I have to leave now. Still, I would like to know the answer to this. If at any time you find out, please phone me. If you're kind enough to do this, then I'll come back a second time to complete the taping."

So I left. —Within an hour, Smith did call me and explained the situation. A week later, I returned and did the job. There's your mystery.

The Black Widowers stared dubiously at their guest. Halsted spoke for all, finally, when he said, "Did that really happen, Brad? Or are you having a bit of fun with us?"

"No, no," said Hume. "It's all true. Every word. Scout's honor. It happened exactly as I described it."

"Well, then, tell us what happened to the cameraman."

Hume shook his head, still smiling. "You wanted a mystery and I gave it to you. You tell *me* what happened. You have all the facts. I'll give you two hints. No one was lying. It wasn't a setup of any kind. The second hint is that it's no tragedy. The cameraman was in no way harmed. Now, where was he?"

Gonzalo said, "Did he have a temporary bout of amnesia and go wandering off?"

Hume said, "No, he was in no way harmed. Neither physically nor mentally."

"See here," said Avalon rather heavily. "You don't really know he was in the hotel at all—or in New York, even. No one saw him there that morning. The pass was sent over the night before, but I'll bet it was just left at the desk for him. Who knows *who* might have been in the room?"

Hume said, "It was someone who signed the cameraman's name in the register."

"Anyone could do that if he knew the name," said Avalon. "The cameraman had a reservation at the hotel and someone knew of it. The someone delayed the cameraman somehow, registered in his name, and had a room for a night at a very posh hotel at someone else's expense. Hotel service found baggage there in the morning, when our imposter had gone about his own business, but no camera equipment. That might just mean that there was no camera equipment in the first place."

Hume said, "Why should anyone do this?"

Avalon said, "I don't know. I could invent motives by the score, perhaps, but I couldn't prove any of them."

Trumbull said, "Someone on the run needed a false name and a secure room just for the night—a spy—"

Drake said, with a tone that showed clearly he was not serious, "A bomb outrage. Needed a room in which to plant a bomb."

"Gentlemen," said Hume, brushing back his mane of hair. "You *are* inventing things. As a matter of fact, it never occurred to us to locate the bellhop who took the cameraman's baggage to the room, but if we had, that bellhop would have told us he had brought up some items that looked as though they might be camera equipment. No, no, it's absolutely certain that the right man registered in the hotel."

"In that case," said Rubin, "he was himself up to funny stuff. He had a girl he had to see, some money matter he had to attend to, something or other in the great city he wanted to do. When he got down to the lobby of the hotel, he checked his equipment, grabbed a taxi, and dashed off. Maybe he thought he'd be back in half an hour and that you would wait that long for him without much fuss. But perhaps it took two hours, because he may have underestimated New York traffic, or gotten into a minor tangle of some sort that delayed him."

Hume said, "I wouldn't think he'd do that. Surely, a job would come first with Old Reliable."

Now there was a long, dank silence, as every face furrowed, and every pair of lips pursed themselves. So it seemed to Hume, until he noticed the exception.

He said, "Henry's the only one smiling. —Henry, what are you grinning about?"

Henry said, "I beg your pardon, sir. I mean no disrespect, but you did say it was no tragedy, and it occurs to me that it was a farce, and so I can't help but smile."

Avalon said, in his rolling baritone, "Do you have a solution, Henry? If so, out with it."

Henry said, "If I have your permission, gentlemen?"

The chorus was immediate and unanimous.

Henry said, "Mr. Hume made it clear that the cameraman was an old, reliable professional who had worked all over the world, and who had, presumably, always given satisfaction. Since he was not found dead in the room, and the police had no report of any accident, we can only assume that in the morning he had gotten ready to do his work, had crossed the street to the office building as he had been instructed to do, and, going to the proper place, had set up his television equipment."

"No," said Avalon. "The receptionist swears he never came in and Mr. Hume has told us the receptionist didn't lie. That means— Mr. Hume, please forgive me the question I am forced to ask. It is merely a matter of the search for a solution? When you told us the receptionist did not lie, may I take it that *you* did not lie?"

"I did not lie," said Hume with equanimity.

"In that case, Henry," said Avalon, "your assumption is wrong."

"Perhaps not, Mr. Avalon," said Henry. "Mr. Hume was supposed to arrive at nine-thirty A.M. and the cameraman was supposed to come at about 9 A.M. in order to be ready by nine-thirty. Isn't that right, Mr. Hume?"

"That's right."

"And the receptionist would have been a very curious receptionist if she had arrived much before nine A.M., which would be the opening of the business day. The cameraman, however, was so reliable, efficient, and professional, that it is quite likely he arrive at eight-thirty A.M. That would account for the fact that the receptionist never saw him. What's more, I expect a new shift came on in the lobby at nine A.M. and that's why no one who is in the next shift down there saw him come in."

"And the door would have been locked," said Avalon, "and he would have had to wait for her."

"Would he, sir? It was a large legal firm, we were told, so there would be many lawyers working there. At least one would have been at work early. He would answer the door, see the cameraman's pass, let him in, go back to his own work, and then forget the whole thing."

Avalon said, "And what happened to the cameraman thereafter? Did he drop through a hole in the floor? Where *was* he? No one saw him."

"Mr. Hume," said Henry, "may I ask you one more question?"

"Go ahead, Henry."

"Considering that it was a large legal firm, did it possess more than one conference room?"

Hume leaned his head back and laughed in sheer enjoyment. "Two, it turned out, Henry. Two!"

"I thought so," said Henry. "The lawyer who let him in took him to the wrong conference room. The cameraman waited in one, and you waited in the other the whole morning, and neither knew where the other was."

"No," said Avalon. "How would that be possible? Wouldn't the cameraman come out and say, 'Where *is* everybody?' "

"In a way, he did," said Hume, choking down his laughter. "He used the phone in his room to call Jones. Jones's secretary answered and said that Jones was away from his desk—which he was, being down in our conference room, wondering where the cameraman was. The cameraman said he had to tape someone, and the secretary said she would tell Jones just as soon as he returned, only Jones didn't return until after I had left. —How did you get it, Henry?"

"In the usual way," said Henry. "Once you and the other two gentlemen in the conference room, and my fellow members of the Black Widowers, too, had cut away all the complexity, the only thing left was something very simple and I just pointed it out."

AFTERWORD

Of all the Black Widowers stories I have written, this one made the
least demand on my imagination. *It really happened.* It happened exactly as I have described it in the story. I must say that it made me
realize how much less clever I am than Henry. I was completely lost
for a solution when it happened to me.

Incidentally, I was very amused at the fact that this story received
more reader flak than any other Black Widowers I had written. A
surprising number of people wrote to object to this or that facet of the
story as improbable. Some even criticized my street addresses, although I gave the actual addresses that the buildings did have.

The conclusion is that in my fiction I am careful to make everything probable and to tie up all loose ends. Real life is not hampered
by such considerations.

The story first appeared in the October 1986 issue of *Ellery Queen's
Mystery Magazine.*

THE OLD PURSE

"William Teller!" said Thomas Trumbull, host for that month's banquet of the Black Widowers, announcing the guest of the evening. He did so, however, with a certain trepidation. His frowning glance fixed itself particularly on Mario Gonzalo.

Gonzalo, gorgeously arrayed as usual, this time in his brown velvet jacket, ignored it. "William Teller," he said delightedly. "Are you a descendant of William Tell, perhaps?"

"Not at all," said Teller agreeably. He had an olive complexion, thick black hair, and a thick black mustache as well. "Actually, William Tell is simply a legend and probably never really existed. However, I'm of Swiss extraction and the first name runs in the family, perhaps in homage to the old fraud. Actually, Teller is an ordinary German word and means 'plate.' "

Geoffrey Avalon, looking down from his seventy-four inches, said, "Parents are often insensitive to the plight of a youngster. I was saved from serious scapegoating by the fact that I always used Jeff as my name. At that I was lucky, since the name alternates with Broderick, and it is my eldest son, not I, who must cope with that. Fortunately, he has always been a muscular youth, as I never was."

"Names can be an inspiration, too," said Teller. "When I was young I dreamed of being a superlative archer. I wanted people to say, 'William Tell was good, but William Teller is better.' I was an assiduous archer at summer camp for that reason."

"Did you make it?" asked James Drake with interest, lighting up the inevitable cigarette.

"No. I was remarkably untalented. The only time I ever hit the target, let alone the bull's-eye, was when I deliberately aimed at something else. Too bad. If I could have won the national archery contest with my name, I would have made every newspaper in the United States; also the 'Believe It or Not' columns, if any exist now."

"You'd have done even better," said Emmanuel Rubin judiciously, "if your name had been Robin Hood."

Roger Halsted said eagerly, "A great many so-called coincidences are manufactured in this way. Someone named Robin Hood would be bound to try his hand at archery and if he were good, saying 'Believe It or Not' misses the point. It would be a natural consequence. In fact, I have a suspicion that the queer things that happen to everybody aren't mystical, but natural. For instance—"

No one ever found out the instance that Halsted was about to give, for Henry, that waiter supreme, chose that moment to announce in his quietly effective manner that dinner was served.

All sat down to tripe madeleine, followed by crisp roast duck in cherry brandy sauce with wild rice and truffles, something that effectively muffled conversation. In fact the dinner pursued a kind of satisfied quiet, in which even Rubin's occasional comments were given out with hushed equanimity, until Trumbull, over the coffee, rattled his spoon against the water glass and appointed Avalon as griller-in-chief.

"Mr. Teller," said Avalon, "how do you justify your existence?"

Teller did not seem to be perturbed by the question. "By making people think."

"And how do you do that?"

"I have a newspaper column called 'On the Contrary.' It does not appear in any of the New York newspapers but it does in one hundred and two papers of moderate size elsewhere in the nation. In my column, I present the unpopular side of any controversy, not necessarily because I passionately support that side but because I think it is apt to be inadequately presented to the public. The public may, after all, be misled, even sometimes dangerously misled, by hearing only one side of a question. Many might not even know that another view exists."

"Can you give us an example of that?" asked Avalon.

"Certainly. In a recent column I presented the view that so-called terrorists have of themselves."

"So-called?" said Drake, in gentle interrogation.

"Yes, indeed. So-called," said Teller. "They don't think of themselves as terrorists, any more than we think of terrorists as such when they are on our side. When we approve their aims, we call them freedom fighters and compare them favorably with George Washington."

"Then you defend terrorism?" said Avalon.

"Not necessarily. I merely try to penetrate the reasoning for the defense. For instance, the United States thinks all conflicts should either take place with missiles, planes, tanks, and all the paraphernalia of war; or by votes, resolutions, arguments, debates, and all the paraphernalia of politics. However, what if there are people who feel they have a just cause, but who lack the paraphernalia of war and are denied the paraphernalia of politics? What do they then do? Surely, they must fight with the weapons they have. Our cry, then, is that they are cowards who strike without warning, and kill innocent civilians at random. But then, is it brave of us to 'fight fair' against forces that are infinitely smaller than our own?"

"I see your point," said Rubin, "but terrorism can be argued against on pragmatic grounds even if you abandon the high moral stand. It simply won't work. Random bombings make headlines and cause private pain and public frustration, but they don't achieve their ends."

"Sure they do, on occasion," said Teller. "The Iranian capture of the American Embassy held the United States up to worldwide ridicule, made Khomeini the hero of the Arab radicals throughout Islam, and destroyed the Carter presidency. And they didn't even kill anybody."

"Yes," said Rubin, "but that was self-defeating, for it led to the Reagan presidency, which has taken a much harder antiterrorist line, and brought about the bombing of Libya, for instance, as punishment for its support of terrorism."

"Yes, but we have yet to see what that will lead to on

the other side. To continue my argument, during war, terrorists are called guerrillas or resistance forces or raiders or commandos, or anything but terrorists, and during World War II such irregular forces in every supposedly conquered nation, notably in Yugoslavia, did much to help defeat the Nazis. Similarly, the guerrillas of Spain did much to defeat Napoleon."

"Perhaps," said Avalon, "you would not be so cold-blooded about it if you had suffered directly at terrorist hands."

"I imagine not, but the argument would exist even if I, out of personal pique, were to refuse to advance it."

Drake chuckled. "You know, Tom, I assume that Mr. Teller is a friend of yours since you've brought him as a guest. Isn't he, with his views, a dangerous friend, considering your government employment?"

"Not at all," said Trumbull. "He's just a professional devil's advocate. He often supports the government strongly, provided it has happened to do something unpopular."

Teller said, "True enough." He stopped and frowned, as though a sudden thought had struck him. Then he said slowly, "You know, this wouldn't have occurred to me if there hadn't been that talk before dinner about odd connections such as that between me and archery, but there's a connection here in the terrorism matter."

"May I ask what connection you are thinking of?" said Avalon.

"Mr. Rubin had pointed out that my views might change if I were a victim. To be sure, I haven't been, but my wife has, and that might be considered close enough. On the very day my column on terrorism appeared—the very day—my wife was the victim of a mild sort of terrorism. She had her purse snatched. Of course, that was the purest of coincidences. However—" He stopped again.

"Yes, Mr. Teller?" said Avalon.

"Nothing apropos. I was just thinking of the sequel to the incident that was really humorous and even mystifying. But never mind that; let's go back to our discussion of my justification for existence. At the time of our misadventure in Lebanon—"

"Wait, wait," said Gonzalo, rattling his spoon on his water glass. "Back up, Mr. Teller. I want to hear about the humorous and mystifying sequel to the purse snatching."

Teller looked surprised and he turned automatically to Trumbull. "Tom—"

Trumbull shrugged. "Go ahead, tell us about the mystifying sequel. If not, Mario will make life hideous for all of us."

"Wait," said Gonzalo. "Wait one minute. Henry isn't here."

"Henry?" said Teller.

"Our waiter." And Gonzalo raised his voice, "Henry!"

Henry entered the dining room. "Yes, Mr. Gonzalo."

"Don't disappear like that," said Gonzalo peevishly. "Where were you?"

"Disposing of dishes and cutlery, Mr. Gonzalo, but I am at your service now."

"Good. I want you to hear this. Mr. Teller, please start at the beginning."

Teller was staring in surprise. He said, "There really isn't much. My wife was in Grand Central Station and on a crowded escalator her purse vanished. She had it slung over her left shoulder, for she was carrying something in each hand, and our guess is that someone behind her carefully cut the strap, held the bag steady till they reached the bottom of the escalator, and then walked rapidly away, with the purse under his arm. She didn't see a thing, she didn't feel a thing. She knows she had the purse in her possession at the top of the escalator, for she shoved it toward her back for greater convenience, and she didn't have it when she was at the bottom. That's all there is to the story. She wasn't hurt, she wasn't shoved, she wasn't threatened. It was a very professional job."

"You don't seem annoyed," said Gonzalo.

"Well, I was, of course, and so was my wife. Such a loss is always inconvenient. She didn't have much money in it—a few dollars—but she had several credit cards, her driver's license, her automobile registration, some personal papers and photographs, and so on. It meant that she had to report the loss of the credit cards and face a few weeks of doing without, or using mine. It meant negotiating with City Hall over her automobile items, and apparently saying good-bye to all the junk she had in the purse.

"Mostly, though, it was her pride that was hurt. The purse was an old one, old and decrepit and on its last legs. This was on purpose. She had any number of new and fancy purses that she used on dress occasions, but this was the battered thing she used on her shopping trips, when she expected to be in crowds. She claimed that no self-respecting thief would dream of taking a purse so disreputable. They would know there was nothing worthwhile in it. Well, they *did* take it, and even though I was careful to make no reference to her earlier statements—she had always been very smug about her cleverness in this respect—she watched me closely and probably knew what I was thinking."

"And what was the mystifying sequel?" asked Gonzalo.

"Well, yesterday, two days after the snatch, I opened the door of my apartment in order to take the rubbish to the compacter—I work at home—and virtually stumbled over a package which had my wife's name on it in straggling letters. I assumed, at first, it was something the mailman had left, even though he perfectly well knew he wasn't supposed to do that without ringing the bell. But when I picked it up I found it had no address and no stamps on it. So it must have been hand-delivered and that rather infuriated me.

"After all, our apartment house is supposed to have tight security and no one should be able to get into the elevator without passing inspection by the doormen and having us called on the intercom to get our consent to have him, or her, sent up. Naturally, this doesn't always work. Someone comes in when the doormen are busy with something else, or tails someone who belongs in the house so that he seems to be a guest— But it still infuriated me.

"I was angry enough to inspect the length of the hall and look into the two stairwells and the compacter room, which wasn't exactly intelligent of me, and found no one. I then called my wife, showed her the package, and asked if she knew what it might be.

"She said at once, and with great conviction, 'It's a bomb.' Naturally, I laughed at this. We are all getting ridiculously terrorist-conscious. It seemed to me too small to hold a bomb and yet I didn't have the nerve to attempt to open it. After considerable indecision, listening to it for some telltale tick, although I don't know if bombs tick these days, and smelling it, and not having quite enough courage to shake it, I called the police. They told us to put it in the center of our largest room and leave the apartment. Down came a bomb squad in virtually no time, with a portable X-ray unit, and, well . . . it wasn't a bomb.

"They opened it for us, and when they called us back into the apartment, they showed us the contents. Damned if it wasn't what had been stolen from my wife two days before. Everything! The package contained all the papers, including the credit cards, all the junk. It even contained every last bit of money down to the little cache of quarters she kept for public transportation and even a few smaller coins. She counted it in amazement and it was all there. They had taken nothing. Did you ever hear of such a thing? I consider that mystifying. Presumably, it was a thief with an attack of conscience."

Gonzalo, who had listened with close attention, seemed disappointed. "Is that the end of it?"

"The absolute end," said Teller. "But then I told you there was nothing much to it, so you mustn't feel annoyed with me."

Gonzalo shook his head, obviously baffled.

Henry, however, said quietly, "I beg your pardon, Mr. Teller, but may I have your permission to ask a question?"

"Well, of course, if you want to, but I don't see what there is to question."

"It's just that you mentioned all the contents, sir, but you didn't mention the purse itself. Was that returned as well?"

Teller looked astonished. "No, it wasn't. I'm glad you

asked. It was the only thing that didn't come back. My wife was annoyed about that, actually. She said that the purse was valuable to her and they might have returned that, too. My own feeling was that it was simply too bulky to fit into a neat little package. Of course, I pointed out that since her scheme of carrying an old purse hadn't worked, it was no great loss, and, equally of course, she gave me the exasperated look that wives always give husbands who descend into mere logic. Anyway, that's it. They returned everything but the purse."

Halsted said, "That *is* mystifying. They could easily have made a somewhat bigger package. If the thief were sufficiently conscience-stricken to return every last penny, he would certainly have been sufficiently conscience-stricken to return the purse."

Rubin said, "Maybe it fell apart, and he felt it was useless to return the tatters."

"No, no, no," interposed Teller. "It was a staunch leather purse. It was old, and weatherbeaten, and looked like hell, but it wasn't going to fall apart."

Trumbull said, "Do you suppose there was a purpose in keeping it? I mean maybe the purse was what they wanted, so they returned everything else."

"Ridiculous," said Rubin. "If they wanted the purse, they could just dump the contents, at least those parts of it they couldn't use."

Drake stubbed out his cigarette and said in his softly hoarse voice, "You can't have it both ways, Manny. Either the thief was not troubled by a conscience and would return nothing, just dumping whatever he didn't want, as you suggest. Or else, he had a conscience and would return everything except what he absolutely needed. The way I see it is that he was reluctantly stealing something he wanted desperately, and he had no intention of stealing anything else."

"You mean," said Avalon, "he was an honest man who had no choice but to steal something he had to have, but not another item was going to sully his tender and gentlemanly soul."

"That's right," said Drake. "Now if that's the case, think it out a bit. He wants to steal a purse in order to get some specific object it contains. But he only sees the purse and nothing else. He doesn't see what's in it. If he wants something that it contains, he couldn't be sure that this particular purse actually contained it. He might have to steal half a dozen purses, examine each, and then, disappointed of his wish, return everything to its owner; or if he finally found a purse with what he wanted inside, he would remove the wanted object and return everything else.

"I don't think an honest man, a man so honest that he would be driven to make a package of what he had taken and run the risk of returning it personally, would steal in so wholesale and cavalier a fashion. If we allow that—"

"Wait," said Rubin. "We don't necessarily allow that. He might be after what any purse might be thought to contain—money, credit cards—"

"Or," said Trumbull, "he might have happened to see Mrs. Teller open her purse and happened to spy something in it that he wanted, and thereafter followed her in order to seize the chance of grasping it."

"Or for some reason," said Gonzalo, "all he wanted was her identification. He just wanted to know her name and address."

Drake considered matters a moment, humming under his breath, then he said, "I don't think so. If he wanted money or credit cards, he would have kept them, but he returned them. If he had spied something in it that he wanted but that wasn't intrinsically valuable, he wouldn't have returned *that*, but he did."

"Wait," said Gonzalo, "how can we be sure he returned everything? There might be some little item that Mrs. Teller didn't notice was gone. Perhaps there was something in the purse that even Mrs. Teller didn't know was there, or had forgotten was there."

"I don't think so," said Teller dubiously. "I can't speak for my wife altogether, but she is a very methodical person with an orderly brain. If she says everything was returned, I'm ready to bet on it."

Avalon cleared his throat and said, "You understand, Mr. Teller, this is a game we're playing. We're trying to work out the implications of this odd event. Please do not be offended, then, when I suggest, merely as a remote possibility, that your wife had, let us say, a letter in her purse that she wanted no one to see. If the thief now has it, and if your wife dare not admit it's gone—"

Teller said grimly, "You are suggesting that the thief now intends to blackmail her. Gentlemen, you'll have to assume I know my wife. She would sooner see the blackmailer—and herself—in hell than pay a penny. Please put blackmail right out of your mind."

Halsted said, "He might return the credit cards but keep a record of the number for later forgery. Or of the car registration."

Teller said, "Useless. My wife has already canceled all those things and will eventually have new ones. The forgeries would be unusable."

"What about the identification?" insisted Gonzalo.

"He had her name and address, and he didn't have to keep the physical objects that gave him the information."

"Why on Earth," said Trumbull, "would he run the risk of purse snatching for that? He might simply have followed her home. He might have struck up an acquaintanceship with her somehow. And why would he want to know the name and address of a woman unknown to him? You'll excuse me, Bill, if I say that she's not a raving beauty?"

Teller smiled. "She's beautiful to me, but to anyone else she is merely a rather ordinary-looking middle-aged woman, I dare say."

Drake was looking from one to another as each spoke, and he finally said, "If we've eliminated all the various reasons for stealing a purse and returning the contents, may I be allowed to finish my thought?"

"Go ahead, Jim," said Avalon.

"Very well, then. You've all played about with complexities and, like Henry, I'm going for simplicity. The thief returned everything but the purse. What's more, all he could see at the time he decided to steal something from Mrs. Teller was the purse, not its contents. Conclusion: He was after the purse itself, nothing more, so he returned all it contained."

Rubin said, "But Jim, that just substitutes one problem for another. Why on Earth should the thief want the purse? —Mr. Teller, are you sure the purse had no intrinsic value?"

"None," said Teller emphatically.

"It wasn't an antique of some sort, was it?"

Teller thought a moment. "I'm not an expert on antiques. My wife bought the purse at least twenty years ago, but it's my impression she picked it up in Klein's.

Nothing Klein's sells would become an antique, would it?"

Gonzalo said, "Mickey Mouse watches, which sold for a dollar apiece to begin with, are now valuable antiques."

"Yes," said Avalon, "but if the man were a collector and recognized that an object might be worth, say, ten thousand dollars, wouldn't he say, 'Pardon me, madam, but your purse reminds me of one my dear, dead wife once had. Would you be willing to sell it to me for ten dollars so that I can have it for its sentimental value?' Even if he were driven to theft, he would *try* to get it legally first."

Drake said, "It looks as though we're driven to the conclusion that he wanted an old, beat-up purse for its own sake."

"Why?" said Avalon.

"Because he couldn't buy one. All those for sale are new ones. Even if he went to a secondhand store, the purses would be furbished to look as good as possible. He had to find one that was already old and beaten up and looked it."

Gonzalo said, "Wouldn't he try to buy it first? 'Hey, lady, you wouldn't sell me that old beat-up, worthless purse for ten dollars, would you, lady?' "

"Besides," said Trumbull, "why would anybody *want* an old, beat-up purse?"

Halsted said, "In the story of Aladdin, the wicked sorcerer went about offering to give new lamps for old, because he wanted Aladdin's old wishing lamp."

Avalon favored Halsted with a haughty stare. "I think we can eliminate the possibility that Mrs. Teller owned a wishing purse."

"Just joking," said Halsted.

"Maybe the thief was a theatrical director who needed an old purse for a play he was doing," said Gonzalo.

"Nuts," said Rubin with contempt. "They would buy a new purse and scuff it up."

Trumbull said, "That eliminates the whole need for an old, beat-up purse. Whatever use one might have, couldn't one buy a new purse, or a good-looking second-hand one and scuff it up and stamp on it and scrape it? Why steal one?"

The conversation came to a dead halt. Finally, Avalon said, "I think we've beaten this to death. There's no logical explanation, and we may simply have to admit that people do illogical things sometimes, and let it go."

"Oh, no," said Gonzalo, "not until Henry has his say. —Henry, what do you make of all this?"

Henry smiled gently and said, "I think, as Mr. Avalon does, that people sometimes do illogical things. However, if we want to continue to play the game, there is one occasion when stealing an old purse is more effective than buying a purse and scuffing it up."

"When is that, Henry?" asked Teller.

"When the thief wants to make sure he is not identified. If the purse is bought, then it is conceivable that something about it can lead investigators to the place where it is purchased, and the seller can then, conceivably, identify the person who bought it. In this case, the thief was not seen and cannot conceivably be identified. Even if it is traced back to Mrs. Teller, she cannot make an identification. He may be so honest a man that he takes the risk of returning everything else, but if he is careful to use a nondescript box and paper for a package, wearing gloves at the time, scrawls a simple name on it, and quietly delivers it without being seen, he is still not likely to be identified."

"But in that case," said Teller, "he would want the purse for a criminal purpose."

"One would suppose so," said Henry.

"Like what?"

"Still playing the game," said Henry, "I can invent a purpose—farfetched, but making a weird kind of sense. The purse was stolen in Grand Central Station and it is well known that there are homeless people who live in the station and who are generally left alone by a society that is too callous to go too far out of its way to help them, but not so callous as to evict them from a warm and secure place.

"No one pays much attention to these derelicts, in fact. The average person tends to avert his or her eyes from these sad individuals, if only because they look dirty and miserable so that the onlooker feels either uncomfortably repelled or uncomfortably conscience-stricken. It would be easy for someone to assume the dirt, the old clothes, and the wretched appearance of a homeless person and count on not being interfered with, or even noticed. Suppose, then, a woman were made up as what is called a bag lady and needs a purse to carry off the deception—"

Gonzalo interrupted. "Hold on, you call them bag ladies because they carry their personal belongings in brown paper bags."

"I'm sure that is the origin of the term, Mr. Gonzalo," said Henry, "but it has become a generic word for such derelicts. I am sure that a homeless woman with a purse would still be considered a bag lady. However, the purse could scarcely be a new one. A bag lady, carrying a new purse, would surely attract attention. It would have to be an old beat-up purse that would fit in with the rest of the costume."

Teller laughed. "Very clever tale-spinning, Henry, but I don't think my wife would take to the notion that she carries a purse suitable for a bag lady. Why would this disguised bag lady need a purse anyway? Why not a brown paper bag?"

"Perhaps," said Henry, "because a paper bag would not be strong enough to contain whatever the bag lady was carrying; only a sturdy, but old purse would do. For instance—and this thought occurs to me only because of the earlier discussion of terrorism—what if the supposed bag lady were carrying an explosive device which she planned to place in the station so as to do a great deal of damage? As Mr. Teller has pointed out, terrorists may look upon themselves as lofty and noble patriots. They would steal a purse that was absolutely essential to their needs, if stealing were the safest way to obtain it, but they would scorn to keep the contents. They are not *thieves*, but patriots. In their own eyes, at least."

Gonzalo said admiringly, "Good Lord, Henry, how nicely you make it all fit."

"Simply a game, sir. Dr. Drake did the real work."

Trumbull said, frowning darkly as he passed his hand over his tightly waved white hair, "You make it all fit *too* nicely, Henry. Is there a chance this is what really happened?"

"I scarcely think so, Mr. Trumbull," said Henry. "There has been no report of an explosion anywhere in the city."

"It's only three days since the purse was stolen," said Trumbull. He turned to Teller. "I don't suppose your wife reported the theft, did she?"

"No, of course not. She couldn't make any identification, not the slightest. She might as well say the purse had disappeared by the wave of an enchanter's wand."

"Even if she had," said Avalon, "what could the police do about it, Tom? And why should they think anything like the story Henry has dreamed up? That only arose out of the fact that everything was returned yesterday."

"And I don't suppose you reported that, either, did you, Bill?" asked Trumbull.

"No, of course not," said Teller.

"Well," said Trumbull, rising heavily to his feet. "This may be crazy, but I'm going to call someone I know. And if"—he looked at his watch—"I catch him watching television or getting ready for bed, that's just too bad."

"He might not be home, Tom," said Avalon.

"I'll get someone," said Trumbull grimly.

He left for the telephone in the next room, while the remaining Black Widowers and their guest remained in an uneasy silence. Only Henry seemed unperturbed.

Finally, Gonzalo said, "Do you really think there might be something to what you've thought up, Henry?"

Henry said, "We had better simply wait for Mr. Trumbull to return."

He did, eventually. He sat down and for perhaps fifteen seconds simply stared at Henry.

"Well, Tom?" said Avalon.

Tom said, "It amounts to this. If ever this gets out, Henry is going to be indicted for witchcraft."

Henry's eyebrows lifted slightly. "If you mean by that, sir, that there *was* a bomb, I think it would be more appropriate to give the credit to the logical minds of the Black Widowers."

"Of *you*, Henry," said Trumbull. "There was indeed a

bomb. It was placed in a spot where it would perhaps not have caused very much in the way of casualties, but it would certainly have disrupted train service for weeks. —What's more, it was contained in an old leather purse."

"But," said Henry, "there was no explosion, I take it."

"No, because the purse was spotted, quite by accident, and because the person who did the spotting lifted it and was surprised by its weight. Then, because these are troubled times, it occurred to him to do precisely the right thing. He called the bomb squad—as you did, Bill."

"That's luck," said Gonzalo. "If it hadn't been found, Henry's analysis would have come too late."

"It's not too late for everything. I'm afraid I told them enough of the story so that your wife is going to have to go there and identify her purse. If it *is* her purse, and I'm ready to bet my last year's salary it is, then they know something important the terrorists don't know they know. They'll start looking at the derelicts in the station and they might well find something. Thank you, Henry."

Teller looked perturbed. "I don't think Jenny is going to enjoy getting involved with this."

Trumbull said, "She has no choice. Just tell her she's got to."

"Yes, that's easy for you to say," said the troubled Teller.

Henry said, "Take heart, Mr. Teller. I'm sure that your professional ability to uphold unpopular points of view in a convincing manner will make it possible for you to accomplish this task with ease."

AFTERWORD

People ask me where I get my ideas, and the answer is: From any place I can.

For the most part I have to think and think before something occurs to me, and that's hard work. (Try it, if you don't believe me.) Therefore, when something comes my way that can be twisted into a story *without* my having to knock myself out thinking, I grab it at once.

A woman told me that her purse had once been stolen, and then returned, rather in the fashion I described in this story. I asked why it was returned, and she said, "I don't know."

Saying "I don't know" sets my antennae to quivering at once. After all, Henry would know. All I have to do is make up a story around the incident. In this case, that was exactly what I did.

The story first appeared in the March 1987 issue of *Ellery Queen's Mystery Magazine.*

THE QUIET PLACE

Emmanuel Rubin, who was host of the Black Widowers banquet that evening, had been at his loudest and most quarrelsome.

He had insisted on the unimportance of algebra to Roger Halsted, who taught the subject in a junior high school; denounced the patent system to Geoffrey Avalon, who was a patent lawyer; denied the validity of quantum theory in connection with molecular structure to James Drake, the chemist; pointed out the uselessness of espionage in modern warfare to Thomas Trumbull, the cipher expert; and finally placed the cherry on the sundae by watching Mario Gonzalo as, with consummate ease and skill, he drew a cartoon of that evening's guest, and telling him he knew nothing at all about caricature.

Trumbull, who, of all the Black Widowers, was least likely to be amused by Rubin in his wilder moments, finally said, "What the devil is wrong with you, Manny? We're used to having you wrong at the top of your voice, and taking on one or another of us with some indefensible point of view, but this time you're tackling us all."

It was Rubin's guest who answered Trumbull in a quiet voice and, at that, it was almost the first time he had spoken that evening. He was a young man, not far gone into his thirties, it would appear, with thin blond hair, light blue eyes, a face that was wide across the cheekbones, and a smile that seemed to come easily and yet had something sad about it. His name was Theodore Jarvik.

"I'm afraid, gentlemen, the fault is mine, if it be a fault to follow professional procedure. I have recently become Manny's editor and I was forced to hand back his latest manuscript with requests for revision."

"For eviscerative revision," muttered Rubin.

"I did offer to cancel out the invitation for this evening," said Jarvik, with his sad smile, "on the supposition that Manny would just as soon not look at me right now."

Gonzalo raised his eyebrows and said, "Manny doesn't mind this sort of thing. We've all heard him say about a thousand times that the true professional writer takes revisions and even rejections in stride. He says that one way you can tell an amateur or a beginner is by noting that he considers his every word sac—"

"Oh, shut up, Mario," said Rubin, clearly chafing. "You don't know the details."

"Actually," said Jarvik, "Manny and I will work it out."

Avalon, from his seventy-four inches of height, said in his grave baritone, "I'm curious, Manny, have you called Mr. Jarvik a 'young punk' yet?"

"Oh, for God's sake," said Rubin, reddening.

"No, he hasn't, Mr. Avalon," said Jarvik, "but he's *thought* it very loudly."

"That is *not true,*" shouted Rubin at the top of his considerable decibel rating.

"Let's wash out this night," said Drake in resignation. "You're going to be in such a foul humor, Manny, that—"

"When have I *ever* been in a foul—" began Rubin, and then Henry, the pearl-beyond-price of waiters, interrupted.

"Gentlemen, please be seated," he said. "Dinner is served."

To do Rubin justice, he did his best to control himself during the dinner. His eyes, behind his thick glasses, flashed; his sparse beard bristled; and he snarled unceasingly; but he managed to say little and leave the conversation to the others.

Gonzalo, who sat next to Jarvik, said to him, "Pardon me, but you keep humming."

Jarvik flushed again, something his fair skin made easy. "I'm sorry, I didn't mean to disturb you."

"It doesn't exactly disturb me. It's just that I don't recognize the tune."

"I don't know. I'm just improvising, I suppose."

"Is that so?" And Gonzalo was quiet for the remainder of the dinner until the rattle of spoon on glass marked the beginning of the questioning of the guest.

Gonzalo said, "May I volunteer to do the grilling?"

"You can, for all of me," growled Rubin, who, as host, had the task of appointing the griller. "Just don't ask him to justify his existence. The editor doesn't live who can do that."

"On the contrary," said Gonzalo, "any editor who has handed back a manuscript of yours has already justified his existence a hundred times over."

Halsted said, "May I suggest we go ahead with grilling our guest and not needling each other?"

Gonzalo brushed some imaginary dust off the sleeve of his loudly checked jacket and said, "Exactly. Mr. Jarvik, during the course of the dinner I asked you what tune you were humming and you said you were improvising. I don't think that's quite right. Once or twice you hummed again after that and it was always the same tune. Now that you are being grilled, you are forced to give full and honest answers, as I hope Manny has explained to you. I therefore repeat: What was the tune you were humming?"

Trumbull intervened. "What kind of stupid question is that?"

Gonzalo turned a haughty face on Trumbull. "As the griller, I am under the impression I can ask any question I choose consistent with human dignity. Host's decision."

"Go ahead, Manny," said Rubin, thus appealed to. "Ask away. —And leave him alone, Tom."

Gonzalo said, "Answer the question, Mr. Jarvik." And when Jarvik still hesitated, Gonzalo said, "I'll help you out. This is the tune." And he hummed a few bars.

Avalon said at once, "I know what that is. It's 'The Lost Chord.' The music is by Arthur Sullivan of the Gilbert and Sullivan operettas. Except for those operettas, Sullivan is known only for the music to two songs. One

is 'Onward, Christian Soldiers' and the other is the afore-
mentioned 'The Lost Chord.' "

"Is that what you were humming, Jarvik?"

"I suppose so. You know how a song gets trapped in
your mind and won't get out."

There was a chorus of agreement from the others and
Avalon said sententiously, "It's a universal complaint."

"Well, whenever I'm trapped in some sort of loud-
ness," said Jarvik, "that song keeps going through my
head."

Drake chuckled. "If you're going to be dealing with
Manny, you'll be humming it till either you or he dies."

Gonzalo said, "Does it have some significance in that
connection? What are the words?"

"I only know a few words, actually."

"*I* know the words," said Avalon.

"Don't sing them," cried out Trumbull in sudden
alarm.

Avalon, whose singing voice was well known to resem-
ble the sound of an alligator in heat, said with dignity, "I
shall recite them. The words are by a lady named Ade-
laide Anne Procter, concerning whom I know nothing,
and the poem goes as follows:" (He cleared his throat.)

Seated one day at the organ, I was weary and ill at ease
And my fingers wandered idly over the noisy keys.
I don't know what I was playing, or what I was dream-
    ing then;
But I struck one chord of music, like the sound of a
    great Amen.
It flooded the crimson twilight, like the close of an an-
    gel's psalm,
And it lay on my fevered spirit with a touch of infinite

calm.

It quieted pain and sorrow, like love overcoming strife;

It seemed like the harmonious echo from our discordant life.

It linked all perplexed meanings into one perfect peace,

And trembled away into silence as if it were loth to cease.

I have sought, but I seek it vainly, that one lost chord divine,

Which came from the soul of the organ, and entered into mine.

It may be that Death's bright angel will speak in that chord again,

may be that only in Heaven shall I hear that grand Amen.

There was a short silence and then Halsted said, "You know, I wonder about that. I don't know how many different chords you can strike on a large organ, considering all the different stops you can push and pull and the things you do with your feet. I suppose it is a very large number indeed and you're not likely to find a particular chord just by fooling around at random."

Rubin said testily, "We'll leave it to your mathematical bent to work out the total number of chords, Roger. As for you, Ted Jarvik, we can at least see why you hum that song when things are noisy. All that talk about infinite calm and one perfect peace and trembling away into silence. Naturally, your mind reverts to the song."

"No," said Jarvik quietly, shaking his head, "that's not it."

"Hah," shouted Gonzalo in triumph. "I knew it. I

knew it. I have a sixth sense about these things. What is it? What does that song mean to you?"

"Quiet, Mario," said Avalon. "Now, Mr. Jarvik, if Mario has managed to touch a sore point, something about which you do not like to speak, please do so anyway. I assure you nothing you say will ever leave this room."

Jarvik looked about at the assembled Black Widowers in bewilderment and said, "How did this ever manage to come up? It's a sore point, certainly, but I can talk about it without trouble. It's just something that's totally uninteresting to anyone but me."

"You can never tell," said Gonzalo, grinning.

Henry refilled the brandy glasses, and Jarvik sighed and began:

I'm a quiet man [said Jarvik] as perhaps you can tell. I'm told it shows. There's something ironic in the fact that I have to live and work in Manhattan, but a man must earn a living.

Still, I'm a single man; I don't have a wife and children to support—not yet, anyway—and I can indulge myself now and then. So, two or three times a year I take a week off and go to a resort up the Hudson River. It's a large rambling mansion, with a Victorian atmosphere. The clientele is composed largely of people who are middle-aged or older and everything about the place is staid and respectable. Even the young people who happen to come there are impressed, or perhaps *oppressed*, by the atmosphere and behave themselves.

It means that it is quiet to some degree and, at night, particularly, it is very quiet. Soothing. I love it and, naturally, I try to escape even the noise that exists. People will talk after all and since there are hundreds in the house at all times, the talk can mount up. There are also vehicles—trucks, lawn mowers, and so on.

However, the place is set in an estate of thousands of acres of hilly woodland laced by roads and pathways, some of which are very rough indeed. It's my particular pleasure to walk those pathways, looking for someplace where I can see only trees and huge glacier-brought rocks, seat myself in one of the gazebos that dot the roads, and look at the wildness of the scenery and listen to the silence. There are, of course, the calling of the birds, the rustling of the leaves—but that is no bother. Such natural sounds simply punctuate and emphasize the silence.

But no matter where I go, where I sit, sooner or later, usually sooner, I can hear human voices. There are groups, tramping on nearby trails, or following along the one I just took. I always found it irritating and would feel invaded. It's silly, I know. After all, I was only one of hundreds, but I felt I ought to be undisturbed. I would get up and keep on wandering, looking always for a quiet place, a really quiet place—and never finding it.

One time, as I was sitting in one of my favorite gazebos, a man passed, looked at me, hesitated a moment, and said in half a whisper, "May I join you?"

I nodded. I couldn't refuse, though I resented him at once; and I couldn't rise and immediately leave without being unbearably discourteous.

After we had been there, in utter silence, some five minutes, the inevitable sound of conversation came from up the road, and there was an explosion of feminine laughter. My newfound companion grimaced and said, "Isn't that annoying?"

My heart warmed to him at once. I shook my head. "You can't get away from it."

He said, "In one place you can," then stopped short as though he had been trapped into saying too much. But I waited with an inquiring look on my face, and didn't say anything, and he said, "There's a place I discovered three, four years ago. —Would you like to see it?"

"Quiet?"

"Oh, yes."

"That would be nice."

"Come with me." He rose, and looked about as if he were taking his bearings. It was a beautifully sunny day, clear blue sky, unclouded, not too warm at all, so when he set off, I followed gladly.

I didn't like to speak, but finally I had to say, "I haven't seen you about."

"I'm usually out on the trails."

"So am I," I said, my heart warming further. "Ted Jarvik is my name," I said, putting out my hand.

He took it and shook it heartily. "Call me Dark Horse," he said.

And at this point, he suddenly walked right into the woods and began scrambling through and around the underbrush. I was glad I had on a pair of slacks. Had it been warmer, I might have been in shorts and I would undoubtedly have been plant-scratched and insect-bitten. As it was, I followed dutifully.

I couldn't make out where he was going. There was no path and we were clambering over boulders as though we were mountain climbing. Despite the coolness of the day, I was puffing, hot, and sweaty before long. Finally, we stopped for a bit under the hemlocks and my companion said, "I usually stop here to catch my breath. It takes me longer these days."

I panted a bit, welcoming the break, and said, "How do you know where you're going?"

"Landmarks. A tree that looks just so. A rock with a particular pattern of moss. I notice these things automatically and don't forget them. It's just a knack, but I never get lost."

I said ruefully, "You're lucky. I have no sense of direction at all. I get irretrievably lost in hotel corridors. Maids have to take me by the hand and lead me to my room."

My companion laughed and said, "I'm sure you have many talents. My inability to get lost is the only one I've got."

"You said your name is Dark Horse. You're not an Indian, are you? A Native American?" I was staring at him. He looked as little an Indian as I did.

"Not at all. It's not my name. I just said to call me that. You see, I believe if you really want to come out on a vacation, you should shuck all the paraphernalia of your ordinary life. I have to give my real name to the hotel, because I have to make a reservation and I have to use my credit card, but while I'm here, I won't be called by my name. Nor will I talk about my business. I simply won't recognize any part of my ordinary self. Whatever I am, officially, is back in Manhattan. It isn't here."

I was struck by that. "Interesting idea. I ought to do the same. Not that I'm very social when I come up here."

He said, "Rested a bit? Let's go, then. We don't have much farther."

I tried to watch where he turned and to observe landmarks, but it was no use. I'm not a noticing man. To me, a tree is a tree and a rock is a rock. —But then we half slid downward into a hollow and Dark Horse whispered, "This is it."

I looked about. The rocks enclosed us on almost every side. There were trees growing between them here and there. Ferns flourished. It was cool, very cool, welcomingly cool.

Above all else, it was quiet. There was not a sound. A rustle of leaves now and then. A faint insect stridulation. Once a brief bird call. But it was quiet, a healing silence in a world which was one large, long, eternal cacophony of noise.

There was a rocky ledge at a convenient height and my companion indicated it silently. We sat down and I let the silence flow into me. What did the poem say? "It lay on my fevered spirit with a touch of infinite calm."

We sat there half an hour, and in all that time I said nothing, and my companion said nothing, and there was not a human sound of any kind. No distant laughter, no crackle of far-off conversation, no vibration of any internal combustion engine. Nothing. I had never experienced anything like it.

Finally, my companion rose and without saying anything asked the question as to whether we ought to go now. Reluctantly, and without saying anything, I answered that we might.

Out we went. We were a quarter mile away before I dared speak. "How did you find the quiet place?" I asked.

"Accident at first. Since then, I've gone back half a dozen times at least. I love it. It's somewhere out of reach of all the trails and, as far as I know, it's not on any of the hotel maps and it's just a hidden undiscovered nook, known only to me, I think—and now you."

"Thanks for showing me. Really," I said, with infinite gratitude. "You wouldn't think there would be a spot untrodden by human feet in a place like this."

"Why not?" said Dark Horse. "I imagine that all over the world there are little areas undisturbed by humanity, sometimes in places that are very busy and crowded overall. There are fewer than there used to be, I'm sure, and perhaps someday they'll be all gone—but not yet, not yet."

He led me back to one of the main trails without hesitation. We scrambled over rocks and roots and through the underbrush again, and to me it seemed it was uphill both ways—but he got us back. I said good-bye and thanked him again and we shook hands. I went back to the room, got cleaned up, and was eventually ready for dinner.

I didn't see him at dinner, though I looked, and, in fact, I didn't see him again during the remainder of the stay. To put it baldly, I have never seen him again from that day to this.

The day after he had taken me to the quiet place, I tried to return on my own. I took a book with me and some sandwiches I had begged at the kitchen, and it was my intention to stay there most of the day if the weather held, but of course I never made it. I had no luck at all. I was wrong from the first turning, I believe.

I didn't give up, though. After I returned to the city, I kept dreaming of the quiet place and as soon as I could manage, I returned to the resort, studied the map, and marked off the area that I felt must contain it. I could make my way to the gazebo where I met Dark Horse and, from there, I set about a systematic course of exploration.

It did me no good whatever. I could never find the place. No matter how I tried to remember the twists and turns, no matter how I kidded myself into believing I recognized one of those blasted trees or rocks, no matter what bogs I slogged through, what crags I stumbled over, I ended up nowhere. I had bites, and scratches, and bruises, and contusions, and sprains. What I didn't have was the place.

I think it's become an obsession with me. I happened to know that passage of "The Lost Chord" and I suppose I began to hear it go through my head with appropriate changes in words: "I have sought, but I seek it vainly, That one lost place divine, From which came the spirit of silence that entered into me."

And I suppose I hum it when things grow loud and chaotic—

There was a pronounced pause when Jarvik concluded.

Finally, Halsted said, "I suppose you simply need this fellow who took you there to take you there again so that you can mark off each twist and turn on the map as best you can."

Gonzalo said hesitantly, "I suppose the fellow really existed. You didn't dream it, did you?"

Jarvik frowned. "Believe me, I didn't dream it. And he wasn't an elf leading me into fairyland, either. It happened exactly as I told you. The problem is that he had a precise sense of direction and I have none at all."

"Then you ought to find him," said Rubin flatly, "if you're that stuck on being in the middle of nowhere."

"Fine," said Jarvik. "I agree. I ought to find him. Now tell me how. I didn't know his room number. I didn't

know his name. It didn't occur to me to try to identify
him at the front desk that evening or the next day."

He shook his head and seemed to debate with himself
whether to go on or not. Then he shrugged and said, "I
might as well tell you how obsessed I've become. The last
time I was at the resort, I spent half the day with the
various desk employees trying to get a list of the people
who had been at the hotel the day on which I was taken
to the quiet place.

"It took a lot of negotiating and a lot of scurrying
through records, and then they were kind enough to
make me up an alphabetized list containing two hundred
forty-nine names. They did it for me because I was a
regular customer and because I spread fifty dollars
among them.

"They didn't include addresses because they said that
was against policy and if they were caught doing that
they would be fired and blacklisted and who knows what
else. I had to make do with the list of names. I made one
last effort to find the place the next day—and failed, of
course, and then spent the remainder of the stay studying the list of names.

"And you know, I've memorized them. Not on purpose, of course. I just memorized them. I can rattle them
off in the alphabetical order in which they were arranged. I happen to have one of those memories." He
brooded a little. "If my sense of direction were as good as
my memory for trivial items on a list—that is, if my sense
of observation could give me small variations I could
then remember—I suppose I wouldn't be in the fix I am
now."

Drake said, frowning through the smoke of his cigarette, "How would the list of names help you?"

Jarvik said, "The first thing that occurred to me was that the false name he used must have some reason behind it. Why would anyone call himself Dark Horse? Possibly because the initials were the same as those of his real name. So I went through the list and there was only one D.H. and the name was Dora Harboard. Well, whatever my friend was, he was not a woman, so that was out.

"Then I thought that perhaps the initials were reversed. So I looked for an H.D. and there was none. Then I looked for unattached males. A great many people were listed as, let us say, Ira and Hortense Abel, to take the first names on the list. It seemed to me I ought to eliminate them, especially if they had children with them. That left me with seventeen unattached males and at first I thought that that was a big advancement.

"But then I realized that Dark Horse gave me no indication that he was unattached. He might well have had a wife and child back in his room, or out attending the mah-jongg game that was being played in the lounge that afternoon."

Trumbull said, "You could try *force majeure*. Follow up every male name on the list and see if one of them is Dark Horse. Who knows, you may strike it lucky the first name you try. And you know he lives in Manhattan. He said so. Try the phone book to begin with."

Jarvik said, "One of the people listed is S. Smith. I dread the thought of how many Smiths there are in the phone book with *S* as the first initial. Besides, if I recall correctly, he said that whatever he was officially was back in Manhattan. It seems to me that meant he worked in Manhattan but not necessarily that he lived there. He could live in any of the five boroughs, or in New Jersey, or Connecticut, or Westchester.

"Listen, I've thought of *force majeure*. Just to show you, I thought that I might hire someone at some small nearby airfield to fly me over the resort so that I could see the spot from above, but I know I wouldn't recognize it. Not from above, in a hurried pass. And even if I did, they'd have to land me back at the airport and if I then tried to reach the quiet place from the ground I'd fail again.

"Then I thought that perhaps I could hire a helicopter and if I recognized the spot, I could have myself lowered by some sort of rope while the helicopter hovered overhead. That's ridiculous, though. I wouldn't have the nerve to dangle from a helicopter even if I recognized the place, and then, after I left it, what if I still couldn't find my way back? I couldn't very well use a helicopter every time, could I?"

Gonzalo said, "Dark Horse! Isn't that a racing term?"

"Originally, yes," said Avalon. "It refers to some horse of unknown potential that might have an outside chance to win, especially if it enters a race in which all the other horses are known quantities."

"Why *dark* horse, then?" said Halsted.

"I presume," said Avalon, "as an indication of how minimal the information is. After all, most horses are dark in coloring. Besides, 'dark' gives the impression of mystery, of the unknown."

"Well," said Gonzalo, "perhaps this fellow has some connection with the racing game."

Jarvik said bitterly, "Fine. Suppose he does. How does that help me find him?"

"Besides," said Trumbull, "it seems to me that 'dark horse' has spread out to mean anyone who enters a contest without being a known item. In boxing, tennis; in politics, even."

"And how does *that* help me find him?" said Jarvik.

Avalon sighed heavily and said, "Mr. Jarvik, why don't we look at 'The Lost Chord' from another angle? Roger Halsted pointed out that a complex organ might have many, many varieties of chords and that one chord could be easily lost among the quantity. But that is surely a way of looking at it that is rather too simplistic.

"Any sensation consists of the sensation itself, objectively, and of the person receiving the sensation, subjectively. The same chord is always the same chord if it is measured by an instrument that analyzes its wave function. However, the chord one *hears* may well vary with the mood and immediate circumstances of the listener.

"The person playing the organ in the poem was 'weary and ill at ease.' For that reason, the chord had a particular effect on him. 'It quieted pain and sorrow' which he may have been feeling. From then on, when he sought the chord again, his mood would be one of anxious expectation, of careful attention. Even if he heard the same chord again, the *same* chord precisely, it would not strike him in the same way and he would not consider it to be the same chord. No wonder he sought it vainly. He was seeking to duplicate not only the chord but himself as he had been."

Jarvik said, "You are saying?"

"I am saying, Mr. Jarvik," said Avalon, "that perhaps you ought to attach less importance to the place. You found it on a perfect day. You found it when someone else was guiding you there so that you were, in a sense, carefree. If you find it again a second time, it may be on a less desirable day—when it is hotter, or colder, or cloudier. You yourself will be seeking anxiously, you will not be at ease. The result is that it may not be the same place you remember. You will be bitterly disappointed. Would it not be better to remain with the memory and let it go at that?"

Jarvik's head bent, and for a few moments he seemed lost in thought. Then he said, "Thank you, Mr. Avalon. I think you're right. If I fail to find the place, I will certainly try to follow your advice and find solace in it. However . . . I would like, if I can, to find it once more, just to make sure. After all, Dark Horse found it a number of times, and enjoyed it each time."

"Dark Horse knew how to get there," said Avalon. "His own mood was fairly constant, and it might be he always chose days of particularly favorable weather to go there."

"Even so," said Jarvik stubbornly, "I would like to find it once more, if there were only a way of finding it."

"But apparently there isn't," said Avalon. "You must admit that."

"I don't know," said Mario. "No one has asked Henry."

"In this case," said Avalon stubbornly, "even Henry can do nothing. There is nothing to seize on."

"What have we to lose?" demanded Mario. "Henry, what can you tell us?"

Jarvik, who had been listening in astonishment, now turned to Rubin and, jerking his thumb over his shoulder, mouthed silently: The waiter?

Rubin put a finger to his lips and shook his head slightly.

Henry, who had been listening with absorption, said, "I must say that I agree fully with Mr. Avalon with respect to the subjective nature of the charms of the place and would hate to have Mr. Jarvik spoil an idyllic memory. Nevertheless—"

"Aha," said Gonzalo. "Go on, Henry."

Henry smiled in his avuncular fashion and said, "Nevertheless, the one thing to seize upon is the phrase 'dark horse,' which everyone has been seizing upon, as it happens. May I ask, Mr. Jarvik, if, by any chance, there was anyone on the list named Polk—not a very common name. A James Polk, perhaps."

Jarvik's eyes opened wide. "You're kidding."

"Not at all. May I take it there *was* such a name?"

"There's a J. Polk, certainly. It could be James."

"Then perhaps that is your man."

"But why?"

"Mr. Trumbull mentioned, I believe, that 'dark horse' is used in politics. That, I suspect, is its most common use these days. A dark horse is some politician who is never thought of in connection with nomination by a major party, but who is nevertheless nominated as a way of breaking what otherwise seems an intransigent deadlock. Nowadays, dark horses rarely show up because the nomination is decided by primary contests. However, as recently as 1940, Wendell Willkie was a dark horse named by the Republican party.

"However, the name is most often used in American history for the very first party nominee who was a dark horse. In 1844, the Democrats were all set to nominate ex-President Martin Van Buren, but he needed a two-thirds majority and intransigent Southern opposition prevented that. Out of sheer weariness, the convention switched to Tennessee's Senator James Knox Polk, whom no one had thought of in connection with the nomination. He was the first dark horse candidate, and went on to win the election. He made a pretty good one-term President."

"He's right," said Rubin. "You do know everything, Henry."

"No, Mr. Rubin," said Henry, "but I had a dim memory of it and while the discussion was going on, I checked our reference shelf. It may be that the J. Polk on Mr. Jarvik's list is a lineal or collateral descendant, which is why he took the name of Dark Horse."

"Amazing," muttered Jarvik.

"However," said Henry, "you may still have trouble finding him, Mr. Jarvik, and even if you find him, he may still be the wrong person, and even if he is the right person, you may still end up disappointed in the quiet place. However—may good luck be with you."

AFTERWORD

My dear wife, Janet, and I have as our favorite resort Mohonk Mountain House, which is located about ninety-two miles from our home, in New Paltz, New York. It has wide acres through which we can wander. Janet does so because she loves to be in the wilderness, and I do so because I love to be with Janet.

And one time we found a place where we appeared to be thoroughly isolated and where, it seemed for a few magic minutes, humanity had not yet been invented.

But there's the difference between Janet and myself. Janet loved that place and those moments for itself and themselves alone, with a pure and holy love that lacked all alloy. I, on the other hand, thought, "I'll bet I can make a Black Widowers out of this." —And I did, and you've just read it.

This story first appeared in the March 1988 issue of *Ellery Queen's Mystery Magazine*.

THE FOUR-LEAF CLOVER

Considering the circumstances, it might have been predicted that when the Black Widowers met at the Milano Restaurant for their monthly banquet, the sole topic of conversation would be the Iran-Contra hearings.

Each of the Black Widowers had something to say, one about Oliver North's hurt-little-boy look and his appeal to middle-aged women; another of John Poindexter's sievelike memory. James Drake, who was host of the banquet, pointed out that, between them, North and Poindexter had badly tarnished the Reagan presidency, something all the Democrats in combination had failed to as much as scratch. Why, then, he wanted to know, was the Republican right making heroes out of that Laurel-and-Hardy team?

It was Emmanuel Rubin who, not unexpectedly,

brought the discussion down to the matter of hostages and principle.

"The thing is," he said, "how does one deal with loss of life, or potential loss of life, or even just a matter of imprisonment? Must the national interest come second to the rescue of hostages? If that is the case, how would we ever dare carry out any armed strike? In any such move, even one as simple and safe as attacking the mighty army of Grenada, or bombing the mighty fortress of Tripoli, we suffer casualties and run the risk of having prisoners taken."

Geoffrey Avalon, staring down at Rubin's sixty-four inches from the height of his own seventy-four, said, "You're talking military action. The hostages are civilians, pursuing a peaceful life, taken without cause by gangsters and thugs. Wouldn't *you* pay any price and abandon any principle to gain the freedom of someone you loved? Wouldn't you pay a ransom to kidnappers if that would keep them from killing your wife?"

"Yes, of course, *I* would," said Rubin, his eyes flashing through his thick spectacles. "*I* would, as an individual. But would I expect two hundred and thirty million Americans to suffer a weakening of the national interest because *I* am suffering? Not even an American president has the right to do that, and *that* was Reagan's mistake. And don't think that hostage-taking is an aberration of peace. It isn't. We're at war with terrorism and the hostages are prisoners of war. We wouldn't think of giving an enemy arms to buy back our prisoners of war. It would have been treason to do that in any other war we've fought."

"Terrorism isn't like any other war," growled Thomas

Trumbull, "and you can't make a point-by-point analogy."

"Actually," said Roger Halsted, "all this talk about national interest is irrelevant. Surely, terrorism is a global problem which will yield only to global action."

Mario Gonzalo said, "Oh, sure. Global! How do you manage a global solution when each nation is willing to make a deal with the terrorists, hoping that it will be left alone and to hell with its neighbors?"

"That's what's got to stop," said Halsted earnestly. "Trying to buy off the terrorists only points out to them how they might make a profit. If hostages sell at a premium, they will take more hostages whenever they run short of funds."

"Of course, and our proper answer to the taking of hostages is making the procedure expensive for the hostage takers. You inflict casualties on them," said Gonzalo.

"Provided you know who the enemy is," protested Avalon. "You can't simply kill people at random."

"Why not? We do that in every war. When we bombed German and Japanese cities during World War II, didn't we know that uncounted thousands of totally innocent people would be killed, including babies? Did we think our bombs were selective enough to kill only villains?"

"All of Germany and Japan was fighting us, even if only by passively supporting the German and Japanese governments," said Avalon.

"And do you think that terrorism can survive without at least the passive approval or acquiescence of the society in which it exists?" demanded Rubin.

At that point, James Drake, who had been listening to the exchange with manifest unease, said, "Gentlemen, my guest is coming up the stairs. Could we suspend the

argument for now, and not return to it, either? Please!"
He then said hurriedly, "Henry, my guest isn't a drinker.
Would you get him a large diet cola? Not much ice."

Henry, the perennial waiter at the Black Widower
banquets, nodded his head slightly just as the guest entered the banquet room.

He was a tall man, darkly tanned, with a large curved
nose, and blue eyes that stood out startlingly against his
dark coloring. His hair, still copious, was graying and he
looked fiftyish.

"Sorry I'm late, Jim," he said, grasping Drake's hand.
"The train did not feel at all bound by the timetable."

"Not too late, Sandy," said Drake. "Let me introduce
you to the Black Widowers. This is Alexander Mountjoy,
gentlemen."

One by one, the Black Widowers advanced to shake his
hand. Last came Henry with his tall drink. Mountjoy
sniffed at it, then grinned. "You warned the waiter, I
see."

Drake nodded. "And I should add that our waiter is
Henry, and that he is a particularly valued member of
our club."

The dinner was a hearty one. Melon, followed by a
thick vegetable soup, a prime rib roast with baked potato
and broccoli, and apple pie with cheese for dessert.

Rubin, having abandoned topical references, chose to
point out Charles Dickens's contribution to the evolution
of the modern detective story with a stern disquisition on
Bleak House, which only he, of those at the table, had read.
Drake, who was quite openly relieved at this new direction of the conversation, pointed out that Dickens's
detective had come a generation after Edgar Allan Poe

and that, if Rubin's descriptions were correct, Dickens had not at all benefited by Poe's work.

This elicited only a snarl of contempt from Rubin, who turned to Wilkie Collins and Émile Gaboriau. At a crucial moment, Drake mentioned Arthur Conan Doyle, at which point Mountjoy plunged in joyously and conversation grew general.

Over the coffee, Drake gave his water glass its ritual tinkle and said, "Manny has done his whole evening's share of talking by now, so if you don't mind, Mario, you take over the grilling. I know I can rely on you to keep Manny quiet."

Gonzalo adjusted his jacket with its subdued green stripe, made sure his tie was seated properly, sat back, and said, "Just how do you justify your existence, Mr. Mountjoy?"

Mountjoy looked satisfyingly replete as he watched Henry pour the brandy, and said, "I'm a Sherlock Holmes enthusiast and a member of the Baker Street Irregulars, which should be justification enough for *this* crowd, eh?"

Gonzalo said, "I don't know about that. Actually, Manny is the only one really interested in mysteries because he writes them, or does something he calls writing them, and makes a living of sorts out of it." He raised his hand, palm held imperiously in the direction of Rubin, who shifted in his seat and gave all the signs of wanting to burst into speech. "Try something else."

"In that case," said Mountjoy, "I might mention that I'm a college president, but I don't know if any perceptible fraction of the world's population would consider that as justifying my existence."

"We are all academic personalities, one way or another," said Avalon, "and we might be willing to consider the matter moot."

Mountjoy grinned. "If college has taught you to speak in that fashion, that's a black mark against me."

Gonzalo said, with clear disappointment, "A college president? Is that all?"

Mountjoy's eyebrows went up. "Well, the post may not justify my existence, but I would scarcely think of it as trivial. Dealing with students and faculty and trustees and potential donors and the general public is quite a bit more than enough. What do you mean, 'Is that all'?"

Gonzalo said, "I mean do you work for the government in any way?"

"No, I'm spared that."

"You haven't been involved in any government investigations?"

"No, of course not."

"Well, then," said Gonzalo, "why is it that Drake asked us not to discuss the matter of hostages in front of you?"

"Oh, for God's sake," exploded Drake. "If I asked you not to, why do you bring the matter up?"

It was impossible for Mountjoy to turn pale, but he took on a rigid look and said angrily, "Jim!"

Drake shook his head. "I'm sorry, Sandy. The conversation was on hostages before you came. It was bound to be, considering what the nation has been going through. But I did ask them to drop it."

"And I want to know why," said Gonzalo stubbornly.

"I can't say why," said Drake. "But I put the matter out of bounds. As host—"

"Even as host you can't do that," said Gonzalo. "The whole point of the club dinners is that there are no holds barred at the grilling. Even the host can't limit the matter. It's—it's unconstitutional."

Avalon, turning the brandy glass in his hand, said thoughtfully, "Mario has a point there. —Mr. Mountjoy, may I assure you that nothing said within these walls is ever repeated outside them. The habit of confidentiality is strong and it includes our excellent waiter, Henry. Does that help?"

"No, it doesn't," said Mountjoy. "I have no secrets, but the government does. I am fully satisfied of the honor and honesty of every person here, but the government is not satisfied as easily as I am."

"You said you don't work for the government," said Gonzalo.

"Nor do I, but I have managed to get entangled with it just the same, and through no deliberate desire of my own."

Thomas Trumbull said gently, "I *am* employed by the government and I have been entrusted with secrets in my time. I vouch for these gentlemen, too. It would have been more convenient all around if we had avoided this matter, but in a free-for-all grilling it would have arisen sooner or later, and perhaps it would have been better if Jim had brought you as guest at another time. But here you are, and Mario's question puts us face-to-face with it. If you feel you cannot discuss the matter, then the rules of the club put an end to the dinner, which we would all regret. Is there anything you *can* tell us? If we decide that it would count as a satisfactory answer to the question we can drop the matter and go on to other subjects."

"The question is this," said Gonzalo. "Why can't we discuss the matter of hostages in front of you? That's just to remind you."

Mountjoy thought for a while, head bent, chin touching his chest. When he looked up, his eyes were friendly and his appearance seemed normal.

"I'll tell you this much, if you'll be kind enough not to ask me names and places and details, which I am not allowed to give you, in any case. I told you I was president of a college. Well, some members of the faculty were kidnapped some months ago by terrorists."

"But there's no secret to that," broke in Rubin. "It was in all the papers. Obviously, you're president of the—"

"Please!" said Mountjoy. "I don't care how certain you are that you know the details of the case. Please realize you may not have them all and that I can't confirm or deny anything. Just listen to what I say. Some faculty members were kidnapped. They are held as hostages. One hostage who was being held, and I am specifically refraining from saying whether he was one of the faculty members or not, was killed. Presumably, he was tortured first.

"Now, then, the subject of hostages is bothersome to me personally since the hostages are known to me, and it is bothersome to me officially since I have been extensively interviewed by government agencies on various aspects of the event. Does that satisfy you, gentlemen? Can we go on to other matters?"

"No," said Gonzalo. "Why were you extensively interviewed? What had you to do with it?"

"With the hostage-taking? Absolutely nothing."

"With anything at all. You said you were interviewed on various aspects of the event. What aspects? Why limit it to hostage-taking?"

"I don't know what you mean."

"What's so hard about the question? I mean why were

you extensively interviewed? If not about the hostage-taking, then about what?"

"I can't answer that question."

"Then I'm not satisfied."

Drake said, "Come on, Mario. Don't be a pigheaded fool."

"I'm not being pigheaded. I have an idea. There's something involved besides the hostage-taking. Mountjoy said the interviews had nothing to do with that, but covered various aspects of the matter. That means aspects besides the hostage-taking. I think there must be some sort of unfinished business in all of this or it wouldn't be so hush-hush. I'll *bet* there's a problem here of some kind, some puzzle, some mystery. How about it, Mr. Mountjoy?"

"I have nothing to say on the matter," said Mountjoy woodenly.

"It so happens," said Gonzalo, "that this club has solved a number of puzzles in the past. We could help you now."

Mountjoy looked toward Drake questioningly.

Drake smashed his cigarette to death and said, "That's true enough, but we can't guarantee we can solve any particular mystery."

Mountjoy muttered, "I wish you could solve this one."

"Ah," said Gonzalo, "then there *is* one. —Hey, Tom, tell him we can help out, and tell him we can be trusted to the death."

Trumbull said, "I've already told him we can all be trusted. —If there's a problem, Mountjoy, and if you're in trouble over it, then Mario is right. Maybe we can help."

Mountjoy said, "Well, let's see what I can tell you."

He stared at the Black Widowers, who, in turn, remained silent. Indeed, they scarcely moved.

Finally, Mountjoy said, "The hostage who was killed was not exactly innocent, at least in the eyes of the terrorists. Usually, the hostages that are taken are simply newsmen, or businessmen, or professors—people whose only value to the terrorists is as pawns. They were handy and the American government and people want them back so they are bargaining points.

"The hostage who was killed—and I can't name him or tell you anything about him— was working for the government, and to the terrorists he could be considered a spy or a secret agent or something like that. They killed him, either because they considered that a just punishment for his crime of being on the other side, or they did so accidentally in the process of torturing him in order to elicit information.

"The question is, how did they know he was worth torturing? They don't torture all their hostages as a matter of course. In fact, they treat them as well as they reasonably can, for a dead hostage has no value to them, and in fact any hostage that is in anything but good condition merely inflames American public opinion and may encourage the United States to more violent reprisals, something for which they are obviously not eager.

"The feeling is that someone fingered him. In short, a traitor of some sort is involved. The dead hostage had confided his true role to someone for some reason, or let it slip inadvertently, and that someone betrayed him. The question, of course, is who? Naturally, the government wants to know, not simply in order to avenge the death by punishing the traitor, but because if the traitor is left at large, he is in a position in which his treason can continue, you understand.

"I come into it because the circumstances of the kidnapping of the faculty members—those particular ones and no others—make it seem clear that the traitor is also a member of the faculty. There is good reasoning behind that, but I can't pass it on to you. I simply say that that is the conclusion—that we have a traitor on the faculty.

"I was interviewed extensively on the matter, and so were others, and it seems that the conclusion come to is that the traitor is one of four members of the faculty, but which of the four— Ah, that's the rub."

Rubin said, "The only safe thing to do is to remove all four from their posts, put them where they can do no harm, and keep them all under surveillance while you continue the investigation."

"And that has been done," said Mountjoy, "but does it occur to you that a great deal of unjustified harm is being done to three innocent people who are loyal Americans and do not deserve such treatment?"

"Casualties of war," said Rubin.

Halsted said, "You're being very callous tonight, Mannie. Are you having trouble with your current novel?"

"That has nothing to do with it," said Rubin. "I say what I think."

"Well, what *I* think," said Mountjoy, "is that it is much more important to absolve the three innocents than to catch the guilty. And there's a way of doing it if only we were clever enough. We assume, for instance, that the dead hostage knew who the traitor was. He would know, after all, to whom he had confided, or let slip, the matter. Now, then, he was forced to write a letter which the kidnappers then released. You know the kind."

The Black Widowers nodded, and Halsted said, "The hostage admits he's a member of the CIA and that he spied on the poor mistreated groups to which the kidnappers belong. He goes on to confess to all sorts of other misdemeanors and then denounces the American government for not giving in to the simple demands of the captors so that he might be released."

"Exactly," said Mountjoy. "Exactly. By then, he had undoubtedly been subject to some torture, so that they wouldn't release a photograph of him as they did in the case of other hostages. Even so, he might not have consented to sign that letter—and it was definitely his signature—were it not that the hostage we're speaking of was hoping to give us information under the nose of his captors. He added at the end of the letter that he hoped he would be lucky enough to have the government arrange his release and drew a four-leaf clover at the end. Very carefully drawn. It was some time after that that he was killed."

Avalon said, "Do you think the four-leaf clover had anything to do with that, Mr. Mountjoy?"

"The government thinks so. He had to choose some sign that would indicate the traitor, yet do so in a sufficiently subtle manner to escape the kidnappers. Unfortunately, it was sufficiently subtle to escape us as well. The government has not been able to work out the significance of the four-leaf clover. However, it may be that the traitor did—that the traitor saw the letter reproduced on television and realized that the four-leaf clover was pointing straight at him. He managed to get a message to the kidnappers, who then tortured their victim further and killed him."

"Well," said Avalon, "a four-leaf clover is a well-known

symbol of good luck. Might it not be that the poor hostage really wanted to have the good luck of being freed and drew a four-leaf clover as a piece of sympathetic magic?"

"It's possible," said Mountjoy. "Anything is possible. The government doesn't give that credence, however. The hostage was an outspoken rationalist, utterly contemptuous of anything that smacked of mysticism or superstition. The people who knew him best say that it is unthinkable that he would draw a four-leaf clover in the expectation of deriving good luck from it."

"Desperation will have people clutching at straws," muttered Avalon.

Trumbull said, "It's an Irish symbol. Are any of the four suspects Irish, or of Irish descent? The traitor could be a member of the Irish Republican Army and be sympathetic to other struggling underground groups."

Mountjoy shook his head violently. "In the first place, the four-leaf clover is not an Irish symbol. The three-leaf clover is. It was plucked up by Saint Patrick, according to legend, to explain to an Irish king how the Trinity could exist—one God in three personifications. The Irish king was converted and the three-leaf clover became the shamrock. And in any case, none of the four suspects are in any way Irish."

Trumbull said, "What can you tell us about the four suspects, then? We can't figure out at whom the four-leaf clover is pointing if we know nothing about them."

"I can't help that," said Mountjoy despairingly. "I can't give you their names or tell you who they are."

"Can you give us their fields of specialty?" asked Avalon.

"I'm not sure. —Maybe I can take the chance." Mountjoy held up his fingers one by one: "One is a historian, one is an entomologist, one is an astronomer, and one is a mathematician. Does that help? It didn't help us."

Halsted said, "Are you sure what he drew was a four-leaf clover?"

"Well, of course it was. What else could it be?"

Halsted shrugged. "I don't know. I didn't see it. But it was something with four things sticking out of it. Right?"

"Yes."

"Then could he have been trying to draw a star? A point with rays of light coming from it? That might indicate the astronomer."

Mountjoy shook his head. "It might be the astronomer, for all I know, but not for that reason. He didn't draw radiating lines, he drew four recognizable clover leaves. The drawing also had a stem. Stars wouldn't have stems."

Drake said, "What kind of mathematician is the mathematician?"

Mountjoy said, "I couldn't tell you. I'm in political science myself and all the mathematics I know barely suffices to enable me to balance my checkbook."

"Could he have done papers on probability?"

"I suppose I could find out, but I don't know it off the cuff."

"Because the thing about four-leaf clovers is that they are rare. I don't know what the chances are of finding one if you look through clover patches at random, but it must be very small. When I was a youngster, I remember lying down in a field of clover and spending hours going over them one by one. I never found a four-leaf clover. So to find one is remarkable and it's the sort of thing that might interest a mathematician who specializes in probability."

Halsted, who was himself a mathematician, said, "That doesn't sound likely at all. What kind of a historian was the historian?"

"Ah," said Mountjoy. "That I can tell you. He wrote a rather well-known book entitled— Well, no, obviously I can't tell you that. It would identify him. Let's say," he added feebly, "that he's a medievalist."

"He specializes in medieval history?"

"Yes. Byzantine Empire. Fatimids. Things like that."

"Anything to do with four-leaf clovers?"

"Not that I know of."

"And what about the entomologist, who obviously studies insects."

"Yes."

"What kind of insects? Bees?"

Gonzalo put in, "Why bees, Roger?"

"Why not? Bees fly from clover blossom to clover blossom collecting honey and spreading pollen. Don't you know Emily Dickinson's quatrain: 'The pedigree of honey / Does not concern the bee. / A clover any time to him / Is aristocracy'? Well, then, a four-leaf clover might easily signify a bee, which would signify our entomologist."

Avalon said, "Why a four-leaf clover in that case? A three-leaf clover would do as well and would be simpler to draw."

Mountjoy said, "It doesn't matter which. The entomologist didn't work with bees. He worked with smaller bugs and I couldn't even give you the name. He told me once and I thought it sounded as though it came straight out of Shakespeare's *A Comedy of Errors*, but I couldn't repeat it."

"Well," said Rubin, "where does it put us? The four-leaf clover doesn't point to anyone. Frankly, I find myself looking with favor on Jeff's original idea that it was just a good luck symbol and nothing more. The poor guy needed luck and didn't have it."

"Poor guy?" said Halsted. "Just a casualty of war, Manny."

Rubin looked annoyed. "I was just speaking theoretically. When we get down to individuals, I'm not any more callous than the rest of you, and you know it."

Drake said, "Well, we chivied and tortured poor Sandy into telling us more than he should have, probably, and putting him under the nervous tension of fearing the government may somehow find out he did, and we haven't been able to help him at all. —I'm sorry, Sandy."

"Hold on," said Gonzalo, teetering his chair back on two legs. "We're not through yet. I notice that Henry is poking his way through the reference shelf."

"Oh, really," said Trumbull. "We'll ask him just as soon as he gets back."

"Whom are we talking about?" said Mountjoy, frowning. "The waiter?"

"We're talking about Henry. The best of the Black Widowers."

Henry returned and resumed his usual place by the service table.

Gonzalo said, "Well, Henry, can you help us?"

"I have had a thought, Mr. Gonzalo, concerning four-leaf clovers."

"Tell us."

"Clovers almost always have three leaves. Occasionally, a clover grows from a seed that is slightly abnormal and it develops four leaves in consequence. Such a sudden change between parent and offspring is called a mutation," said Henry politely.

"So it is," said Halsted.

"Mutations take place now and then in all species. You can get a white blackbird, or a two-headed calf, or a baby with six fingers. I daresay the list is endless."

"Probably," murmured Avalon.

"For the most part, mutations are unfavorable and are viewed as deformities and monstrous distortions. The four-leaf clover is an example of a mutation, however, that not only does not strike people as a deformity but is valued and treasured by them—by almost all of them—as something very desirable, as a symbol and bringer of good luck. That makes it very unusual as a mutation and it is one mutation that can be easily drawn without repelling people and can be made to seem as nothing more than a natural way of calling down good fortune. It can therefore symbolize the idea of mutation unmistakably and yet escape detection by people without a certain degree of education. However, to those who know the hostage's strong rationality, they would—or should—dismiss the good luck and cling to the symbolization of a mutation."

"Where does all that get us, Henry?" asked Trumbull.

"To change the subject slightly, Mr. Mountjoy mentioned Shakespeare's *A Comedy of Errors*. There are two characters in it named Antipholus. They are twin brothers, one from the city of Syracuse in Sicily and one from Ephesus in Asia Minor. Does the name Antipholus bring anything to your mind, Mr. Mountjoy?"

"Yes," said Mountjoy. "The insects the entomologist

was working with. I still can't give you the exact name, though."

"Was it Drosophila?"

"Yes! By God, yes."

"It is more commonly known as the fruit fly and it is the classic insect used for the study of mutations. It seems to me, then, that the four-leaf clover may have been drawn to signify mutations and that that was meant to point rather precisely to the entomologist as the traitor. At least, it seems so to me."

"Heavens!" said Mountjoy. "It seems so to me, too. —I'll get in touch with—with some people in Washington first thing in the morning and suggest it. Drosophila. Drosophila. I'll have to remember the name."

"Fruit fly will be sufficient, sir," said Henry, "and if the suggestion is accepted, I would suggest you allow it to remain understood that it occurred to you quite independently. No need to admit you spoke of the matter to the Black Widowers."

AFTERWORD

Sometimes, if I feel really lazy, I think of some one thing and see if I can't build a story around it. Thus, I was in a grassy place at Mohonk (see the previous Afterword) and I noted that it was rich in three-leaf clovers. As is my wont, I looked about to see if there was a four-leaf clover and after about two and a half seconds I decided there wasn't. (I have never found a four-leaf clover in my life, but I have had enough good luck even without it.)

So I thought: Let's write a story about a four-leaf clover, and I did.

This time, though, Eleanor Sullivan, the beautiful editor of *Ellery Queen's Mystery Magazine,* turned it down. She thought the point of the story was sufficiently arcane to be unfair to the reader. I didn't agree (I never agree with a rejection) but the editor's word is law, and I present the story here as the second in this collection to make its first-time appearance.

THE ENVELOPE

Emmanuel Rubin arrived at the Black Widowers banquet in a foul mood. This was not much worse than his usual attitude, to be sure, but his eyes, magnified behind the thick lenses of his spectacles, flashed dangerously.

"Uh-oh," said Mario Gonzalo, host of the occasion, "someone has received a well-deserved rejection."

"I have *not* received a rejection," snapped Rubin, "well-deserved or otherwise. It's much worse than that."

Geoffrey Avalon stared down from his seventy-four-inch height at the diminutive Rubin and said in his stately baritone, "Much worse than a rejection? For a free-lance writer like you, Manny? Come now."

"Listen," said Rubin furiously, "I walked into the local post office this morning and asked for a roll of twenty-five cent stamps. That irks me to begin with. I can remember when it cost two cents to mail a letter, but the price keeps going up and up without seeming to affect the eternal deficit—"

"At least," said Roger Halsted, "the service gets worse to balance the increase in rates."

"You say that because you think it's funny, Roger," said Rubin, "but you happen to be dead right. —Thank you, Henry."

Henry, the unsurpassable waiter of the Black Widower banquets, recognizing the demands being made on Rubin by his passion, had brought him a refill of his drink.

James Drake, lighting his perennial cigarette, said, "I remember when stamps were two cents, too, and the morning newspaper was two cents, and a pack of cigarettes was thirteen cents—and my weekly salary was fifteen dollars. So what?"

"I haven't finished," said Rubin. "So I asked for a roll of twenty-five-cent stamps and the confounded idiot at the window looked me right in the eye and said, 'We don't have any.' I was stunned. It was a post office, damn it. I said, 'Why not?' And he just shrugged and shouted, 'Next!' I mean, no sign of regret or embarrassment. They might have put up a sign to say the rolls were temporarily out. I had to wait half an hour in line to be told I couldn't have one."

Gonzalo said, "Suppose we cool you down to your usual state of semi-sanity, Manny, so that I can introduce my guest—Francis MacShannon. He's a good friend of mine."

Rubin shook hands loftily. "Any good friend of Mario's, Mr. MacShannon, is highly suspect in my eyes."

"Which is what you'd expect," said Gonzalo, "from someone who falls into a tirade over a roll of twenty-five-cent stamps. —I'll give you a few to tide you over, Manny. No charge."

"No, thanks," said Rubin. "I got my roll later in the day. It's a matter of principle."

"I apologize for Manny's dubious principles, Frank," said Gonzalo. "He makes one up whenever he can't get his way."

Francis MacShannon laughed. He appeared sixtyish, with a round and jolly face above a short, plump body. He had a ruddy complexion and a gray chin-beard, giving him the appearance of a semi-shaven Santa Claus.

"I'm on your side, Mr. Rubin," he said in a high-pitched voice that rather spoiled the Santa Claus image. "I have complaints about the post office, too."

"Doesn't everyone," growled Thomas Trumbull, who had arrived a moment before and who had seized upon the scotch and soda that Henry held out for him.

There was a pause while MacShannon was introduced to the final newcomer, and then he said, "My own complaint is with the matter of postmarks. Nowadays, they are only dirty smudges, but when I was young, postmarks were legible and beautifully clear. They were geography lessons. In fact, I built up a huge collection of postmarks."

Avalon's formidable eyebrows raised. "How does one do that, Mr. MacShannon?"

"To begin with, my parents gave me the envelopes they received in the mail. So did the neighbors up and down the street, once they learned how serious I was about it. The best part of it, though, was finding discarded envelopes in the street, in backyards, under bushes. You'd be surprised how many envelopes it was possible to find. Each new postmark I had never before encountered was a treasure and I'd look it up carefully in the atlas. I made lists of them by states and nations and pasted the envelopes into notebooks in organized fashion. I became an aficionado of envelopes such as you could scarcely imagine. In fact, it was my interest in envelopes that led to my—"

It was at this point that Henry's softly authoritative voice said, "Dinner is served, gentlemen."

They sat down to their melon prosciutto, followed by cream of asparagus soup and a mixed green salad. The conversation dealt with the new Russian probe designed to study the Martian satellite, Phobos, and over the roast capon, the discussion grew heated over whether a joint Soviet-American Mars expedition was desirable or not. The post office and its manifold sins dwindled and vanished in the fire of the new controversy. Down went the chocolate almond pie and the coffee and, over the brandy, Gonzalo called for the grilling.

"Manny," he said, "you be the griller, and I invoke host's privilege and tell you that the subject of the post office must not be mentioned."

Rubin scowled and said, "Mr. MacShannon, how do you justify your existence?"

MacShannon said amiably, "I'm a computer programmer and designer. These days I think that speaks for itself."

"Maybe," said Rubin. "We might get back to that later. Obviously, your present labors have nothing to do with your activities as a child—I mean your postmark collection. You had said—"

"Manny," said Gonzalo abruptly, "I ruled out the post office."

"Fire and brimstone," exploded Rubin. "Who's talking post office? I'm talking postmark collection. I appeal to the membership."

"All right. Go ahead," said Gonzalo resignedly.

"Now, then," said Rubin, after an unnecessarily protracted glare at Gonzalo, "you said that it was your interest in envelopes that led you to your— And then, before you could finish your sentence, you were interrupted by the announcement that dinner was ready. Now, then, I would like to have the sentence finished. What did your interest in envelopes lead to?"

MacShannon frowned thoughtfully. "Did I say that?" Then his brow cleared and a look of almost comic self-satisfaction crossed his face. "Oh, yes, of course. Back in 1953, it was through my interest in envelopes that I caught a spy. A real honest-to-Pete spy."

"In 1953?" said Avalon, frowning suddenly. "Don't tell me you were one of the young men working for Senator Joseph McCarthy."

"Who? Me?" said MacShannon, clearly astonished at the suggestion. "Never! I never had any use for McCarthy at all. Of course—" he pondered the matter a moment, "he did make the nation spy-conscious and traitor-conscious, and that couldn't help but affect me, I suppose. You couldn't help thinking in that direction even if you disapproved of McCarthy's tactics, as I did."

"National paranoia, I call it," said Rubin seriously.

"Maybe," said MacShannon, "but anyway, whatever you call it, I suppose that that's what put the whole melodrama in my mind. In a quieter, less frenetic time, I would have seen that envelope and never given it a thought."

"Tell us about it," said Rubin.

"Certainly, if you wish. After thirty-six years, it can't be sensitive. Besides, I don't know the details, only the general outline. I was just starting out in the world, had my engineering degree, had a small job, was living by myself for the first time. I was twenty-four years old, though, and still a little uncertain of myself.

"There was another person, living across the hall from me—Benham was his name. I don't remember his first name. He was about thirty, I think, and I would occasionally see him going in or out. He was a scowler, if you know what I mean, unfriendly, never addressed me. I said hello once or twice, in passing, but he would give me the curtest possible nod and freeze me with his expression. I grew to dislike him intensely, of course, and since I was a great reader of thrillers in those days, I fantasized that he was something villainous—a criminal, a hitman, or, best of all, a spy.

"Then, one day, as we were both waiting for an elevator to take us to our two apartments on the eighth floor, he tore open an envelope he was carrying, which I assumed he had just picked up from his letter box. I had checked mine earlier and it was empty, as it almost always was in those days, except when my mother wrote me. I watched my neighbor out of the corner of my eye, partly because I would naturally watch someone I was fantasizing to be a mysterious villain, partly because I envied anyone who got a letter, and even partly because I never quite got over my childhood fascination with envelopes.

"Having torn open the envelope, he extracted the letter, unfolded it, read it without the slightest expression on his face, then crumpled it and tossed it into the trash basket that stood by the elevators in the hall. He then, still without expression, placed the empty envelope inside his inner jacket pocket. He did it very carefully and patted the front of his jacket as though to assure himself it was well-seated."

Trumbull interrupted. "How did you know it was an empty envelope? There could have been an enclosure along with the letter. A check, for instance."

MacShannon shook his head amiably. "I told you I had this quasi-professional attitude concerning envelopes. It was a flimsy kind, semi-transparent. He had held it in the hand near me while he scanned the letter and I could tell it was empty. No mistake was possible."

"Odd," said Halsted.

"The odd thing about it," said MacShannon, "was that at first I *didn't* think it was odd. After all, people frequently discard envelopes and keep letters, but I had never seen anyone discard a letter and keep an empty envelope and yet I didn't think it was odd. I said to myself, 'Gee, he's collecting postmarks,' and for a moment I was a ten-year-old again and remembering the thrill of the chase. In fact, for a little while I recognized this Benham as a fellow postmarker and I could feel myself warming to him.

"Maybe it was just as well, for if I hadn't had the postmark thought, I might not have kept the envelope in mind. But as it was, I did keep it in mind, and by the time I reached the eighth floor, I had other thoughts. As usual, my neighbor had not addressed a word to me, or cast me a glance, and my heart hardened toward him again. He couldn't be a postmarker, I decided, because postmarks had already deteriorated past the point where collecting could be profitable. Already, one never saw a clear postmark except on the occasional commemorative envelope.

"Why, then, did he save the envelope? It took me only ten seconds to convert the matter into a spy thriller and I had it. He had received a casual, meaningless message anyone could see and dismiss, but the *real* message was on the envelope where no one would look for it, and which he therefore kept for later study.

"By the time I had thought of that, I was in my apartment. I waited there for about half a minute, then peered out into the hall to make sure my neighbor wasn't lingering there. He wasn't, so I got back into the elevator, went down to the lobby, and retrieved that crumpled letter."

Rubin said, "Which, I suppose, turned out to be completely uninteresting."

"Well," said MacShannon, "at least it *seemed* to show Benham in a more human light. The letter was in a feminine handwriting, but by no means a cultivated one—a semi-legible scrawl."

Avalon said with a sigh, "That is about the best you can expect in these degenerate days."

MacShannon smiled. "I suppose so. In any case, I studied that letter so closely over the next few days that I still remember it thirty-six years later—not that there was much to remember. It wasn't dated and it just started, 'Dear Mr. Benham, I had a very good time and it was kind of you to promise to check the matter of the job opening. Please let me know, and thank you.'"

"I see what you mean," said Halsted. "This neighbor might freeze you out, but his female correspondent thought him a kindly man."

Trumbull said, "Many a curmudgeon will unbend to a young woman to achieve the usual end."

MacShannon said, "I didn't think of anything like that. All it seemed to me was that the letter seemed totally innocuous, as I had thought it would have to be. The whole thing about job openings and kindness might just be a matter of writing at random, so to speak. To me, it meant that the envelope was all the more likely to be the important item. The question was, what ought I to do about it? I dithered for several days, and then finally took action. —Please remember that I was young and naive in those days, because in the end I went to the local office of the FBI."

Drake smiled and fingered the ashtray before him. "You risked making a fool of yourself."

"Even I knew that much," said MacShannon. "In fact, I remember that as I told my story to an apparently politely bored functionary, I felt more and more foolish, as I sounded less and less convincing in my own ears. I had several things on my side, though. Senator McCarthy had made it impossible for any agent to ignore any tale of spies. After all, it would be his neck if he let one go that he should not have."

"I can see that," said Halsted. "An agent dismissing something wrongfully would probably be accused of being a spy himself, or a card-carrying member of the Communist party."

"Yes," said MacShannon. "The FBI has to investigate anything brought to it even in easygoing times, but at the height of the McCarthy mania— Then, too, it turned out that Benham, this neighbor of mine, had a post in the infant computer industry and was in a position to know a few things the Pentagon distinctly wanted to have kept secret. In fact, it was my eventual understanding of this that roused my own interest in computers, so that I owe my present career to Benham, in a sense. In any case, I was listened to and the letter was taken from me. I was given a receipt, even though it wasn't my letter."

"It was in your possession," said Rubin, "and it belonged to you, since its previous owner had thrown it away and abandoned it, making it the property of anyone who picked it up."

"In a way," said MacShannon, "I entered into a distant partnership with the FBI, for I was asked to keep an eye on Benham and report anything further I thought unusual or suspicious. It made a common spy out of me, which, looking back on it, makes me feel a little awkward, but I honestly thought I might be dealing with an enemy agent, and I was a bit of a romantic in those days."

"And you might have been infected by the times," said Avalon.

"I wouldn't be surprised," said MacShannon agreeably. "At the time, of course, I didn't know exactly what the FBI was doing, but eventually I became friendly with the agent I had first spoken to, especially as it slowly turned out that Benham was indeed more than he seemed, so that the agent couldn't help but think highly of me."

Rubin said, "Then the hidden envelope turned out to be important, I suppose."

"Let me tell you how things worked out in order," said MacShannon. "They investigated the letter I gave them for some sort of code. What seemed nonsignificant to me might contain a hidden meaning. They could find none. Nor could they find hidden writing, or anything technically advanced, and that just made my story the more persuasive, since I, of course, had stressed the importance of the envelope from the beginning.

"They took to intercepting Benham's mail and opening it, reading it, resealing it, and sending it on. I watched the process on one occasion and it gave me a grisly feeling. It seemed so un-American. There was no way of telling at the conclusion that the letter had been opened, or in any way tampered with, and I have never been able to trust my own mail entirely since then. Who knows who might be studying it without my knowledge?"

Rubin said dryly, "For that matter, phone calls can be listened to, rooms can be bugged, conversations in the open can be overheard. We live in a world devoid of privacy."

"I'm sure you're right," said MacShannon. "In any case, they were particularly interested in any letters that Benham got from the young woman whose letter I had myself picked up. These had their own points of interest to a nosybody, for, as I was eventually told by my friend the agent, it was plain that there was a burgeoning love affair going on there. The letters grew more impassioned and devoted, but the woman's letters, at least, were always scrawled, brief, and continued to show no great intellectual capacity."

Drake grinned. "Intellectual capacity is not necessarily what a man might be after."

Halsted asked, "How long did the investigation go on?"

"Months," said MacShannon. "It was an on-and-off affair."

"Say," said Gonzalo, "if this was a love affair, the letter might not be significant in any case. If agents are in the business of collecting and transmitting information, they're not going to fall in love."

"Why not?" said Avalon sententiously. "Love comes as it pleases, sometimes to the most unlikely participants in the most unlikely situations. That's why Eros, the god of love, is often pictured as blind."

"That's not what I mean," said Gonzalo. "Of course they can fall in love, but they wouldn't use their official communications, if I may call them that, as a vehicle. They'd make love on their own time, so to speak, in their own way, and leave the important messages alone."

MacShannon said, "Not if the real messages were on the envelope. The more immaterial the letter itself, the better. Why not carry on a love affair, even a sincere love affair, in the letter itself? Who would think of looking at the envelopes in cases where the letter itself seems so all-important to the writer and reader? If I hadn't seen him save that first envelope—"

"Well," said Trumbull, a little impatiently, "get on with it. I have some connection with counterintelligence myself and I'm sure they investigated the envelopes."

"They did, indeed," said MacShannon. "Every one of them, whether they were from the young lady or not. At least, the agent told me they did, and I had no reason to think he was lying. Of course, I wondered, at the time if what they were doing was legal. It seemed un-American to me, as I have already said."

"Undoubtedly it was illegal," said Trumbull. "They had no evidence of wrongdoing. Saving an empty envelope may be puzzling, but it is not a crime. Still, national security purifies a multitude of sins and a bit of illegality here and there is winked at."

"Bad in principle," growled Rubin. "A bit of illegality

leads to a lot, and in no time we'd be at the Gestapo level."

"We aren't yet," said Trumbull, "and there's a tight rein placed on these organizations."

"Yes, when they're caught," said Rubin.

"And they're caught often enough to be kept within bounds. Come on, Manny, let's let MacShannon proceed. You were telling us they inspected the envelopes."

"Yes, they did," said MacShannon. "They removed the stamps to see what might be underneath. They studied every bit of writing on the envelope to the last detail and they subjected the paper to every known test. They even substituted new envelopes which they made just like the old except that they made small nonsignificant changes. They wanted to see if the new envelope had something distorted that would reduce its message to nonsense."

Drake said, "That's a lot of trouble to take for anything as thin as your story.

"You can thank McCarthy," said MacShannon briefly. "But they never did find anything either in the letters or on the envelopes."

Rubin said, "Hold on, Mr. MacShannon, when you started this story, you said that as a result of your interest in envelopes, you caught an honest-to-Pete spy. Did you or didn't you?"

"I did," said MacShannon urgently, "I *did.*"

"Are you going to tell us," said Rubin, "that as a result of the investigation, a different person altogether was trapped as the spy?"

"No, no. It was Benham. *Benham.*"

"But you said the letters and the envelopes showed nothing. You did say that, didn't you?"

"I didn't quite say they showed nothing, but I did say

the FBI found nothing in the correspondence. However, they didn't confine themselves to that. They worked at the other end—his job. They inspected his work record, kept him under hidden surveillance, and eventually found out what he was doing and with whom. I gathered that quite a substantial spy ring was broken and I got some nice words from the bureau. Nothing official, of course, but it was the big excitement of my life and I owed it all, in a way, to my having collected postmarks as a boy."

There was perhaps less satisfaction on the faces of the assembled Black Widowers than there was on MacShannon's.

Avalon said, "What about the young woman? Benham's light o' love? Was she picked up, too?"

For a moment, MacShannon looked uncertain. "I'm not dead sure," he said. "I was never told. My impression at the time was that there was insufficient evidence in her case, since they got nothing out of the letters or envelopes. —But that's the one thing that bothers me. I got Benham because he had saved that envelope. Why couldn't they find anything on the envelopes, then? If Benham and company had some secret communication system that the FBI didn't penetrate, who knows what damage has been done since then by its means."

Halsted said, "Maybe the FBI found nothing on the envelope because there was nothing to find there. Even spies can't be spies every minute of the day. Maybe the love affair was only a love affair."

MacShannon's good humor, until then unfailing, began to evaporate. He looked a little grim as he said, "But then why did he save that envelope? It always comes down to that. We're not talking about an ordinary person, but about a spy, a real spy. Why should he discard a letter so casually that anyone could pick it up, and save an empty envelope. There has to be a reason. If there's an innocent reason that has nothing to do with his profession, what is it?"

Avalon said gently, "I take it that you yourself have never thought of an adequate reason, Mr. MacShannon."

"None, except that the envelope bore a message of some sort," said MacShannon.

"I suspect," said Rubin, "that you haven't tried thinking of what we have been calling an innocent explanation, Mr. MacShannon. Perhaps you have been too satisfied with your message theory."

"In that case, *you* think of an alternate reason, Mr. Rubin," said MacShannon defiantly.

"Now wait," said Halsted, "the spy thing was *not* Mr. MacShannon's original assumption. At first he thought that Benham was collecting postmarks—or possibly stamps, for that matter. Suppose that very first thought was correct."

MacShannon said, "Don't underestimate the FBI. I had mentioned my original thought and, on one occasion, they managed to search his apartment. There were no signs of any collecting mania of any kind. Certainly, there were no envelope collections. They told me so."

"You might have told us that," said Rubin.

"I just have," said MacShannon, "but it's not important. The chance of his saving the envelope for collecting purposes was so small that it made no sense to dwell on it. —Well, then, have you come up with some other explanation for saving the envelope, Mr. Rubin? Or any of you?"

Drake said, "It could have been a thoughtless action.

People do things out of habit, all sorts of silly things. Your Mr. Benham meant to save the letter and discard the envelope and, without thinking, he did the reverse."

"I can't believe that," said MacShannon.

"Why not? It's called being absentminded," said Drake. "Later, when he found he had saved the envelope, he may have gone downstairs to recover the letter and found it gone."

MacShannon said, "A man whose career is espionage is surely not absentminded. He wouldn't last long if he were. Besides, he knew what he was doing. He read the letter and crumpled it at once and discarded it. Then he looked at the envelope thoughtfully and put it away carefully. He knew what he was doing."

"Are you sure?" said Drake. "It happened thirty-six years ago. With all due respect, you may be honestly remembering what you want to remember."

"Not at all," said MacShannon frigidly. "It was the big excitement of my life and I spent a lot of time thinking about it. My memory is accurate."

Drake shrugged. "If you insist, it's impossible to argue, of course."

MacShannon looked about the table from face to face. "Now, then, who has an alternate explanation? No collection. No absentmindedness. What else? —And no sentimental attachment for the writer. There might have been a love affair afterward, but that letter Benham discarded was clearly the first one he had received. He had just met her. And even if it was love at first sight, something he didn't strike me as subject to, he would have kept the letter, not the envelope."

There was silence around the table and MacShannon said, "There you are! It's bothered me for all these years.

What was there about the envelope that defeated the FBI? I guess I'll just have to keep on wondering for the rest of my life."

"Wait," said Avalon, "the communication, if there was indeed one, may have been on the first envelope only, the one he saved and the one that the FBI presumably never saw. All the others may have been clean and irrelevant."

MacShannon's little beard quivered at that. "I'll leave it to Mr. Trumbull," he said. "He said he was with counterintelligence. Does a conspirator of some sort give up a method of communication once it has been proven successful?"

Trumbull said, "It's not a cosmic law, but successful gambits are not lightly abandoned, it's true. However, it might no longer have been particularly successful. That envelope he kept may have just happened to be the last of a line of such things that was using a technique that had grown risky. It could then have been abandoned."

"Might! May have! Could have been!" said MacShannon, his voice rising to a squeak. "We have two actual facts. The man *was* a spy. The man *did* keep an empty envelope. Let's find an explanation as to why a spy should keep an empty envelope, an explanation that isn't pure speculation."

Again there was silence about the table and MacShannon smiled sardonically and said, "There is no such explanation, except that it bore a message."

At this point, Henry, from his post at the sideboard, said mildly, "May I offer a suggestion?"

MacShannon whirled at this unexpected entry into the conversation and said in annoyed fashion, "What is it you want, waiter?"

Gonzalo immediately held up his hand in a stop gesture and said, "Henry is a member of the club, Frank. He's expected to contribute."

"I see," said MacShannon, without any noticeable easing of his manner. "What is it you wish to say, then, my man?"

"Only, sir, that saving an empty envelope is something so reasonable that any of us might do it and that each of us may, in fact, have done so at some time or another."

"I deny that," said MacShannon.

"Consider, sir," said Henry quietly, "that the letter you obtained from the trash can was, as you yourself have said, the first between them. They had been out together on a date or, perhaps, as the result of a casual meeting. They talked. She told him of her difficulties in locating a suitable job, and he offered to help her. Since he was not an agreeable character from your description of him, Mr. MacShannon, he must have been attracted to her and strove to be agreeable against his natural bent. We don't know if she was young and pretty, but that's a reasonable assumption. She must have been attracted to him, too. Certainly the letter expressed gratitude and encouraged a continuation of the correspondence. She said, 'Please let me know.' And, in fact, there *was* further correspondence and there is apparently no question but that a certain romance eventually began between them. Would you judge me correct in all this?"

"Yes," said MacShannon, "but what of it?"

"We might further reason," said Henry, "that Mr. Benham would want to continue the correspondence with a woman who may have been young and pretty and was certainly being grateful and inviting. Now you told us the contents of the letter, Mr. MacShannon, and said you remembered it word for word. It was not a long letter and I accept your memory. It was the letter of a pleasant, but not well-organized, young woman, for you said it was undated, and almost anyone with any sense of order would date a letter."

"Yes," said MacShannon. "It was undated, but I still don't get what you're driving at."

Henry said, "Someone casual enough to leave a letter undated may well have omitted other things as well. You said it started, without preamble, with a 'Dear Mr. Benham.' I take it then that there was no return address included on the letter sheet."

MacShannon's frown smoothed out and he said, with a note of surprise, "No, there wasn't."

"Then," said Henry, "since the letter was not a love letter and Benham was not the type, perhaps, to place even a love letter next to his heart, he crumpled it and threw it away. However, he did want to answer it and perhaps encourage a relationship he suspected might be sexually satisfying. People who don't put the return address on the letter itself often do place it on the envelope. So Mr. Benham looked at the envelope, noted that it carried the return address, and naturally saved it so that he could answer the young lady. Surely that is a reasonable explanation."

A wave of brief applause swept the table, and Henry, flushing slightly, said, "Thank you, gentlemen."

MacShannon, clearly taken aback, said, "But in that case the envelope had nothing to do with Benham's espionage."

"As Mr. Halsted said earlier," said Henry, "a spy needn't be a spy every second. There are bound to be intervals of normality. However, he did break a cardinal rule of the profession, I think."

"What was that, Henry?" asked Trumbull.

"It seems to me that anyone engaged in the difficult profession of espionage must, above all, refrain from attracting attention of any kind. The envelope should not have been saved and the letter discarded in front of a witness. It should not even have been opened and read in front of a witness. —Of course, Mr. Benham had no way of knowing that the young man he always studiously ignored had once collected postmarks and was therefore sensitized to envelopes.

AFTERWORD

My favorite time for writing Black Widowers stories is when I'm on vacation. Every once in a while, Janet and I go on a cruise to Bermuda. For seven days, I'm away from my typewriter, my word processor, and my reference library. What I do, under such abysmal conditions, is smuggle a pad of paper and some ballpoint pens into my luggage, and then I write fiction. This story and the following one were written on the Bermuda trip in July of 1988, together with a third story that was not a Black Widowers, so the vacation was not entirely a waste of time.

Incidentally, it was not till I was putting the stories together for this collection that I noticed that the central point of "The Envelope" was used as a subsidiary point in "Sunset on the Water." That sort of thing is bound to happen once in a while, especially when one writes as much and as assiduously as I do, but it makes me feel bad just the same.

This story first appeared in the April 1989 issue of *Ellery Queen's Mystery Magazine*.

THE ALIBI

Emmanuel Rubin was in an uncharacteristically mild mood during the cocktail hour preceding the Black Widowers' banquet. And uncharacteristically thoughtful, too. —But characteristically didactic.

He was saying to Geoffrey Avalon (though his voice was loud enough to reach all corners of the room), "I don't know how many mystery stories—or suspense stories, as they tend to call them these days—have been written, but the number is approaching the astronomical and I certainly haven't read them all.

"Of course, the old-fashioned puzzle story is passé, though I like to write one now and then, but even the modern psychological story in which the crime is merely mentioned in passing, but the inner workings of the criminal's tortured soul occupies thousands of tortured words, may have its puzzle aspects.

"What it amounts to is that I'm trying to think up a new kind of alibi that is broken in a new kind of way, and I wonder—what are the odds of my thinking one up that has never been used before? And no matter how ingenious I am, how can I possibly know that someone long ago, in some obscure volume I never read, did not use precisely the same bit of ingenuity? I envy the early practitioners in the field. Almost anything they made up had never been used before."

Avalon said, "What's the odds, Manny? If you haven't read all the suspense stories written, neither has any reader. Just make up something. If it's a repeat of some obscure device that appeared in a novel published fifty-two years ago, who will know?"

Rubin said bitterly, "Somewhere someone will have read that early novel and he'll write to me, very likely sarcastically."

Mario Gonzalo, from the other end of the room, called out, "In your case, it won't matter, Manny. There are so many other things to criticize in your stories that probably no one will bother pointing out that your gimmicks are old hat."

"There speaks a man," said Rubin, "who in a lifetime of portraiture has produced only caricature."

"Caricature is a difficult art," said Gonzalo, "as you would know if you knew anything about art."

Gonzalo was sketching the evening's guest in order that the sketch might be added to those that marched along the wall of the room at the Milano Restaurant in which the banquets took place.

He had what seemed an easy task this time, for the guest, brought in by Avalon, who was host of the evening, had a magnificent mane of white hair, thick and lightly waved, shining like spun silver in the lamplight. His regular features and spontaneous, even-toothed smile made it quite certain that he was one of those men who grew statelier and more handsome with age. His name was Leonard Koenig and Avalon had introduced him merely as "my friend."

Koenig said, "You are making me look something like a superannuated movie star, Mr. Gonzalo."

"You can't fool an artist's eye, Mr. Koenig," said Gonzalo. "Are you one, by any chance?"

"No," said Koenig without further elaboration, and Rubin laughed.

"Mario is right, Mr. Koenig," said Rubin. "You can't fool an *artist's* eye."

With that the conversation grew more general, breaking off temporarily only when the soft voice of that peerless waiter, Henry, announced, "Please take your seats, gentlemen. Dinner is being served." —And they sat down to their turtle soup, which Roger Halsted, as the club gourmet, sipped carefully before giving it the benediction of a broad smile.

Over the brandy, Thomas Trumbull, whose crisply waved white hair lost caste, somehow, against the brighter, softer hair of the guest, took up the task of grilling.

"Mr. Koenig, how do you justify your existence?" he asked.

Koenig smiled broadly. "In view of Mr. Rubin's problems with the invention of alibis, I suppose I can most easily justify my existence by pointing out that in my time I have been a breaker of alibis."

"Your profession has not been announced by Jeff," said

Trumbull. "May I take it, then, that you are on the police force?"

"Not quite. Not on an ordinary police force. I am in counterespionage, or, to put it more accurately, I was. I retired early and moved into the law, which is how I met Jeff Avalon."

Trumbull's eyebrows shot up. "Counterespionage?"

Koenig smiled again. "I read your mind, Mr. Trumbull. I know of your position with the government and you're wondering why you don't know my name. I assure you I was a minor cog, who, except for one case, never did anything notable. Besides, as you know, it's not department policy to publicize its members. We do our work best in obscurity. And, as I said, I retired early, and have been forgotten in any case."

Gonzalo said eagerly, "That alibi you broke. How did you do that?"

"It's a long story," said Koenig, "and not something I should talk about in detail."

"You can trust us," said Gonzalo. "Nothing that's said at any Black Widowers meeting is ever mentioned outside. That includes our waiter, Henry, who's himself a member of the club. Tom, tell him."

"Well, it's true," said Trumbull reluctantly. "We are all souls of discretion. Even so, though, I can't urge you to talk about matters that should not be talked of."

Avalon pursed his lips judiciously. "I'm not sure we can take that attitude, Tom. The conditions of the banquet are that the guest must answer all questions and rely on our discretion."

Gonzalo said, "Well, look, Mr. Koenig, you can leave out anything you think is too sensitive to talk about. Just describe the alibi and don't tell us how you broke it, and *we'll* break it for you."

James Drake chuckled. "Don't make rash promises, Mario."

"We can try, anyway," said Gonzalo.

Koenig said thoughtfully, "Do you mean you want to make a game of this?"

"Why not, Mr. Koenig?" said Gonzalo. "And Tom Trumbull can disqualify himself if it turns out he remembers the case."

"I doubt that he will. The whole thing was on a 'need to know' basis and he was not part of the same organization I was." Koenig paused to think for a moment. "I suppose it's possible to play the game, but it was almost thirty years ago. I hope I remember all the details." He cleared his throat and began.

"It's interesting," said Koenig, "that Mr. Rubin mentioned the tales that talk about the psychology of the criminal, because in my old business a lot depended on the psychology of the spy. There were people who betrayed their country for money, or for spite, or out of sexual infatuation. These are easy to handle, in a way, because they have no strong underpinning of conviction and, if caught, give way easily."

"Greed is the thing," said Halsted feelingly, "and you don't have to be a spy. The corrupt politician, the tax-finagling businessman, the industrialist who defrauds the armed forces with overcharges and shoddy work, can damage the country as badly as any spy."

"Yes," said Rubin, "but these guys will shout patriotism all over the place. They can steal the government and the people blind, but as long as they hang out the flag on Memorial Day and vilify foreigners and anyone to the left of Genghis Khan, they're great guys."

"That's why," said Avalon, "Samuel Johnson pointed out that patriotism was the last refuge of the scoundrel."

"Undoubtedly," said Koenig, "but we're veering from the point. I was going on to say that there are also spies who do their job out of a strong ideological feeling. They may do so out of admiration for the ideals of another nation, or because they feel they are serving the cause of world peace, or in some other way are behaving nobly in their own eyes. We can't really complain about this, for we have people in foreign countries who work for us for similar idealistic reasons and, in fact, we have more of these than our enemies have. In any case, these ideologues are the really dangerous spies, for they plan more carefully, are willing to take greater risks, and are far more resolute when caught. A man of that sort was Stephen. Notice that I'm using only his first name, and Stephen is not the true first name, either."

Stephen lived a quiet life [Koenig began]; he did not draw attention to himself. He did not make the mistake of trying to cover his true purposes by an unrealistic profession of patriotism. It's just that he had available to him, in the way of his work and of circumstances, a great many items we did not want the enemy to have. Still, there are many people who know matters that had best be confidential, and the vast majority of them are thoroughly dependable. There was no reason to suppose that Stephen wasn't as dependable as any of them.

However, there were certain data that the enemy would particularly want to have, data to which Stephen had access. He could easily pass it along to the enemy, but if he did, circumstances were such that he would surely be suspected. In fact, there would be what would amount to a moral certainty that he was the culprit. Yet such was the importance of the information that he *had* to obtain it.

Notice, by the way, that I don't tell you anything at all about the nature of the data in question, about the manner in which he had access, or the manner in which he would make the transfer. All that is irrelevant to the little game we are playing. Now let me try to put myself into Stephen's mind—

He knew he had to perform the task, and he knew he would instantly be suspected, strongly suspected. He felt that he had to protect himself somehow. It was not so much that he feared imprisonment, for he might be exchanged. Nor, I imagine, did he fear death, since the circumstances of his life were such that he must have known that he lived with the possibility of death, even unpleasant death, every day.

Nevertheless, as a patriot—I suppose he could be considered that if viewed through his own eyes—he did not want to be caught because he knew he could not easily be replaced. Furthermore, if he could somehow be absolved of suspicion, our department would have to look elsewhere. That would waste our energies and place any number of innocent people under suspicion, all of which would work to our disadvantage.

But how could he avoid being caught when he was, of necessity, the obvious culprit? Clearly, he would have to be in two places—in the city, where he could carry through his task, and, at the same time, in a far away place so that it would seem he could not possibly have had anything to do with the task. The only way he could achieve this was to be two people.

Here is the way he managed it, as we eventually found out. The country Stephen worked for provided a look-alike, whom we might call Stephen Two. I imagine that if Stephen and Stephen Two stood next to each other it would be easy to distinguish between them, but if someone saw Stephen Two and then, a few days later, Stephen himself, it would seem that he had seen the same person.

It also seems logical to suppose that Stephen Two's resemblance to Stephen was reinforced. He would be given Stephen's hairstyling, would cultivate Stephen's thin mustache, would practice Stephen's voice as given on recordings, and his signature as recorded on documents. He would even have learned to make use of some of Stephen's favorite expressions. Naturally, he would have to be someone who spoke English and understood the culture as well as Stephen did.

All this must have taken considerable time and effort, but it is a measure of the importance of what the enemy country was after that the time and effort was spent.

We eventually pieced together what it was Stephen did and are satisfied that the account is essentially correct. As the time approached, Stephen let it be known, in as casual a manner as seemed appropriate, that he would be going to Bermuda for a week's vacation by way of a cruise ship. When the time came, he went into hiding and changed his appearance slightly, so that he would not readily be recognized while he carried out the theft and transmission of the data as quietly and as obscurely as possible. It was Stephen Two, of course, who took the ship to Bermuda.

Stephen himself, as it happened, had never been to Bermuda, and that struck him as a useful fact. Having been there but once would account for the fact that he might not know all there was to know about the island. He had, however, to know what he himself had done on the island, and for that purpose, he had Stephen Two send him, by way of a simple code and a secure accommodation address, a condensed but detailed account of what he did and saw on Bermuda. In particular, Stephen Two must do a number of unimportant things that he would have to recount in detail, so that Stephen could use them as proof of having been in Bermuda. A casual reference to the unimportant could be made to seem convincing evidence.

We are quite certain that Stephen ordered Stephen Two to make friends with some reasonably attractive woman on the ship and get along with her well enough so that she would be certain to remember him—yet not so well that she could detect some difference between the two Stephens.

In particular, he did not want Stephen Two to get intimate and start a romance. I imagine that Stephen did not want to be handed a situation that might make him uncomfortable, and a woman who imagined they had been lovers, when that was something he would not be able to deny without great danger to himself, would certainly represent something uncomfortable.

The week during which Stephen Two was in Bermuda must have been a period of great suspense for Stephen. He carried through his own task, but what if the cruise ship foundered, or Stephen Two fell overboard, or had an accident in Bermuda and was hospitalized, crippled, or even killed? Or suppose Stephen Two were fingerprinted for some reason, or had turned traitor (or had, from our point of view, defected). Anything like that would have ruined Stephen's alibi and made his jailing certain.

In actual fact, of course, none of these things took place. Stephen Two sent his letters faithfully, numbering each so that Stephen could be certain that none had been lost. Stephen carefully memorized each letter as well as he might.

Eventually, Stephen Two returned from Bermuda, and with quiet skill faded out and went back to his own country, while Stephen resumed his identity.

It was two weeks after the end of the Bermuda trip that we had reason to suspect that the data Stephen had been after had been tampered with. A quick investigation proved the case, and the finger of suspicion pointed forcefully and without question at Stephen.

A group of us descended upon him.

He was quite admirable in his way. His distress at the loss of the information seemed quite sincere and he admitted ruefully that he was the logical suspect, and indeed the only one.

"But," he said with gentle patience, "I was on the *Island Duchess* from the ninth to the sixteenth, and I was in Bermuda between the eleventh and the fourteenth. If the loss took place during that period, I simply couldn't have done it."

He gave us full details and, of course, had ample records to the effect that he had bought tickets, embarked, disembarked, paid his bar bill and some other expenses, and so on. All seemed in order. It didn't even seem suspicious that he could produce this all on demand. He said, "I'm going to claim part of this as a business expense, so I'll need records for the IRS."

There seemed to be a disposition among my confreres to accept this and to wonder if there might be other suspects after all. I held off. Stephen seemed, for some reason, to be too smooth to me, and I insisted on continuing to question him while others tackled other angles of the case. That was my big achievement as a spy catcher, of course. If I had had one or two more like that, the department might not have been so willing to let me go when I asked for retirement, but I didn't. This was my one and only.

In a second interview, I said to him, "Were you on the ship or on Bermuda every moment from embarkation to disembarkation?"

"Yes, of course," he said, "I was at the mercy of the ship."

"Not entirely, sir."

He frowned a bit, as though trying to penetrate my meaning, then said, "Do you mean that I might have flown from the ship to here and then back to the ship and, in that way, have been here for the job and there for an alibi?"

"Something like that," I said grimly.

"I couldn't get on a plane without identifying myself."

"There are such things as deliberate misidentifications."

"I understand that," he said, "but I suppose you can check as to whether any helicopter encountered the ship at any time. I suppose you can check every passenger on every plane between here and Bermuda during the time I was on the island and see whether any passenger is unaccounted for, or is anything but a real person distinct from myself."

I didn't bother to tell Stephen that such checks were actually under way—and in the end, they uncovered nothing.

Our interviews were recorded, of course, with Stephen's permission. We had read him his rights, but he said he was perfectly willing to talk and required no lawyer. He was the very model of an innocent citizen confident of his innocence, and that simply raised my suspicions somehow. He seemed too good to be true, and too confident. It was about then that I began to wonder if he had a twin brother so that he could seem to be in Bermuda even while he was at home. That was checked out, too, and it was established he was a single birth and, indeed, an only son—but the idea of a look-alike remained in my mind.

I said, in a later interview, "Did you stay on the ship while in Bermuda? Or at a hotel?"

"On the ship."

"Had you ever been to Bermuda before? Are you a well-known figure there in any way?"

"It was my first trip to Bermuda ever."

"Is there anyone who can vouch for your presence on the ship each day? Is there anyone who can vouch that you were indeed in Bermuda at those times you were off the ship?"

He hesitated. "I was on the cruise alone. I didn't go with any friends. After all, I had no idea, no faintest notion—how could I?—that I would have to prove I was on the ship."

I half smiled. That seemed a hair too ingenuous.

"You're not going to tell me," I said, "that you were a recluse, skulking in corners and speaking to no one."

"No," he said, looking a little uncomfortable. "As a matter of fact, I was friendly enough, but I can't guarantee that any of the people I interacted with casually would remember me. Except—"

"Go on! What is the exception?"

"There was a certain young woman I grew friendly with at the start of the cruise. She became my steady companion, so to speak, at ship's meals, and for much of the time on Bermuda. —Don't get me wrong, Mr. Koenig. There was nothing improper about the relationship. I'm not a married man, but even so it was just a casual friendship. I think she might remember me. We danced on board ship and, in Bermuda, we visited the aquarium, went on the glass-bottom boat together, took tours, ate at the Princess Hotel. Things like that. She went to the beach alone, though. I tend to avoid the sun."

"Did you see her every day?"

He thought a moment. "Yes, every day. Not all day, of course. And not at night. She was never in my room and I was never in hers."

"We're not concerned with your morals, sir."

"I'm sure you're not, but I don't want to say anything that would unfairly reflect on *her* morals."

"That's very considerate of you. What was the young woman's name?"

"Artemis."

"Artemis?" I said, rather in disbelief.

"That's what she told me her name was, and that's what I heard others call her. She was a very pretty woman, in her early thirties I should judge, with dark blond hair and blue eyes. About five feet six in height."

"And her last name?"

He hesitated. "I don't remember. She may not even have mentioned it. It was shipboard, you know, very informal. She called me Stephen. I don't think I ever mentioned my own last name."

"Her address?"

"I don't know. She spoke as though she were a New Yorker, but I don't know. You can always look at the ship's records for the week. She'd be listed, and I'd say the chances were virtually zero that there would be two Artemis's. They would surely have her last name and her home address."

I turned off the recording device at that and warned him that, as had been established, he would continue to be confined to his apartment for the duration of the questioning, but that anything necessary would be brought to him, and any reasonable errands would be run for him.

I was determined to prove if I could that whoever had been on Bermuda, it was not Stephen, but for that I would clearly need the woman.

It took three days to arrange matters, and each day was an annoyance. Obviously, I could not keep Stephen under wraps indefinitely, and once he began to complain loudly enough, we would have to come up with something definite or let him go.

But he did not complain. He continued to be a model citizen and once I had Artemis in tow, I arranged to have her see him when he did not know she was looking at him. She said, "It certainly looks like Stephen."

"Let's meet him, then. Just act naturally, but please keep your eyes open and let me know if, for any reason, you think it's not the man you met on the ship."

I brought her into the room and Stephen looked at her, smiled, and said without hesitation, "Hello, Artemis."

She said, a little hesitantly, "Hello, Stephen."

She was no actress. She looked at him anxiously, and Stephen would have had to be far less intelligent than he clearly was not to guess that, under instructions, she was trying to tell whether he might not be an imposter.

Finally, she said, "He certainly looks like Stephen, except Stephen had little tufts of hair on the back of the rear end of his fingers. I thought that was so virile. I don't see them now."

Stephen didn't seem to mind being discussed in the third person, or to be offended that the woman searched for difference. He merely smiled and held up his hands. "The hair is there."

She said, "It should be darker." She didn't sound definite about it, though.

Stephen said, "Remember the time when I tripped over my own two left feet while we were dancing and my hand slipped out of yours and you said it was because they were so smooth? That doesn't sound as though you were so terribly impressed over their hairiness, does it?"

Artemis's face lit up. She turned to me and said, "Yes, that did happen."

"And you remember I apologized for being a clumsy dancer, and you kept saying I was a good dancer, but I knew you were just being sweet, and trying to make me feel better. Remember, Artemis?"

She said happily, "Yes, I remember. Hello, Stephen. I'm glad it's you."

He said, "Thanks for recognizing me, Artemis. I'd have been in considerable trouble if you hadn't."

I interrupted a bit irritably, I suppose. "Wait, Miss Cataldo. Don't rush to conclusions."

He said, "Is that your last name, Artemis? They asked me, but I didn't know. You'd never told me."

I waved him quiet. I said, "Ask him some questions, Miss Cataldo; little things that he ought to get right."

Artemis flushed. "Did you ever kiss me, Stephen?"

Stephen looked a little embarrassed. "I did once—just once. In the taxi, Artemis. Remember?"

I didn't give the woman a chance to reply. I said sharply, "The details, Stephen. And no hesitation."

He shrugged. "We were in the taxi being driven to a place called Spittal Pond, a bird refuge that Artemis wanted to see. Artemis teased me because I said how pleasant it was to be going with a young woman who wanted to see bird refuges and not nightclubs and she said that by the next week, I would have forgotten her completely, and I wouldn't even remember her name. So I said gallantly, 'What? Forget Artemis, the chaste huntress?' I reached over her and wrote the name on the car window on the left. It was a humid day and there was a thin film of moisture on it."

"Where does the kiss come in?" I demanded.

"Well, I was seated on her right," said Stephen, "and I reached across her chest with my right arm to write her name. My left arm was on the back of the seat." He showed me how it was, stretching his left arm behind an imaginary companion, and then pushing his right hand across in front, so that his arms nearly enclosed that companion. "I had just finished writing her name when the taxi lurched, for some reason. My elbow nearly collided with the driver's head so I grabbed Artemis's shoulder to steady myself—pure reflex—and there I was embracing her." He was still demonstrating. "I found the position so irresistible that I kissed her. Only on the cheek, I am sorry to say."

I looked at the woman. "Well?"

Her eyes were shining. She said, "That's exactly how it happened, Mr. Koenig. This is Stephen, all right. There is just no question about it." She added dramatically, "I identify this man as the man on the ship and in Bermuda."

Stephen smiled with just a touch of triumph, it seemed to me, and I said, "Very well. You can leave now, Miss Cataldo."

And that's it.

Koenig stopped talking and looked at the Black Widowers with his eyebrows raised.

Gonzalo said explosively, "That's *it*? I thought you said you cracked his alibi."

"So I did. But you wanted me simply to tell you about the alibi and that *you* would then break it down."

"And you haven't left out anything?"

"Nothing essential," said Koenig.

Avalon cleared his throat and said, "I presume you found Stephen Two. That would break the alibi."

"So it would," said Koenig cheerfully, "but we never found Stephen Two, I'm sorry to say."

Halsted said, "Is it possible that Miss Whatsername was paid off? That she was lying?"

"If she was," said Koenig, "we found no evidence to back it. In any case, the alibi was broken quite apart from anything she said or didn't say. —Have any of you gentlemen visited Bermuda?"

There was a general silence and finally Gonzalo said,

"I was taken there when I was four years old or so. I don't remember anything."

Trumbull said, "Are you hinting that Stephen got some of the places in Bermuda wrong? Was it that there was no bird refuge of the kind he mentioned or no Princess Hotel or something like that?"

"No, he got all the places correct. No mistake that we could find as far as the geography or sights of the place were concerned."

Again there was a silence and Drake finally said, "Henry, is there anything about this that strikes you as making sense?"

Henry, who was just returning from the reference shelf, said thoughtfully, "I can't speak through firsthand knowledge because I, too, have never been on Bermuda, but it's possible that what Mr. Stephen said may have proved that he was never on Bermuda, either."

Drake said in surprise, "Why, what did he say?"

Henry said, "Mr. Koenig ended his tale with the account of the kiss in the taxi, so I thought that perhaps something about that account broke the alibi. Now, Bermuda is a British crown colony and it strikes me that it may follow British custom as far as traffic is concerned. I have just checked the Columbia Encyclopedia on the reference shelf and it says nothing about that, but it is a possibility.

"If, in Bermuda, traffic is always on the left, as it is in Great Britain, the automobiles must have the steering wheel, and, therefore, the driver, on the right side of the front seat as in Great Britain; whereas in the United States, with traffic on the right, steering wheel and driver are on the left. If Mr. Stephen was sitting to the young woman's right and reaching over her to write her name on the left window as he said, he could scarcely have nearly struck the driver when the taxi lurched. The driver would have been on the other side.

"I imagine Stephen Two told Mr. Stephen about the kissing incident, but neglected to mention the matter of the steering wheel or the driver, taking that for granted. Mr. Stephen added the matter of the driver for added verisimilitude and that was his great mistake, for, undoubtedly, Mr. Koenig saw the point at once."

Koenig sat back in his chair and smiled admiringly. "That's very good, Henry."

"Not at all. The praise is yours, Mr. Koenig," said Henry. "I knew you had broken the alibi; I knew you had done it by reason; and I knew that the reasoning had to be deduced from the facts you gave us. You, in breaking the alibi, did not have the advantage of that special knowledge."

AFTERWORD

The influence of my having been on my Bermuda vacation (see the previous Afterword) shows itself clearly in this story, which first appeared in the September 1989 issue of *Ellery Queen's Mystery Magazine.*

THE RECIPE

Roger Halsted said in a whisper to Geoffrey Avalon, "He's my plumber."

Avalon stared at him for a moment or two, more in incredulity than in disapproval. "Your plumber?"

"Used to be, actually. He's retired and moved to the suburbs. He's a nice fellow, and if you want to judge by the usual criterion of American success, he has always made a lot more money than I have."

"I'm not at all surprised," said Avalon. "A master plumber—"

"He was that. And I just teach algebra at a junior high school. No comparison. But, you know, Jeff, we always get professional men as guests at these Black Widower banquets and I thought it would be rather refreshing to have someone who works with his hands."

Avalon said, rather unconvincingly, "Far be it from me

to indulge in social snobbery, Roger, but *he* may find *us* uncomfortable."

"You can't tell. —And it may give us a chance to find out about plumbing."

In another part of the room, Thomas Trumbull nursed his scotch and soda and said, "I've just read *The Third Bullet* by John Dickson Carr, Jim."

James Drake squinted at Trumbull and said, "That's an oldie."

"It's about half a century old, according to the copyright notice. I read it decades ago, as a matter of fact, but I didn't remember it well enough to spoil my fun. It's one of those locked-room mysteries, you know."

"I know. That was Carr's specialty. No one did them as consistently, or as well, as he did."

"And yet—" Trumbull shook his head. "Something bothered me."

Emmanuel Rubin had gravitated toward the pair at the first mention of a mystery. He said, "Let me guess what's bothering you, Tom. Carr is terrific, but he has his faults. For one thing, his writing tends to be overdramatic so that the reader is always uncomfortably aware that he is reading fiction. Then, when Carr finally gets to the solution, he has devised one that takes at least twenty pages. What's more, it is so intricate that the reader can't follow it without reading it several times, which he never does. And that means that it's all unconvincing."

"That's the point," said Trumbull. "That last bit. It's unconvincing. A locked-room mystery is usually so tortured in its construction and in its solution that you just can't accept it. I mean, has there ever been a locked-room mystery in real life? Somehow I doubt it."

Drake said, "We'd have to ask someone who is a connoisseur of real-life mysteries. Manny?"

"Don't look at me. I confine myself strictly to the fictional variety. I've never tried a locked-room mystery because, frankly, I think Carr killed the market for them. I can't bring myself to undertake thinking up a new variation."

Mario Gonzalo joined the group at this point. He said, "That reminds me of a game you can try sometimes. It's called, 'What's the greatest not by.' "

"What does that mean?" said Rubin suspiciously. "Assuming you know."

"Easy. It's asking a question like, what's the greatest Elizabethan tragedy not by Shakespeare?"

"The usual answer to that," said Rubin, "is Webster's *The Duchess of Malfi*, though I never liked it."

"All right. What's the best waltz not by Johann Strauss?"

" 'The Merry Widow Waltz' by Franz Lehár, I would say," said Rubin.

"What about 'The Skater's Waltz'?" demanded Gonzalo.

"A matter of taste," said Rubin.

"What's the greatest comic opera not by Gilbert and Sullivan?"

"How about Strauss's *Die Fledermaus*?" said Rubin.

"Or anything by Offenbach?" suggested Drake.

"And now," said Gonzalo, "what's the greatest locked-room mystery story not written by John Dickson Carr?"

There was a tremendous silence, followed by three people beginning to talk at once and others joining. In the increasing babble, Henry, that imperturbable waiter, announced that dinner was served.

Halsted's guest, the plumber, was Myron Dynast. His aging had not been entirely graceful. His hair was mostly gone, he had pouches under his eyes, a corrugated neck, and a pronounced paunch. His eyes, however, were sharp, his voice was not harsh, and his vocabulary was reasonably good. Avalon consequently said in a whisper to Halsted, "He doesn't *sound* like a plumber."

Halsted said, "What you really mean, Jeff, is that he doesn't sound like your mental stereotype of a plumber."

Avalon drew himself to his full height and brought his formidable eyebrows downward to affix Halsted with an offended glare. But then he thought better of it and said mildly, "Perhaps you're right, Roger."

Dynast, however, did not talk a great deal. Whether he was abashed at finding himself in intellectual company, or whether he was simply interested in the topics of conversation that enlivened the meal, he listened quietly, for the most part, his quick eyes darting from speaker to speaker.

Finally, over the brandy, Halsted rattled his spoon against his water glass and said, "Jeff, will you do the honors with respect to our guest."

"Gladly," said Avalon. With a somewhat exaggerated courtesy, he turned to Dynast and said, "It is customary at these, our banquets, to begin by asking our guest to justify his existence. How do you justify your existence, Mr. Dynast, or, in other words—"

"I don't need other words, Mr. Avalon," said Dynast. "Just being a good plumber is all the justification I need. Has anyone ever awakened in the middle of the night and realized that he suddenly needed a hotshot nuclear physicist? Think of all the emergencies in which you would be a lot happier if you lived next door to a plumber like me than to a professor like—like—"

"Like any of us," said Avalon, and cleared his throat. "You are quite right, Mr. Dynast. I accept your answer. Tell me, how long have you been a plumber?"

Dynast suddenly looked anxious. "Is this what it's going to be? Are you going to ask me all about plumbing?"

"Possibly, Mr. Dynast, we might."

Halsted interrupted in his soft voice. "I told you, Mike, that the conditions of the banquet are that you must answer all the questions we ask."

"I will, Rog, but I've got something more interesting to say—if you'll let me."

Avalon paused thoughtfully for a moment, then said, "It is not our intention to hamper you unduly, Mr. Dynast. You may tell us what it is you want to say, but if we go back to plumbing, you must accede to that. That is—"

"I know what you said, Mr. Avalon, and it's okay with me," said Dynast. "What I want to say is that before the banquet I heard you talking about locked-room mysteries. I heard you say you didn't know if a locked-room mystery could happen in real life. The thing is that I have one."

That brought the table to a frozen moment of immobility. Even Henry, who was quietly and efficiently clearing the last remnants of the banquet, looked up in thoughtful surprise.

Finally, Trumbull said in what was almost a hushed tone, "Do you mean you've heard of one, or that you've experienced one? Are you saying that you yourself have been involved in one?"

"Not me. My wife. *She* was."

Mario Gonzalo, at the other end of the table, was leaning forward in his seat, a look of unholy glee on his face. "Wait awhile, now, Mr. Dynast, are you going to tell us there was a locked room and someone was killed inside and it wasn't suicide and there was no murderer inside and your wife was there and knows all about it?"

Dynast stared in horror at that. "Murder? I'm not talking about murder. Good Lord, there was no murder. Nothing like *that*."

Gonzalo deflated visibly. "Then what are you talking about?"

Dynast said, "There was this room that was locked. And something happened that *couldn't* happen, that's all. And it involved my wife. It doesn't have to be murder to be a locked-room, does it?"

Avalon raised his hand and said in his deepest baritone, "I am doing the grilling, gentlemen, so let's have order. This may well be interesting and it may supersede our probing of the plumbing profession, at least temporarily, but let's go about it reasonably."

He waited, frowning, for silence, then said, "Mr. Dynast, exactly what happened in the locked room that couldn't have happened?"

"Something was stolen."

"Something of value?"

"To my wife, it had a great deal of value. Can I explain? I can't really talk about it without some explaining."

Avalon looked about the table. "Are there any objections to our listening to Mr. Dynast?"

Gonzalo said, "I have objections to *not* listening to him."

"Yes, Mario, I should suppose you have. Very well, Mr.

Dynast, but you must understand we will interrupt with questions at such times as we have any."

"Sure, go ahead." Dynast turned to Henry, who had taken up his accustomed position at the sideboard. "Waiter, could I have more coffee?"

Henry obliged, and Dynast said, "My wife, gentlemen, was born in a small town. She married me when she was thirty-three and, as it happened, we never had children. We spent some twenty years in the city, but she never got over being a small-town girl. Old-fashioned, too, if you know what I mean."

"I'm not sure we do," said Avalon. "What *do* you mean?"

"I mean she went out for church socials, and picnics, and all kinds of neighborhood activities. You couldn't really do much of that in the city, you know, but once I retired and we moved out of town, and bought a nice little house with some land, she went right back into the swim. It was as though she were trying to be a girl again. With no children, and no money problems, she could spend all her time at that sort of thing. And I'm willing —as long as she doesn't drag me into it."

"I take it, then, you're not a small-town boy," said Rubin.

"Definitely not. I'm a boy out of the concrete canyons."

"Don't you find it rather dull in the suburbs, then?"

"Oh, sure, but in the first place, I'm not so far from the city that I can't come in, now and then, to fill my lungs with the foul air. Ginny—that's my wife—doesn't mind. And then, too, I'm not entirely retired. I take on plumbing jobs when someone needs it, and that fills some of my time. You know, each plumbing job is different, each one is a challenge, especially if you want to do it well. And the plumbing in the suburbs is just different enough from that in the city to be interesting. Besides—"

He paused and flushed a little. "Besides, Ginny has been a good wife. She stuck it out in the city when things weren't so hot sometimes and didn't complain any more than she had to. Now it's her turn and she's happy—or *was* happy—and I wasn't about to spoil it for her.

"She keeps busy. Not having children, she sort of makes up for it by always being ready to do some baby-sitting. Half the time, the house has kids in it, running around and making noise. She loves it."

"Do *you* love it?" asked Trumbull, scowling.

"No, I don't, but it's *her* job. She doesn't ask me to help out. I know nothing about kids."

"Does your wife? If she has none of her own—" said Avalon.

"Oh, Lord. She just hasn't had any—uh—biologically, but she was the oldest of six. She spent practically all her life till she married me being a kind of assistant mother. Me, I had one big brother and we never got along. Kids are a closed book to me, but I don't miss them. Once we talked about adopting, but I was sort of against it, and she didn't force it on me."

Gonzalo said, with a touch of impatience, "Are we getting to the locked room?"

"There's one more point I have to explain. What makes my wife popular at these church socials is that she's a great cook. I can't explain it myself. I'm just an eater and I don't know what makes food special, but hers *is* special and I spent my whole life trying not to get fat on her food." He looked down at his abdomen with some chagrin as he said that.

"Listen, if she were a bad wife, I'd still stand her for the sake of her cooking—but she's a *good* wife. I don't say her cooking is fancy. She doesn't turn out the kind of food you get in fancy restaurants. Hers is plain stuff, but it melts in the mouth. Just to show you, her specialty is blueberry muffins. That doesn't sound like much because you can get them anywhere, but once you taste Ginny's blueberry muffins, you'll never buy them again. Compared to hers everything else is trash.

"She's got dozens of little things she does better than anyone else. I don't know how. Maybe it's spices, or how she mixes them, or how long she cooks, or who knows—She's just a genius at it, like I'm pretty good at plumbing. When she brings in her creations to one of these socials or picnics she goes to, everyone stands around with their tongues hanging out. And she loves it. It's her passport to fame and success. But what she's proudest of, what's nearest her heart, are those blueberry muffins. `

"No one can get any recipes out of her. She doesn't have them except in her head, and that's where she keeps them. Secret! They're her crown jewels. She never lets anyone into her kitchen when she's cooking except me, because she knows I don't know what's going on."

Drake said, "I remember my mother used to be a bit like that. When cooking is your expertise, you don't want anyone competing with you by making use of your own discoveries."

"That's right," said Dynast. "But you know, people kept talking to her about writing down all the recipes and making a book out of it. One of the ladies brought in a friend who worked at a publishing house and she talked to Ginny and said that cookbooks made money, and that a good cookbook of plain food could be a gold mine. She also said that someday Ginny would pass on and it wouldn't be right that her cooking secrets should die with her. She flattered Ginny right out of her shoes, and I could see Ginny was beginning to think there was something to it.

"To tell you the truth, I was sort of in favor, too. I would have liked to have her known far and wide for her cooking. I would be proud. So I pushed her, and she began thinking about it even more.

"Not that it was easy, you know. She talked about it and she would say things like, 'I just cook. I do things without even thinking about it. I add and mix and it's all in my fingertips, not in my brain. If I sit down to write a recipe, I would have to figure each one out.'

" 'Do it anyway,' I said. "Even if it's hard, you do it. Writing any kind of book is hard. Why shouldn't a cookbook be hard, too?'

"So she started to work at it now and then, and she'd keep all the recipes she worked out in a little fireproof box, which locked up with a key, and she would say to me, 'I just can't include the blueberry muffin recipe. That's my secret.' I would say, 'Come on, Ginny, no secrets,' but I knew what she meant.

"Those blueberry muffins were the one thing that created hard feelings against Ginny. They were *so* good and all the husbands loved them so much that all the wives had their noses out of joint. The other things lots of them could do almost as well, but Ginny's muffins were just out of reach. There was a lot of sentiment that she ought to put the recipe up on the church bulletin board and that it was a lack of Christian charity to hog it like that. But Ginny wouldn't be moved.

"Anyway, now you have the explanation. One day,

they were having some meeting at the church and, for a wonder, Ginny didn't feel she had to attend. She explained she wanted to stay home and work on her recipes and she said she would take care of some of the younger kids for those who attended the meeting to make up for not going. She ended up with five kids in the house for about three hours. In those three hours, the house was locked up, even the windows, because we had air-conditioning. There was no one in the house but Ginny and five little kids. That was it."

"Where were you, Mr. Dynast?" asked Avalon.

"I was in the city. To tell you the truth, I always try to be elsewhere when the kids get too thick. Ginny doesn't mind. Glad not to have me underfoot, I suppose."

Gonzalo said, "Is this the locked room you're talking about, Mr. Dynast? Your house locked up with just your wife and the five children in it?"

"That's right."

"I should have thought," said Avalon, "that Mrs. Dynast would get very little work done with five children underfoot."

"It wasn't bad," said Dynast. "Four of the children were old-timers, so to speak, who'd been in the house lots of times. They knew Ginny and Ginny knew them. They were all three or four years old and they had cookies and milk, and toys, and games. One of the children was new, but he was the best one. He belonged to a cousin of one of the regular mothers. The cousin and her husband were both going to the meeting with the mother, and Ginny was glad to take on the new child. His name was Harold and he was maybe almost five, very well-behaved and good-natured, according to

Ginny. He helped take care of the other children, in fact. He was very good with them.

"So Ginny kept working on her recipes and, for the first time, she actually wrote down the recipe for her blueberry muffins. She hated to do it, she said, so she wrote it down in pencil, lightly, as though that were equivalent to only half writing it down. Even so, she lost heart because just before it was all over and the children were taken away, she tore the card into confetti.

"That was what was so impossible to explain. She had written down the recipe near the start of her babysitting stint; she had torn it up near the end. It had existed maybe two and a half hours in that closed house, with no one inside but her and the five children, and during that two-and-a-half-hour period the recipe was stolen. —Wouldn't you call that a locked-room mystery?"

Trumbull said, "The recipe was stolen? I thought you said she tore it up."

"I didn't say the piece of paper was stolen. The recipe *on* it was stolen. The next day that recipe was on the church bulletin board, word for word, as she had written it. Poor Ginny. She was devastated. Since then, she's just been a different woman. She's not going to do the cookbook now, and she's not going to have anything to do with the church anymore."

"She's angry with the whole church?" said Gonzalo. "Who did the stealing?"

"She doesn't know, and I don't know. We don't know who stole it and we don't know how it was stolen. If we did know, she might get over it. She might have some specific person to be enraged with. She might see it was her own carelessness. As it is—" He shook his head. "That's why I was so interested when someone said there were no locked-room mysteries in real life. What do you call this?"

There was a silence, and Rubin said, "You were away the whole time? You saw none of this?"

"Almost the whole time, Mr. Rubin. I came home just as everything was breaking up. The others were milling about, taking their kids, and thanking Ginny. There was the cousin and her husband, the parents of little Harold. They were both quite short—about five feet tall each—but friendly and pleasant. I saw their boy for a moment. He was introduced to me and shook hands like a little man. It was all the height of pleasantness but, by that time, Ginny had already torn up the recipe and it had already, somehow, been stolen."

Halsted leaned back in his chair, hands clasped across his abdomen. "How sure can you be, Mike, that the house was really the equivalent of a locked room, that there was no window open and no way of getting in?"

Dynast shook his head. "That really doesn't matter, does it? All the doors and windows *were* locked, because Ginny is very careful, and as long as the kids are in her care, she wants none of them falling out a window or wandering out of the house. But never mind that. The fact is that she and the recipe were in this particular room and no one entered that room during all the time the recipe existed. It's just not possible that someone might have gotten in without her noticing."

"Even if she was absorbed in her recipes?" demanded Rubin.

"She wouldn't be that absorbed. The children came first. She would be on the alert at all times."

Gonzalo said, "And she never left the room at any time? She didn't go to the bathroom?"

"Listen," said Dynast. "We talked about this and I asked her that particular question. No, she didn't have to go to the bathroom, but she did leave the room. She left the house, in fact."

"Ah," said Gonzalo. "Why?"

"She remembered she had promised to deliver something to the neighbors who lived across the way, and she was afraid she would continue to forget if she didn't bring it over right then. It was only a matter of fifty feet and it would only take a minute. So she ran over, rang the bell, the husband came out, she shoved it into his hands with an explanation—his wife was at the meeting —exchanged two sentences, and dashed back. The whole thing took two minutes at the most."

Gonzalo said, "You weren't there, Mr. Dynast. A woman may feel she took only two minutes, and actually take twenty."

"Never," said Dynast indignantly. "She had a houseful of kids to take care of. She wouldn't take more than two minutes. She had no reason to take more than two minutes."

"Did she lock the door when she left?" asked Gonzalo.

"No, she didn't like to. Without being there, she was afraid that if something happened to her, and then something happened to the children, and there was a locked door to delay people getting in, well— But that doesn't matter. She had the front door under observation at all times. No one approached it. No one came anywhere near it. When she got back, and locked the door again, she asked little Harold if anything at all had happened when she was gone and he said nothing had. Certainly nothing was disturbed and the children seemed perfectly contented."

Gonzalo said, "Just the same, it's not really a locked room if it was open at some point."

"Let's not be legalistic, Mario," said Avalon. "If the story is accurate, then the house is still the equivalent of a locked room. I must admit, though, that the story is secondhand. I wish we could interview Mrs. Dynast firsthand."

"Well, we can't," said Rubin.

Trumbull said, "Now wait awhile. If we were talking about something material that was stolen, then the house might be considered a locked room. However, nothing material was stolen. The card on which the recipe was written was destroyed by Mrs. Dynast herself. All that was stolen was the information on the card, and that makes the situation different. —Mr. Dynast, I believe that you implied that Mrs. Dynast's friends, her church-social associates, knew that she was preparing recipes."

"Oh, yes, it was big news."

"And would they know that she was working on those recipes at this particular time, when the rest attended the church meeting?"

"Yes, I believe I mentioned that she had told them so, as her excuse for not going."

"And in preparing the recipes, she would label each and identify it, wouldn't she?"

"Certainly. In fact, the blueberry muffin recipe would be labeled 'Grandma's Blueberry Muffins' because that's how she always referred to them to me and to everyone else. Her grandmother had apparently taught her the recipe and she had then improved on it."

"And I presume the room in which she worked had windows."

"Yes, of course."

"In that case," said Trumbull, you certainly didn't have a locked room. People might not have been able to reach into it physically to steal a recipe card, but they could surely look through a window and read what was on the recipe card, couldn't they?"

"No, I don't think so, Mr. Trumbull," said Dynast. "The front of our house was street level, but the ground slanted downward as one moved away from the street. That left room for a basement and garage with openings at ground level in the backyard and with a driveway going back there. But the back rooms, in which Ginny was working and had the kids, was one story high. You couldn't very well look into the windows unless you were ten or eleven feet high, or unless you used a ladder. And I rather think Ginny would have noticed in either case."

Trumbull wouldn't let go. "He might have been in a tree, if the room faced a backyard."

"He might have been—or she—but there was no tree within twenty feet of those windows. Besides, as I had said, Ginny had been irresolute and had written the recipe very lightly in pencil. I don't think anyone could have read it even if his or her nose had been pressed right up against the glass of the window. And then, to make matters worse, in order to keep it even more secure, Ginny had slipped the recipe under a book after she had written it. It was still under the book when her heart failed her and she took it out to tear it up."

Drake said, "Was that the only time the recipe was written down?"

"The only time."

"And was it really quoted word for word? It couldn't have been a merely similar recipe that someone else had independently invented, could it? After all, I must tell you that even the greatest scientific discoveries are sometimes independently thought up by two different scientists at more or less the same time. These things do happen."

"The same words," said Dynast intransigently. "Ginny swears to it and I believe her. At one point, she said, 'Stir furiously till your hand is in danger of falling off. Then count ten rapid breaths and—' All that was right there. That's the way she talks about cooking when she talks to me. No one else is likely to talk that same exact way."

There was silence around the table and Avalon said, "I'm afraid, Mr. Dynast, that I don't see how it could have been done. You're not making this up as a joke, I suppose."

Dynast shook his head. "I wish I were, Mr. Avalon, but it's no joke to Ginny, and if we don't find out how it's done, I wouldn't be surprised if, in the end, we'll have to sell our house and move away. Ginny can't bear the thought of living near the people who did this to her."

Drake said, "Would you say that your wife has really told the entire truth?"

"I'd stake my life on it," said Dynast.

"Then with a room containing one woman and five young children you have to conclude that the woman herself stole her own recipe. Do you suppose it is possible that Mrs. Dynast arranged the whole thing herself as an excuse to be able to move away?"

Dynast said, "If she wanted to move, she would just have to say so. She wouldn't have to arrange a big, fancy trick. And if you knew Ginny, you'd know how impossible it would have been for her to play tricks with her blueberry muffins. You can't imagine what they meant to her."

Rubin said, "Well, it's the damnedest locked-room mystery I've ever heard. There's no solution."

At this point, Henry said half apologetically, "Gentlemen?"

Rubin looked up. "Come on, Henry, are you trying to tell us there *is* a solution?"

"I can't guarantee it, but I would like to ask Mr. Dynast a question."

Avalon said, "Would that be all right with you, Mr. Dynast? Henry is a valued member of our organization."

"I suppose so," said Dynast. "Sure."

"In that case, the oldest child—Harold."

"Yes?"

"How old did you say Harold was?"

"Five at the most."

"How do you know, Mr. Dynast?"

"Ginny said so."

"How did she know, Mr. Dynast?"

"I suppose she asked him."

"Did she say she had asked him?"

"N-no. —But I saw him myself when I came home. I told you. He was a little fellow. Five at the outside."

"But, Mr. Dynast, you also said that you saw Harold's parents and that each was five feet tall. You wouldn't say that because they were each five feet tall they were teenagers."

"No. They were just short."

"Exactly. And short parents may well have short children. It is possible that Harold may look five, judging by his height and size, and yet be eight years old. And, for all we may know, he may be uncommonly bright for eight."

"Good Lord," said Avalon. "Do you really think that could be so, Henry?"

"Consider the consequences, Mr. Avalon, if it *is* so. One of the women of the neighborhood desperately wants the recipe. She has a short sister who has married a short man, and the two have an uncommonly small boy, who happens to be a prodigy. He is a bright eight-year-old who can easily pass for an unremarkable five-year-old. This bright boy is placed in your house, Mr. Dynast, and told what to look for.

"Mrs. Dynast would feel no concern if this little boy were watching her, or staring curiously at what she is writing. He is, after all, to all appearances, a preschool youngster who cannot read. He might see her do a recipe for 'Grandma's Blueberry Muffins' and place it under a book. Then, when she leaves on her errand, even if it is only for two minutes, the boy can take the recipe out from under the book, read it, memorize it, and put it back. It would not be a terribly long thing to memorize, and particularly bright children can pick up such things as though their minds were blotting paper. I remember that well from my own childhood."

Gonzalo said triumphantly, "Sure. That explains it, and there's no other explanation possible."

Henry said, "It is merely a possibility. However, if you can find out the name of the cousin and her husband, it would be simple to find out how old the boy is, what school he is going to, what grade he is in, and how well he is doing. If the woman refuses to give you any information about her cousin and her nephew, then that in itself would strongly imply that our theory is correct."

"Who'd have thought it?" said Dynast blankly.

Henry murmured, "There must be a rational explanation to everything, sir, and, as usual, the Black Widowers had carefully eliminated all possible explanations and left me to point out what remained."

AFTERWORD

I was reading *The Third Bullet* by John Dickson Carr, as Trumbull did in the story, and it occurred to me that I had never written a Black Widowers story involving a locked-room mystery.

Naturally, I was at once overwhelmed with a desire to do so, but it didn't seem possible to me to think up a new gimmick involving a locked room. John Dickson Carr had simply done it all, and other writers had filled in what inconsiderable gaps might remain.

However, I hated to give up. Could I possibly think of some new way of explaining a locked-room mystery? And to my astonishment, I found I could.

In great excitement, I sat down and wrote "The Recipe" in one sitting—the whole thing. I don't think I ever enjoyed writing a story more.

And now that this collection is done, may I tell you once again that I'm still in reasonably good health and have no intention of stopping. The Black Widowers, I assure you, will continue as long as I do.

ABOUT THE AUTHOR

Isaac Asimov is the author of over four hundred books of fiction and nonfiction, including the recent bestseller *Prelude to Foundation.* His previous collections of mystery stories include *Tales of the Black Widowers* (1974), *More Tales of the Black Widowers* (1976), *Casebook of the Black Widowers* (1980), and *Banquets of the Black Widowers* (1984). He lives in New York City.